"I don't want you sleeping in there... with me,"

Casey said.

Reid held her gaze. "I was sent here to *guard* you twenty-four hours a day. If I sleep in another hut, how can I protect you?"

Anger sizzled through Casey. "I can take care of myself, Reid."

"I can't let you be alone, Casey. And I don't need you looking at me like I'm an enemy, too. I'm not."

Casey tried to force herself to speak, but he stood too close to her. Did he have any idea how much he affected her? When she twisted up a look in his direction, she swallowed hard. The nakedness of the pain in his features told her everything.

He really *didn't* know how she felt about him.

* * * *

"Ms. McKenna is an expert at making our hearts beat faster with her intriguing plots and unforgettable lovers."
—*Romantic Times Magazine*

Dear Reader,

It's the most festive time of the year! And Special Edition is celebrating with six sparkling romances for you to treasure all season long.

Those MORGAN'S MERCENARIES are back by popular demand with bestselling author Lindsay McKenna's brand-new series, MORGAN'S MERCENARIES: THE HUNTERS. Book one, *Heart of the Hunter,* features the first of four fearless brothers who are on a collision course with love—and danger. And in January, the drama and adventure continues with Lindsay's provocative Silhouette Single Title release, *Morgan's Mercenaries:Heart of the Jaguar.*

Popular author Penny Richards brings you a poignant THAT'S MY BABY! story for December. In *Their Child,* a ranching heiress and a rugged rancher are married for the sake of *their* little girl, but their platonic arrangement finally blossoms into a passionate love. Also this month, the riveting PRESCRIPTION: MARRIAGE medical miniseries continues with an unlikely romance between a mousy nurse and the man of her secret dreams in *Dr. Devastating* by Christine Rimmer. And don't miss Sherryl Woods's 40th Silhouette novel, *Natural Born Lawman,* a tale about two willful opposites attracting—the latest in her AND BABY MAKES THREE: THE NEXT GENERATION miniseries.

Just in time for the holidays, award-winning author Marie Ferrarella delivers a *Wife in the Mail*—a heartwarming story about a gruff widower who falls for his brother's jilted mail-order bride. And long-buried family secrets are finally revealed in *The Secret Daughter* by Jackie Merritt, the last book in THE BENNING LEGACY crossline miniseries.

I hope you enjoy all our romance novels this month. All of us at Silhouette Books wish you a wonderful holiday season!

Sincerely,
Karen Taylor Richman
Senior Editor

Please address questions and book requests to:
Silhouette Reader Service
U.S.: 3010 Walden Ave., P.O. Box 1325, Buffalo, NY 14269
Canadian: P.O. Box 609, Fort Erie, Ont. L2A 5X3

LINDSAY McKENNA

HEART OF THE HUNTER

Published by Silhouette Books
America's Publisher of Contemporary Romance

To my editor,
Lynda Curnyn, who is as fast as I am.
Thanks for your help, direction,
laughter and great sense of humor.
Whatta gold medal team!

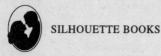 SILHOUETTE BOOKS

ISBN 0-373-24214-X

HEART OF THE HUNTER

Copyright © 1998 by Lindsay McKenna

Printed in U.S.A.

LINDSAY McKENNA

is a practicing homeopath and emergency medical technician on the Navajo Reservation in Arizona. She comes from an Eastern Cherokee medicine family and is a member of the Wolf Clan. Dividing her energies between alternative medicine and writing, she feels books on and about love are the greatest positive healing force in the world. She lives with her husband, David, at La Casa de Madre Tierra, near Sedona.

Dear Reader,

Just as they've grown on you, Morgan Trayhern, his family and his career have grown on me in the nicest of ways. It is always a joy to write another series of books about him and the men and women of his team, Perseus. Perseus is a wonderful platform from which to launch even more stories of the mercenaries who work for Morgan—their lives, the danger and adventure they encounter…and the love they find, whether they were planning to or not!

I said I would not attempt to write another four-book series, but thanks to your enthusiasm and that of my editors, how could I say no? This time, MORGAN'S MERCENARIES features the four Hunter brothers. Book one, *Heart of the Hunter*, is Reid's story. He's a Marine Corps officer whom Morgan calls upon for help because of his chilling specialty: biohazard warfare. Reid is a bit of a throwback to the males of yesteryear, so you can imagine his frustration when he is paired with a real nineties woman—scientist Dr. Casey Morrow. From the moment they meet, their lives are in danger, but that doesn't stop them from falling in love.

Love mixed with danger is the underlying theme of this four-book gift to you. It takes special men and women to battle on these two fronts simultaneously.

I hope you will enjoy this ongoing series as much as I am enjoying writing it. I hope you will eagerly anticipate each brother's adventure and his ultimate meeting with the woman who matches him in every way.

I always love to hear from my readers, so drop me a note in care of Silhouette Books. Let me know your thoughts on future books in the MORGAN'S MERCENARIES series!

Warmly,

Lindsay McKenna

Chapter One

What the hell am I doing here? Marine Corps Captain Reid Hunter almost mouthed the words out loud as he followed a stiffly moving, armed sentry toward a special elevator located in the heart of the Pentagon. He'd been called from Camp Reed, California, to make an urgent military flight back to Washington, D.C. Wiping his watering and burning eyes with the back of his darkly haired hand, he realized that whatever he'd been summoned for was serious. He watched the marine sentry present a special pass to the two armed guards stationed at the elevator. These men meant business; their eyes were hard, assessing, and the M-16 rifles they carried were locked and loaded.

The words *level Q* reached his ears. Yes, Reid had heard this whispered term before. Who hadn't? Level Q in the Pentagon was above Top Secret. It was the level known for its compartmentalization, its hush-hush, global network of secrets. It was well known that even those working at level Q only got information on a need-to-know basis. No one got told the whole picture—only the part they needed to know in order to operate and complete their assigned objective or mission. Which explained the mystery surrounding the call he'd gotten.

As he moved into the brightly polished brass elevator, which reflected the image of him in his tan uniform, hat beneath his left arm, he compressed his full lips. He had a Top Secret clearance, not a Q clearance. The air pressure in the elevator as it plummeted downward caught his attention momentarily. It felt as if he was moving five or six stories down into the bowels of the Pentagon.

What the hell did they want with him? What was going on?

He had a lot of questions and no answers. Six hours before, he'd been out in the boonies of Camp Reed with his Recon team, on patrol. The call had come in on a communications satellite link. A marine general from the Pentagon had told him to cease his activities and board the first transport heading east, pronto. That was it.

As the elevator doors whooshed open to reveal a well-lit marbled hall, Reid scowled. His three older brothers, all graduates of military academies like himself, had left the service as soon as their six-year hitch was up. They'd hired on with a supersecret government organization known as Perseus—a dark, covert branch of the CIA, as he understood it. Ty, Devlin and Shep hadn't said much about their line of work except that it was global and dangerous. As he followed the smart-stepping sentry down the hall, Reid wondered if one of his brothers was in trouble. Maybe that's what this meeting was all about?

The old fear nagged at him. His brothers had had no problem leaving the military. He did. He'd wanted to follow them, but something about civilian life scared the hell out of him. He liked the comfort of the military, which, like a nurturing mother, took care of all his needs. In civilian life, that didn't necessarily happen. Yes, the civilian world was an emotionally dangerous place for a man used to the rigorous discipline of military life. Reid didn't like the idea of risking himself emotionally. There was something about the cool, mechanical environment within the military that made him comfortable. It was a world where black was black and white was white. A world he could count on without having to expose his vulnerability like people did on the "outside." After all, it was far easier to go to war than risk his heart, as he'd once foolishly done.

Gut tightening, Reid halted at a double oak door with polished brass handles. The sentry stepped to one side.

"Please enter, sir," the marine said as he briskly pulled open one door.

Nodding briefly, Reid did as he was instructed. The door closed quietly behind him. The large, low-lit conference room held a long, oval maple table with at least twenty red leather chairs situated around its expanse. Eyes narrowing, Reid saw ten military officers seated there and one man in a dark pinstripe suit sitting at the other end. Talk about fruit salad! The quantity of colorful ribbons on their uniforms documented acts of heroism from the Korean War to the present day. It was impressive. Intimidating.

They were all studying him with the same keen, curious intensity. Hunter realized with a sinking feeling that he was a lowly captain compared to all the scrambled eggs and brass he saw in this assembly. Every armed service was represented, from admiral to general. Most of them he did not recognize as he snapped to rigid attention and announced himself to the prestigious group.

"Captain Hunter reporting as ordered, sir."

The man at the other end of the table, the civilian, rose slowly. He was the first to speak.

"At ease, Captain."

Reid relaxed a little, his gaze pinned on the man as he approached, his hand outstretched.

Whoever he was, the civilian clothes couldn't hide his

decided military bearing, the way he squared his shoulders or that measuring look of a warrior in his eyes. Reid wasn't swayed at all by the expensive black pinstripe suit, the white silk shirt or the conservative red paisley tie he wore. Not at all. But he was immediately impressed by the man himself.

Reid extended his hand, roughened and callused by many months out in the field at his marine base. As the civilian shook it firmly, Reid studied him, noticing the scar on his face that ran from his hairline down to the hard line of his squared jaw. He should know this man, Reid realized. Where had he seen his picture? Where? The man's lips twisted a little. "Welcome to Perseus, Captain. I'm Morgan Trayhern. I trust your flight here was adequate?"

Reid nodded slightly and released Trayhern's scarred hand. "Yes, sir. Adequate." Reid halted a smile before it pulled at the corners of his generous mouth. He knew exactly who Morgan Trayhern was. His life as a marine was legendary. Reid's brothers had nothing but admiration for him. To be able to meet him face-to-face was something Reid had never dreamed of. Feeling a little heat steal into his cheeks, he murmured, "It's a real pleasure, sir, to meet you."

Morgan matched his sour grin with one of his own. "No autographs, Captain."

"No, sir. Wouldn't think of it, sir."

Turning, Morgan lifted his hand to the awaiting officers. "Captain, you are here with us because the Pentagon computer said that, out of all the services, you were the best at what you do. Frankly, looking at your education, I'm not surprised." His eyes gleamed with humor. "And I'm not surprised it was a marine who came in top dog. Come and sit down. We've got a lot of ground to cover in a very little time." Morgan scowled as he took Reid's arm and led him toward a chair next to where he'd been sitting.

The serious expressions on the faces of the generals and admirals in attendance quickly dampened Reid's elation at meeting Morgan Trayhern. The lights were dimmed until the room was dark. A screen in front of them lit up. Morgan stood off to one side.

"Black biology, Captain. It's not a term lost on you, is it?"

"No, sir, it's not."

With a nod, Morgan lifted his head and looked over the attentive assemblage. "Unfortunately, it's the newest buzzword in our terrorist vocabulary, and it seems to be growing more and more out of control every day. Black biology, for those of you here who are not quite as up to speed as Captain Hunter, is about the illegal use of biological bacteria and viruses. These deadly agents can either be used as a lethal threat or dispersed readily and easily as a 'bomb' in one of many convenient ways."

Morgan scowled once again. "There's aerosol transmission, which is a nice way of saying that the germ can be loaded on board an airplane or any other airborne device, and deliberately spread over an unsuspecting populace. Or—" his voice deepened with concern "—the said germ can be put into a water supply, such as at a sewage treatment plant. Then any poor, unsuspecting bastard who drinks that water is infected and dies of the disease sooner or later. Depending, of course, on what the germ is."

"Morgan," Admiral Turner interjected, "humor me on this. Exactly *which* germs are we talking about?"

"Specifically?"

"Yes."

Morgan turned to Reid. "Captain?"

Hunter tensed slightly. He was surprised to be included in such a high-ranking discussion. Normally, lowly lieutenants and captains were there to perform on cue like trained dogs and keep their mouths shut otherwise. His fingers moved around his cap, which sat in his lap beneath the table.

"Specifically, anthrax is one of several of the most lethal threats from terrorists who utilize black biology. It's an infectious disease caused by a deadly bacterium. Sarin, a chemical warfare agent that disrupts nerve impulse transmission and ability to breathe, was used by a terrorist organization in the subways of Japan. That same organization tried to buy the Ebola virus in vitro from Russian scientists who were testing it on monkeys in Moscow, but they were refused. They turned to sarin, a neurotoxin, instead."

"Does anthrax have an antidote, Captain?" Morgan inquired.

"Yes, sir, it does. If caught in time, antibiotics can be utilized to save the person's life. They are considered moderately effective. Penicillin and tetracycline may not be effective as the organism becomes resistant to them. Right now, the sop—standard operating procedure—here in the U.S., should there be an anthrax attack, would be to utilize amoxicillin, ciprofloxacin, erythromycin and gentamicin, all of which are preferred, third-generation antibiotics."

Turner grunted and rubbed his jaw. His silver hair glinted in the low lighting. "And sarin has no antidote?"

Hunter turned his attention to the high ranking navy official. "No, sir, it does not." He cleared his throat. "However, the *amount* of sarin one inhales will determine whether you live or die. It is a colorless liquid and has a fruitlike odor. There were cases that survived because they had low levels of sarin inhaled into their respiratory tract. Recovery in such a situation takes about two weeks. Atropine injections on site, along with artificial respiration and the delivery of pure oxygen, can increase a person's chance of survival, sir. Administration of injected muscle relaxants also proved helpful in this type of black biology attack." Reid's gaze moved swiftly to the right. He saw a pleased look on Trayhern's face.

"Go on, Captain. Your knowledge is impressive."

Reid wished someone had told him he'd have to give a lecture on what he knew best, biological warfare—what had come to be known of late as black biology in the hands of terrorists. Nervousness shot through him. "Permission to stand, sir?"

Morgan nodded. "Of course, Captain."

Placing his hat on the highly polished table, Reid faced the determined, somber faces of the elite officers from each of the five services. Sweat trickled down the sides of his rib cage. He kept his voice steady as he pointed to the slide projected up on the screen and discussed sarin and other nerve gases as well as bacterial forms such as anthrax and Bubonic plague.

When he was finished, Morgan said, "Thank you, Captain. Your information is most sobering."

Reid nodded and sat down. His hands were sweaty. Helluva way to lose his chance at major's leaves if he blew this little impromptu exercise in front of these brass hats. Above it all, Trayhern had a knowing gleam in his eyes; it was as if he knew Reid could deliver the goods.

"One more thing, Captain," Morgan said in a deep voice, "your knowledge of the sarin attack in Japan is more than book-learning deep, isn't it?"

"Yes, sir, it is. I was on the primary NBC—nuclear, biological and chemical—warfare team sent over there at the invitation of the Japanese government. We gave educational information to their medical people, as well as to their law enforcement officials. We were there for six weeks bringing them up to speed."

Hunter saw a number of heads nod. Intuitively, he felt as if the group had accepted him without any more questioning. He was, in fact, one of a handful of military people who understood the horrible consequences of what was

going on in the world with black biology. At times it gave
him nightmares.

Another slide appeared—of two men in civilian clothes,
probably in their late thirties. They were standing near a
portable table with lush jungle behind them. South American? Reid wondered.

"Gentlemen," Morgan continued, "this is the late Dr.
Vincent Gilroy and his lab assistant, Stan Howard. Both
were from OID, the Office of Infectious Diseases. Two
weeks ago, they were kidnapped and then murdered—by
terrorists."

Hunter felt his chest constrict. Although he was part of
the national NBC warfare team, he wasn't privy to this
high level of information unless he was called in to assist
in the cleanup. The heaviness in Trayhern's voice sent a
frisson of fear through Reid. Clamping his teeth together,
he stopped himself from launching into a barrage of questions. Trayhern would fill them in soon enough.

"This doctor was one of three U.S. scientists who are
considered experts on the virus Ebola. Dr. Gilroy was over
in Zaire, Africa, looking for the reservoir—the animal, insect, reptile or bird—that Ebola makes its home within.
The World Health Organization, the OID and many other
countries have been teaming up and sending groups of
scientists and virologists to Africa to try and locate it. To
date, we haven't found it."

Morgan pressed a button on the table and another slide
came into view. It showed the bodies of the men, blood-
soaked and lying facedown on the muddy floor of the jungle, their hands bound behind them. "Two weeks ago, Dr.
Gilroy made an excited call by comsat to the OID. He told
his supervisor, Dr. Morrow, that he *thought* he'd finally
located the Ebola reservoir. He was calling to report that
the slides and samples containing Ebola were going to be
sent out by airplane from the capital two days later."

Reid watched as the third slide appeared. It looked like

worms, but he knew better. Because of his training, he knew he was looking at the deadly Ebola virus, magnified many times beneath the OID electron microscope.

"This is the virus that Dr. Gilroy collected from a species of bird. One of the slides, probably broken by the terrorists when they overran the camp, was found jammed into the mud. The NBC warfare team discovered it later on a grid search of the area."

"Gilroy was hit shortly after the comsat call?" Turner demanded.

"Yes, within a couple hours, from what the team estimates. The samples were gone, except for this broken slide. Luckily, Dr. Morrow was able to not only identify it, but to determine that the bird wasn't a reservoir, after all."

"Any leads on the terrorist group? Any ID?" Turner asked.

Morgan looked at them grimly. "Black Dawn."

Whispers started among the group. Hunter held his breath momentarily. *Black Dawn.* It made sense. He saw the worry on the faces of the officers at the table as they murmured in low voices to one another. He saw the sadness and anxiety in Morgan Trayhern's icy features.

"Most of you know a little about Black Dawn. We don't know a whole lot, collectively," Morgan continued. "It's an international amalgam of terrorists. They come from all walks of life, all nationalities and both genders. One thing they share in common is the belief that the present-day governments of the world need to be toppled. Secondly, they are highly motivated, zealous, well-trained professionals from academia. This is no hothead, knee-jerk operation. They are a collection of cold, precise and careful thinkers planning meticulously what they are doing and how they are going about it. Their weapon of choice is black biology. Every law-enforcement agency and government in thirty countries is scrambling to try and connect the dots on this terrorist group. To date, we have very little to go on." Morgan looked over at Hunter. "Do you have anything to add about them, Captain?"

"They were implicated in the attack in Japan. It is believed that they have set up several small-scale scenarios in what was once known as the Soviet Union. The Kurds have paid the price, too. Black Dawn is utilizing any government that will cooperate in building several types of black biology weapons. One is a medium-range missile that can carry a warhead filled with a particular germ such as anthrax. It's no larger than a suitcase and will kill tens of thousands of people. There's another payload known as a UAV, an unmanned aerial vehicle. They can take something as nonthreatening as a single-engine biplane, fill the crop-dusting receptacles with anthrax and then fly it over a city, spraying it on the populace. These planes have already been flown, according to CIA reports. Pilotless, they are ground controlled by radio and fitted with a programmed computer."

"How much can they carry?" an army general asked.

"Up to a ton can be delivered," Hunter said. "And it could be dropped by a highly unsophisticated delivery system."

"Missile range," Turner commented, "is known to be at least four hundred miles."

"And," Morgan said, "as little as two pounds of anthrax can do a lot of damage."

Reid added, "Two pounds, if dispersed properly over two hundred and fifty acres, can kill everyone within that area."

"My God," Turner said in exasperation, "and we thought nuclear war was the end-all nightmare."

"This is just as bad," Morgan agreed. He shook his head and put another slide on the screen. "We've got problems. Black Dawn is gearing up. They want Ebola. I'm sure Captain Hunter would agree that Ebola is the virus of choice, would you not?''

"Yes, sir, I would.''

"Why?'' Turner demanded. "Why not anthrax?''

Reid shrugged. "Sir, Ebola has been proven to have mutated to the aerosol stage. That means that if I was infected with this virus, and you touched my perspiration, you would contract the infection. There's scientific evidence to suggest that it's also capable of being passed from one animal to another simply by breathing. In my outfit, we treat it as if it is completely aerosol active. Ebola has many advantages over sarin and VX nerve gas. Eight weeks after a victim dies, the virus has been found in the bloody mattress filling and fiber, alive and well. Not many viruses have that kind of half-life.''

"Anthrax has a long life, too,'' Morgan remarked.

"Yes, sir, it does, but there's medicine available that can stop it from killing you if we get to you in time. There is *no* antidote for Ebola. Once you've got it, you will die from it. No amount of antibiotics will save your life.''

"So,'' Army General Patterson groused, "you're expecting that whoever we send over to Zaire will meet the same fate as that poor bastard, Gilroy?''

"We are,'' Morgan said grimly. "The OID is working with all the major scientific organizations, and there's a stringent international effort among scientists to locate this reservoir for Ebola. This is such an important criteria that the OID is sending Dr. Morrow to Zaire in two days.'' Morgan pinned Hunter with a dark look. "And you're going to accompany her, Captain. Dr. Morrow is the assistant supervisor in emerging diseases at the OID. She took this post just a year ago. Dr. Gilroy was her assistant.''

Reid grimaced inwardly as a color photo of Dr. Morrow was flashed on the screen. Compared to all the other lethal and harrowing images they'd just seen, she was like a breath of life being injected into the tension-filled room.

Hunter tried to throttle his reaction to the mop of red hair that gleamed with gold and burgundy highlights. In the close-up photo, Dr. Morrow looked very, very young. The dusting of freckles across her smiling face and those lively green eyes that danced with laughter touched him. Deeply. Inexplicably.

She had a triangular face, a broad brow indicating her high intelligence, her green eyes huge and set far apart. Reid liked her prominent nose; it had a bump on it. Most of all, he liked her wide, smiling mouth. There was such a carefree sense about Dr. Morrow, he thought as he studied the photo, noticing her hands stuffed casually in the pockets of her lab coat. Reid recognized the redbrick OID building in the background. He'd been there on a number of occasions for training, but he'd never run into Casey Morrow.

Her winsome smile made his heart beat harder in his chest. She was part girl, part woman, he decided—tall, lean and wearing no makeup or jewelry at all. Of course, in her business, jewelry wasn't something to be worn because it, too, could become infected. She looked so happy. Hunter found himself jealous of her joy. It had been a long time since he had been able to smile like she was smiling. As if she hadn't a care in the world. Life hadn't touched her—yet—to mar her, to make her serious or somber, as it had him.

Hunter moved uncomfortably in his chair. Frowning, he placed his hand near his cap, which lay on the table. *She looks like she's eighteen. Young and naive. And that's what she is—a kid. A kid who's out for a lark in life. She wouldn't be smiling if she knew what kind of a snake pit she was entering by going over to Africa with Black Dawn shadowing her—and my—every move.*

"Sir…" Hunter began, his voice oddly rough with emotion, "with all due respect, Dr. Morrow is, well, a woman, and this situation is dangerous."

Morgan smiled thinly. "Captain, if my wife were standing here, she'd be more than a little miffed at your attitude."

Reid compressed his lips. "Sir, my response is not sexist. If I'm going out in the field, I'd at least like to have someone who can handle a side arm—"

"She can, I assure you," Morgan rumbled. He gazed up at Morrow's photo on the screen. "She may look young and wet behind the ears, but this woman has faced death so many times it makes most of us look like weak sisters. You've heard of the hot zone, Captain?"

"Yes, sir. It's a lab specially built for working with the most lethal viruses we have on this planet."

"That's right. Dr. Morrow is in the hot zone every *week*, Captain, handling some kind of deadly, infectious material. One wrong slip and she's dead. She's been doing this work for the OID for five years, and she's still alive. Besides, she lost her fiancé to Ebola and she's got a score to settle with this virus on that account."

"I understand that, sir," Reid muttered, "but Black Dawn is not a virus and is more deadly. Judging from that slide of the two dead OID officials, I'd say they endured a lot of torture before their brains were blown out." His eyes hardened, as did his voice, and he dared to look around the room. Reid knew he was way out of line, but his protective mechanism toward women was winning this battle inside him. "If Dr. Morrow is *that* valuable to the OID, then her knowledge of Ebola and other emerging diseases is too precious to risk out there in the jungles of Zaire, don't you think?"

His palms were sweaty. Hunter wanted desperately to rub them against his pants, but he didn't dare. Somehow, his gaze kept ranging back to Dr. Morrow. The photo showed her standing outside under a blue sky with autumn leaves forming a colorful backdrop to a highly manicured green lawn. Bright sunlight enveloped her like lover's arms, and the white lab coat she wore made her look more like an angel than a flesh-and-blood human being. Hell, she looked like an ingenue fresh out of high school, not a world-class virologist handling some of the most deadly material on the face of this earth. Reid couldn't stop his protective mechanism from working overtime.

Morgan gave him an amused smile. "I understand your concerns, Captain, but Dr. Morrow volunteered for this assignment. She knows the score and she's got a score to even on a personal playing field. Normally, I'd never support sending out on a mission someone who had an emotional vendetta but I know Casey Morrow well and I know she won't allow her own feelings to overshadow the mission's important agendas. She also is a very courageous person. She deserves someone of equal courage. That's you…if you want to take the assignment. With your background and degree in microbiology, you can double as her lab assistant, plus be her eyes and ears—her guard."

Reid wanted to add "dog" to the end of Trayhern's sentence, but resisted. Barely. His heart was beating hard in his chest. And it wasn't from adrenaline. He was scared! Him! Of all things! All he had to do was stare up at her larger-than-life image on that screen, and he felt his heart opening up as if doors were being flung wide open. In his thirty years of life, Reid had never experienced such a startling sensation. He was scared—of her.

Wrestling inwardly to recapture his unraveling emotional response, Reid rasped, "Sir, I'm not questioning her courage. But there's a big difference between a bullet and torture, and getting nailed by a virus."

With a slight shrug, Morgan smiled a little more. "Captain, I think Casey Morrow would probably take you to task on that last comment. Suffering is suffering. We agree that torture by Black Dawn is a risk. But it's a risk she's willing to take. We don't question your credentials or your abilities as a marine." His gaze became assessing. "And if I don't misread your concern, my sense is you're feeling protective about Dr. Morrow? Because she's a woman?''

Damn! Reid almost mouthed the word, but snapped his mouth shut just in time. Well, he'd heard that the legendary Morgan Trayhern could pin a man on his real intentions from a mile away, could read him like a book. And sure enough, Trayhern had effectively gotten inside him and read him dead to rights. Sitting up stiffly, Reid said, "Yes, sir, you're reading me correctly on my concern."

"I know Casey Morrow," Admiral Turner growled, "and I realize you don't, Captain. She's a capable woman. An incredible resource to us. Her knowledge about emerging viruses makes her one of our top people in the U.S as an expert on the topic. She's a scrapper and a fighter. No, Captain, you've got a woman warrior on your hands, not a weakling, as you believe." Turner pointed toward the photo on the screen: "She may look vulnerable and incapable of taking care of herself, but I assure you, she's just the opposite."

Morgan chuckled. "Maybe another way to put this to rest is to say that no book should be judged by its cover, Admiral?"

Turner pursed his lips. "Exactly, Morgan. Exactly."

Reid felt heat stealing into his cheeks. It was disconcerting at his age to blush, but that's exactly what he was doing. Thankfully, the low lighting didn't give his teenage response away—except to the sharp eyes of Morgan Trayhern, who glanced at him and then, mercifully, allowed his gaze to drift away.

That was just his style, Reid thought with admiration, remembering some of the things his brothers had told him about Trayhern. Well, Reid had hoped to meet this famous man someday, but certainly not like this.

Morgan moved back to the podium. His hands wrapped around the edges of the lectern. "Gentlemen, let's give

Captain Hunter some time to think this through. Shall we break for lunch? Captain, if you'll come with me?''

The silken tone in Morgan's voice wasn't to be confused with friendliness toward him, Hunter realized as he shot up out of the chair at stiff attention as the brass began to leave the room.

Chapter Two

"Captain, there's someone I want you to see," Morgan murmured as he paused at a door leading from the main conference room they'd been meeting in minutes earlier.

Quelling his disgruntled state, Reid nodded. "Yes, sir." Compressing his lips into a thin line after Trayhern exited and quietly shut the door, Reid looked around the small alcove he'd been left alone in. Tossing his hat on the rectangular desk made from dark cherry wood, he placed his hands on his hips. *Helluva fix to be in. A woman, of all things…*

Reid's thoughts were interrupted by a swift, sharp knock on the door.

"It's open," he muttered as he looked toward it. His eyes opened wide.

"Ty!"

Ty Hunter entered, his tall, muscular frame looking almost too large to fit through the door. He grinned engagingly. "Hey, Morgan said I'd find you fuming in here. He said you'd probably be pacing the floor like a caged lion or some such thing.'' Thrusting out his hand, he shook Reid's with a pumping action. ''Good to see you. You look surprised to see me.''

''You could say that,'' Reid said, swallowing his surprise as his brother, who was just a year older than he, shut the door behind him. Ty wasn't dressed like a man who worked as a mercenary for Morgan Trayhern and the government outpost known as Perseus. The navy blue blazer and tan chino pants looked casual, but Reid knew his brown-eyed, dark-haired brother too well to judge him by his clothes. Ty was dangerous and good at the undercover work he did. Reid had tried to get his brothers to remain in the service, but they'd all bolted at the end of their promised tour. Having met Morgan Trayhern, Reid could see why his brothers had swung their allegiance to this mysterious, legendary man. There was no doubting Trayhern's obvious leadership and charisma.

Releasing his hand, Ty moved his long, thick fingers around the collar of the starched white shirt he wore beneath his sport coat. ''Give me jungle utilities any day,'' he said with a grin as he went over to the coffee machine and poured himself a cup. ''Coffee? Or maybe a stiff drink, from the look on your face?''

Reid scowled. ''Yeah, I could use some. And yes, a shot of whiskey is preferable, but under the circumstances, a no-can-do. Thanks.''

''You're not lookin' real happy, brother. Bad news?''

''Travels fast, doesn't it?'' Reid said as Ty handed him a ceramic cup with a navy symbol on the side of it. ''Thanks.''

''Hmm, don't mention it.'' Ty poured a hefty dose of sugar and milk into his own coffee. ''I'm between assignments. Morgan thought he might need me.''

Snorting softly, Reid watched his brother walk to the desk and sit down behind it. ''Really?''

Sipping the coffee gratefully, Ty eyed him over the raised cup. "He was right."

"I suppose you know all about what was discussed back in there?" Reid demanded, motioning with a thumb over his shoulder. He lifted the cup to his lips and gulped quickly, the coffee scalding his tongue.

"Most of it."

"Why don't you take the mission?"

"Because I'm not as qualified in black biology as you are, that's why. I know a lot about this area because Mom and Dad are both involved in it from different ends of the spectrum, but you're the expert."

"Bull."

"Well, maybe a little," he said, a grin starting to crawl across his wide, well-shaped mouth. "But Morgan has other plans for me, and I can't take on two assignments at once. I was the one who suggested you. They ran a quick computer check on NBC specialists in the service, and your name popped up at the top. I told Morgan to get you in here. You're the man for this job."

Glaring down at Ty, Reid snapped, "This is not a military assignment."

"True, it's spook ops, no doubt about that." Raising his arched, thick eyebrows, he studied Reid. "This will look good on your jacket. Should make major leaves really easy to come by after this little mission is completed."

With a roll of his eyes, Reid sipped his coffee more cautiously this time. There was too much glee in Ty's dark, cinnamon-colored eyes to suit him. It was as if he knew something Reid didn't. One thing Reid didn't like was not knowing the turf he was standing on. That implied lack of control over the situation, and in his business, control was everything. It meant the split-second difference between life and death at times.

Ty lost his genial, easygoing smile and sat up, his large, scarred hands encircling the mug of coffee sitting before

him on the desk. "Okay, here's the scoop. I know and
have worked with Dr. Casey Morrow before. I warned
Morgan that due to previous bad luck in your personal life
with women, you really wouldn't be all that thrilled about
an assignment that engaged a woman as your partner. But
Morgan really wants you for this assignment so he thought
it best I fly down here and tell you that Casey Morrow is
up to the job. She won't be a pain in the ass to you, Reid.

"She's smart, savvy and doesn't take any BS from any-
body— especially a man. So—" he wagged his finger at
Reid, a smile breaking at the corners of his mouth
"—you've got to practice your gender-neutral terminology
big-time with this lady. Or else you'll be in *her* gun sights.
And I can guarantee you from personal experience with
her it is *not* where you want to find yourself, even on a
good day."

Reid's anger rippled, but he didn't allow it to show. "I
don't care for you speaking of my personal life to strang-
ers, Ty."

"Don't get tied up in knots. I wasn't specific, Reid.
Morgan Trayhern is a mind reader of sorts. He got the
picture loud and clear. Once he saw your jacket and your
professional education in NBC warfare, he wanted you—
only you—for this assignment." Sipping his coffee with a
pleased look on his square features, Ty murmured, "Morgan usually gets his way with the Joint Chiefs of Staff."

"Women are women."

Ty shook his head. "Brother, you have met your match
with Casey Morrow. Now, I know you saw a slide of her
in that little program Morgan put together in there, and I
agree, at first glance, she looks weak…but she's not. This
gal has lived half her life in Africa. That's no small thing
to do, given that half the people over there die at a young
age from snake bites, disease or malnutrition. Casey
thrived in that place. She's a backpacker, a hiker, and just

for fun, she climbs El Capitan once a year to keep herself in top-notch physical condition.''

El Capitan was the huge butte in Yosemite National Park. Reid knew what kind of skill it took to make it up that slate gray, granite slab, which rose thousands of feet vertically. Very few people could say they'd climbed El Capitan once, much less once a year. Sitting on the edge of the desk, he studied Ty, who seemed to delight in this whole fiasco. ''Okay, so she can hang off sheer rock walls and not plummet to her death. So what?''

Sipping the coffee again, Ty murmured, ''She's pretty...not that you'd be interested in that after your last tango with Janet. Hey, I know you're still smarting over it all, but maybe Casey is just what you need—a diversion.''

''Don't you think Black Dawn is *enough* of a diversion?'' Reid growled.

Ty nodded and became serious. ''You're not kidding. They're spreading like a disease in their own right over the world, Reid. I didn't realize how powerful an organization they were until I started working with Casey. She more or less interfaces between the OID, the feds and us. Of course, that's private information and not for public consumption.'' Setting down his cup, he slowly stood up. ''Twelve-hour flights are hell,'' he muttered good-naturedly, and stretched to his full six-foot-five-inch height.

''Having a woman involved in this is our Achilles' heel,'' Reid said in a warning voice. ''Morgan Trayhern *has* to realize that.''

Ty arched an eyebrow at his brother and rounded the desk. Jamming his hands into the pockets of his chinos, he stopped before him. ''Don't let Morgan hear you say that. Fifty percent of the mercenaries in his employ are women. They do as good a job as we do—if not better. He's got the stats to prove it, too. They pay attention to a lot of little details.'' Ty jabbed a finger at Reid's shoulder. ''And you know how important little details are in our line of work.''

''So I'm a damn throwback to the Ice Age.''

Chortling, Ty said, ''Casey would call you a Neanderthal to your face, brother.''

''She would?''

Grinning, he nodded. ''Casey doesn't suffer fools gladly—male or female. That's why she's the assistant in her hot-zone department. She didn't get that position because she was pretty lookin' but dumb.''

Frowning, Reid said, ''Trayhern said she could shoot straight. True?''

''Her real name is Annie Oakley.''

A sour grin edged Reid's lips. ''What's she qualified in?''

''Ask me what she isn't qualified in. It's a helluva shorter list.''

Reid studied his brother in silence. Ty was a joker of sorts, but when the chips were down, he was rock solid. ''Why would she be so qualified in that many weapons?''

''Because,'' Ty said lightly, ''she's been in Africa too many times. With all the warring tribes and nationalities over there, the rebellions and changes of government, she learned a long time ago how to shoot whatever was handy. Give that woman an SKS with metal-piercing bullet capability and I wouldn't want to be her target.''

''She ever kill anyone?''

''Not that I know of.''

''Would she?''

Ty nodded. ''I believe if she had to, she would.''

Rising, Reid rubbed the back of his neck. ''Damn it.''

''Hey, give her a chance, will you? Casey isn't your worst nightmare like you think. Black Dawn sure as hell *is*.''

Moving slowly to the corner of the alcove, Reid studied

Ty's features. He began to realize his brother had gray smudges beneath his eyes, indicating fatigue. "So you made a special trip here to convince me to take this assignment with Dr. Morrow?"

"Yes. I think if Morgan could find one more person of your education, experience and knowledge about NBC warfare, he'd have opted for him, but that's not in the cards." Ty shrugged his broad shoulders, as if to rid them of some unnamed weight he carried. "Casey fits the bill perfectly. Morgan can't help that she's a woman and you're still in the middle of your own woman problems. I told him you were capable of rising above all of it and taking this mission." Frowning, Ty studied him across the room. "This Black Dawn...it's dangerous. I know you don't need to be told that...but Casey has seen what they can do firsthand. It was her doc and assistant that bought the farm over there. She's madder than a wet hen. She's always been a red-headed spitfire, but now I think there's a bit of revenge in her soul on account of the death of her people. She's feeling guilty right now, judging from the call I had with her earlier. She feels that if she'd been over there instead, it wouldn't have happened."

Reid snorted. "It can happen to *any* of us. A terrorist group like Black Dawn doesn't let gender stand in the way of putting a bullet through someone's head. Or worse..."

Ty lightened a little, his gaze assessing. "Then...you'll take the mission?"

Releasing a breath of air, more out of frustration than anything else, Reid rasped, "Do I have a choice?"

"No," Ty answered with a chuckle, "you don't. Morgan just wanted you to think you did."

Running his long, strong fingers through his short dark hair, Reid said, "Marines know the score. I knew mine when I walked into that room. They need cannon fodder. If we get lucky, we'll nail Black Dawn before they nail us. Otherwise, we'll just be two more notches on their international gun belt, is all.''

Ty held his dark look. "Morgan cares what you think," he said slowly. "If he didn't, he wouldn't have taken me out of the mission I was on and flown me straight here to talk with you about Casey. I think he saw trouble coming and he knows Black Dawn well enough to get the very *best* people involved at this escalating stage of things. If Black Dawn gets ahold of the Ebola virus or any other deadly germs, there's going to be a lot of people dead in one helluva hurry. They can trot that virus around the world in forty-eight hours, hit so many major cities in that time span that this globe will shake like a dying dog. You know that and so do I. Even more, Casey knows it. She's a warrior, Reid, just like you and me. Don't let the fact that she happens to be in a woman's body fool you, okay?''

The lethal quality in Ty's voice caught Reid off guard.

His brother had tremendous persuasive skills, though he was the jokester and trickster in their family, while Dev was the hellion, and Shep the ultimate risk taker. Reid was the conservative, straight-arrow brother. He had to be; he was the youngest and was expected to toe the line. Finally, with an effort, he whispered, "Okay, it's a go. Tell Trayhern I'm on the team.''

Brightening, Ty came over and slapped him good-naturedly on the back. "You won't regret your decision.''

"Oh, yes, I will," Reid retorted as he put his arms around his brother's shoulders in a hug. It had been nearly six months since he'd last seen Ty, between undercover assignments. As they parted, Reid asked, "Where are you off to now?''

"Hopefully, twenty-four hours of uninterrupted sleep at my apartment in New York City," Ty teased as he opened the door. "Good luck on this mission. I told Morgan I wanted to keep tabs on you and Casey while you're out in the field...."

Reid nodded. "I feel safer already."

Chuckling indulgently, Ty lifted his hand. "Hang around. I'll get Morgan. He'll probably give you some last-minute details, your airline tickets, and you'll be off to meet Casey Morrow at the Washington National Airport."

As Casey sat in National Airport, ceaseless traffic ebbing and flowing by her, she felt the back of her neck prickle in warning. It was a feeling she'd experienced far too often to ignore. She lowered the book she had in hand—*Emerging Plagues,* written by herself. Someone was looking at her, gauging her like a quarry. But who? The thought had barely registered as she quietly closed the thick, hardback volume and looked up—up into relentless gray eyes narrowed at her like a predatory eagle.

He stood across the thoroughfare in a dark brown leather bomber jacket, a pair of jeans, a cranberry-colored polo shirt and hiking boots. His hair was walnut brown and short—close cropped to his skull. The square jaw jutted out and reminded her of the granite hardness of El Capitan, which challenged her yearly. Judging by the way his eyes crinkled in the corners, she figured him to be in his early thirties. Although his features were filled with frank disapproval, he had a handsome face, in a rough-hewn way, one that instantly sent a shiver of awareness through Casey.

His hands were thrust into the pockets of his jeans, and he was leaning casually against a pillar, just watching her. Kind of like a bug under an electron microscope, she thought, smarting at his bad manners. Morgan Trayhern had told her a Captain Reid Hunter from the Marine Corps would be joining her shortly before her flight to Zaire. This *had* to be him. He stood out like a sore thumb among the casually dressed passengers around him. His eyes were too alert; his shoulders, broad and strong, were thrown back in obvious pride, and that confidence in his face was something to behold. The good captain obviously thought a lot of himself.

Quelling a grin that wanted to blossom on her lips, Casey relaxed beneath the marine's scrutiny. Fine, he wanted a look. Let him take a good, long look. She wasn't going anywhere and she certainly was not intimidated by the likes of him. Ty Hunter had warned her earlier that his younger brother was a little backward when it came to women. Might as well let the arrogant captain, who apparently thought male testosterone was the be-all and end-all, know that she didn't think so. Casey met and held his scalpel-like stare with one of equal frankness and intensity. She saw his eyes widen momentarily, and then those thick, straight brows dip in consternation over his large gray eyes.

Laughing to herself, she uncrossed her legs beneath the pale pink silk skirt that revealed the slenderness of her ankles and the sensible white shoes she wore. There was no doubt a power around this marine officer. It radiated around him like sunlight. If Casey had to put a name to it, she would say charisma or natural leadership ability was just oozing off the good captain. She wanted to dislike him for his sneakiness; he could have come up and pleasantly introduced himself. But no, he had to steal upon her unannounced and check her out to his satisfaction before deciding to come forward. *The cad.* And then Casey laughed, the sound bubbling up through her slender, long throat as she tilted her head back to release it.

Reid scowled. Dr. Morrow's bell-like laughter feathered across his sensitized, taut nerves like water being sprayed across a hot fire. When she tilted her head back, something old and hurting broke loose in his chest. Automatically, he rubbed his hand across his heart in reaction. What the hell was happening? This woman with her mop of red hair and sparkling green eyes that positively glowed with laughter shouldn't be able to reach him like this.

There was nothing to dislike about Casey Morrow, he thought sourly, as he watched her laughter die away, those intense, green eyes challenging him once more. She had moxie, he'd give her that. And he liked the shape of her face and the sprinkling of freckles across her nose and upper cheeks. Maybe it was the fullness of her lips, that soft tilt at the corners, that engaged him. For a moment, before he squashed the feeling, he felt like a hormone driven teenager being hurtled headlong into a morass of emotions and confusion. Once was enough!

But he couldn't help staring at her, at her soft, wind-blown hair. She didn't use hair spray, that was for sure. Short, bright red with gold highlights, the strands curved around and accented her skull to a decided advantage, falling softly just below her delicate earlobes, and looking like someone had playfully ruffled it. The thin gold chain around her throat, the white silk blouse opening in a V just provocatively enough to reveal the soft swell of her breasts, engaged all his senses, whether he wanted them to or not. His brows knitted more deeply as Casey Morrow stood up, book in hand, and strolled slowly across the walkway, straight toward him. Just the way she walked roused him. She swayed like a willow being stroked by a loving breeze. The silk of the pale pink skirt fell across her hips and flowed around her long thighs and lower legs like water. Swallowing his surprise, he realized Casey was a lot taller than he'd ever imagined her to be. He was a solid six foot three inches tall, and he'd have to guess she was nearly six feet herself. And he couldn't help but notice her obvious athletic form; nothing was wasted about her movements. but the laughter in her gaze was what really got to him. She didn't have a smile on her luscious mouth, but he saw it in her eyes—that Irish gleam of playfulness in their sparkling green-and-gold depths. Feeling heat in-

vade his neck and cheeks, he realized he was blushing.
Taking his hands out of his pockets as she boldly approached him, Reid couldn't help but grin a little.

Casey liked his unabashed grin. He was like a little boy
who was caught with the goods and had the grace to admit
it. "Captain Hunter, I presume?" she asked in a husky,
softened tone.

"One and the same, Dr. Morrow." His smile broadened
despite his desire to maintain that stern exterior. He found
he couldn't help himself. What *was* it about this red-haired
she-devil that literally grabbed him and wouldn't let him
go? She stood almost at eye level with him, and the seriousness on her face belied the laughter glinting in her
green-and-gold-flecked eyes.

"I think you got caught with your hand in the cookie
jar?"

Chuckling and properly embarrassed, Reid looked down
at his newly bought hiking boots and then back up at her.
The stinging heat in his cheeks, he was sure, could be seen
like red lights on a Christmas tree now. "That's one way
of putting it."

"Am I that daunting that you couldn't approach me directly?"

Her throaty voice was nearly his undoing. Reid had met
few women who had beauty, confidence and guts in this
combination.

"I thought I could watch you without being spotted."

"Honesty. That's a good sign. You're a throwback to
Neanderthal days, I see." Her eyes narrowed on him
thoughtfully. "Honest to a fault?"

He scratched his head. Though he smarted internally
over the Neanderthal label, Reid had been duly warned by
Ty earlier, so he had no one to blame but himself. Foot-
in-mouth disease was his forte upon occasion. "Unfortunately, yes." His attitude about women hadn't served him
at all in his last relationship, but Reid couldn't be some-

thing he wasn't. He wasn't equipped to play games. It just wasn't in his genes.

"Another point in your favor." Casey looked down at her watch and then over at the check-in counter for their flight. "Sneakiness isn't something I condone."

"I don't call what I was doing sneaky."

A smile edged her lips. She was enjoying the good captain's unease. He was blushing profusely, and Casey felt sorry for him. It was obvious he was painfully aware that he'd been caught red-handed at something he thought he was quite good at. He'd never taken on an African brat, though. She'd learned a long time ago to have the proverbial eyes in the back of her head in order to stay out of the danger that abounded in the bush.

"Oh!" she said, pouting playfully. "Then you thought you wouldn't get caught because…?"

Reid straightened up to his full height. Ty had warned him about this. "I thought I could get away with it because you were a woman."

Laughing fully, Casey said, "You are honest, to a fault." She held out her hand toward him. "Well, now that we've more or less met, you can call me Casey."

Reid grinned again. She was impossible to dislike, he decided, as he took her hand. He was surprised that her grip was strong, firm and slightly rough feeling. But then, he reminded himself, she climbed rocks for the hell of it in her free time.

Casey heard the flight attendant give the call for first-class passengers. "That's us they're calling."

He nodded, not wanting to release her hand. But he forced himself to do just that as Casey gave him a fleeting, intense look once again. Now he knew how a bug under a microscope felt. Her hand had been cool and firm. His was moist and embarrassingly hot. As she turned and began to walk over to the line of people waiting to board, her airline ticket in hand, he hurried to catch up with her.

Digging in his back pocket, he produced his ticket. If Ty had been here, he'd have been rolling on the floor with laughter. Well, his brother had warned him that Casey Morrow wasn't to be trifled with.

Reid hurried ahead of her to scoop up her briefcase. "Let me get that," he said.

"Thanks, but I'll carry it on," Casey said.

Stymied, Reid held out his hand as she straightened up, her dark brown leather briefcase, which had obviously seen a lot of wars itself, by the look of it, at her side. "Your ticket?"

"Yes, I have it." She saw the quizzical expression on his features. "Captain, I really am capable of boarding a plane by myself—without your help."

Reid felt helpless. "It's my job...."

Gently, because she could see he was truly at odds with her independence, she smiled and whispered, "I thought Army Rangers had other, more important jobs to perform?"

Reid realized she was teasing him. Falling into step with her, he murmured, "Good doctor, I'm a Recon Marine, not from the doggy army. There *is* a difference."

Chortling, Casey handed her ticket to the awaiting flight attendant at the door. "Really?"

Once in first class, up in the top of the jumbo jet, Reid noticed to his satisfaction that they were alone. The flight wasn't full and he was glad. Just ahead of them, the door to the cockpit was open, one of the male flight attendants having brought the crew hot coffee.

Reid and Casey sat down in two large seats separated by an area for drinks. He tried to be discreet as he gazed at Dr. Morrow, while she took off her sensible shoes and wriggled her toes with decided pleasure on the nubby carpet.

"The only thing missing on this grand adventure is a

hot tub,'' she said with a sigh, then rested her head against the plush seat.

''Where we're going, there aren't going to be many amenities,'' he groused, laying the seat belt across his lap. Watching as the flight attendant closed the cockpit door and then quickly left, Reid met Casey's half-closed eyes.

She smiled a little. ''Tell me about it, Captain.''

Irked, he said in a low tone, ''You can call me Hunter. Or Reid, if you like.''

''You have a strong name.'' She sighed and closed her eyes as she brought the seat back into a semiupright position.

Reid sat there, knocked off balance by her warmth and familiarity with him. There was no shyness to Casey Morrow. None. She acted as if she had known him all her life. He ruminated about how he was the exact opposite: it took him time to let down his guard and open up to people. And then he grimaced. Maybe his trial with Janet had burned him so badly he couldn't open up. Was he always this closed? This inaccessible?

As the jumbo jet slowly eased out of its loading dock, Reid slid deeper into his own tortured morass of emotions. Looking at Casey, who now had her eyes closed, her hands folded against her abdomen, he felt like a concrete wall in comparison. She was vulnerable. Accessible. Unlike him. And he recalled his ex-fiancée's words: *Hunter, you're heartless. I mean it.*

I've never seen a man so out of touch with his emotions and less willing to share them with someone he's supposed to love. What's wrong with you, Reid? Why can't you share how you feel with me? Moving uncomfortably in his seat, he scowled unhappily.

''What's wrong?''

Casey's direct question surprised him. But then, Ty had warned him about her directness. ''Nothing...just trying to get comfortable," he muttered defensively. "Why don't you go to sleep?"

Prying one eye open, Casey studied him. "What? And miss all the fun and excitement?" Her lips curved ruefully. She hoped the starched and pressed marine officer would relax a little, let down his considerable guard and just be himself. The guy was really uptight. Instead, Casey saw his lips flatten at her words. "I was just teasing," she added, realizing he hadn't taken it as teasing at all. Great. Her trip to Africa, complete with the threat of Black Dawn, was with an officer who was like a bow that was strung too tightly. And he was a Neanderthal on top of it all.

Looking down at his hands, she decided she liked them. He had long, lean fingers with large knuckles and there were plenty of small, pale scars all over them. She saw no wedding ring on his hand and only a watch on his left wrist. Marines didn't tend to wear a lot of jewelry, anyway. Casey felt badly for the man and opened both eyes and sat up. They were alone in the hump of the jumbo jet, and she was grateful for the privacy.

"Did you just get out of the field, Captain—I mean Reid?"

The husky warmth of her voice covered him like a blanket.

Reid stopped fidgeting with his lap belt and glanced over at her. "You might say that."

"They gave me your personnel record just before I hopped my flight from Atlanta up to D.C. And as you've already revealed, you're a Recon Marine and not from the doggy army."

He had the good grace to grin slightly. "That's right."

"How long?"

Reid knew she was making small talk for his sake. That was another nice aspect about Dr. Morrow—a sensitive awareness of others. Sometimes scientists were so caught up in their microscopic world that they rarely connected on a human or social level with normal people out of their field specialty. And he'd had many opportunities to socialize with scientists as an NBC warfare specialist.

"I've been in the corps since I graduated from college."

"That would be something like seven years? Give or take one?" She forced a bit of a smile. Though his face was rock hard, his eyes gave him away; they had turned a warm slate color as she engaged him in conversation. He'd also quit fiddling with his lap belt. Despite his tenseness, Casey liked him. She had no idea why. There was just something about the man that gave her a very protected feeling; it radiated out to her like the arms of a lover.

"Yes."

Casey smiled inwardly. "Small talk isn't your thing?"

Glancing at her, he snapped, "That's an astute observation, Doctor."

"As an officer, I'm sure you've had to cultivate it just a little?"

"Not as much as you might have hoped, Dr. Morrow." And then, defensively, he growled, "I don't think it's right that a woman be put in danger. I argued against you going on this mission."

Casey's eyes narrowed speculatively on the hard-faced officer. "Well," she began in a rigid tone of voice, "fortunately you don't have a say-so on who does or doesn't go on this mission."

Reid held her intense stare. He was getting a taste of her tough side, he realized. "Terrorists aren't your forte, Doctor. They're mine. You aren't trained for this."

"That's all right," Casey rasped. "I've got a score to settle, and right now, I've got a very sweet taste in my mouth because I *am* on this mission. Whether you like or approve of it or not, it's out of your hands." She felt her heart pumping with grief as the words flowed from her lips. Anger bubbled dangerously beneath her sorrow. She saw the marine's eyes widen momentarily, and then grow to slits as he studied her in the sudden, tension-filled silence.

"Revenge isn't the right reason to dive headlong into this mission."

The terseness in his voice made her even more determined to even the score. She'd fought for and won the right to go back to Africa for many reasons. She wasn't about to let this arrogant, unfeeling marine officer in on why, either. It was none of his damn business. But Casey couldn't help sparring with him, especially with the gut full of emotions she was feeling presently. "I'm a little shy on sleep, Reid, so don't mind me. I get giddy and silly on less than two hours...."

"Why are you short on sleep?" he asked, suddenly concerned. Reid wanted to dislike her, but somehow she had the ability to effortlessly engage him with her husky voice. A warmth flowed through him and he felt it settle in his chest. If he didn't know better, he'd say it felt like a flower had just opened to the sun's rays. Only Casey was the sun and he the flower. It was an absurd thought and Reid cursed silently. What *was* it about this mop-haired woman with sparkling green eyes that captured his tongue and made him sound like a heartless, snarling, growly old bear? She obviously wasn't going to jump his bones, although that thought had crossed his mind, making Reid wonder briefly about his sanity. The fiasco with Janet was a year old and he thought he was over it. Or maybe the carefree Dr. Morrow, whose girlish good looks, warmth and ability to set him too much at ease, was making him panic. *Why?*

Casey closed her eyes and smiled softly. "Getting ready for this trip to Africa was last minute." Her smile disappeared and she opened her eyes and looked at Reid. "Two of my best friends were just murdered in Zaire, Reid. I'm still in shock over it. Shocked and angry. Ever since it happened, a little over three weeks ago, I haven't slept well. Nightmares..." She waved her hand helplessly.

"Yes, I have revenge in my heart. I want to even the score for the sake of my friends—and someone I loved. I want to outwit those terrorists who think they can get away with this."

He studied her. The pain in her voice was real and it touched him deeply. No woman—indeed, no *one,* had ever reached inside of him the way Casey was right now. Wrestling with this unsettling discovery, Reid muttered, "I'm sorry for you, Dr. Morrow. Sorry for their families, and for your loss...."

Sitting up, Casey felt the jumbo jet slowly trundle down the runway toward the take-off point. So the robotlike officer could be vulnerable. She saw the sincerity in his eyes and heard it in his halting voice. If she didn't know better, she might believe Hunter was deeply affected by what she'd just said, but he was having an awful time wrestling with the emotions of it, much less expressing them. His apology was halting, and terribly shy and awkward. In some ways, he appeared to be like a little boy who was a bundle of violent feelings, but simply didn't have the ability to deal with them like most people did.

Stymied by her observation, Casey was intrigued by him even more. Because she was very intuitive, she felt people, felt their emotions, and many times sensed a lot about them even when they might not talk directly to her. That's how she felt about Reid. It wasn't that he was a cold automaton; it was that he was somehow disconnected from his feelings. And when he got around someone like her, who was all feelings, it put him at a decided disadvantage. In the military, emotions were suppressed and destroyed in preference to a clear head and clear thinking in dangerous circumstances. The only problem with that, Casey knew, was that emotions weren't that easy to get rid of—or to ignore. And right now, she was watching Hunter wrestle with that very problem.

His sadness for her loss was there in his eyes. His struggle to connect with the feeling was wrenching to her. Emotionally, he was like a fish out of water. Realizing this, she said very gently, "That's what I've lost sleep over—their families, Reid. At the OID, we're like a big family of sorts. You get close in our business. Losing Vince and Stan... and...someone else earlier..." she rubbed her face with her hands "...was horrible. A shock."

"So they were friends, not just employees?" Reid asked, studying her tear-filled eyes. He was surprised at her ability to express her emotions so quickly and without reservation or apology.

"Vince had two kids. I was at the hospital, with his wife, Maureen, helping her deliver them when they were born. And Stan..." Casey sniffed and leaned over and retrieved the large leather bag that served as both purse and briefcase "...he was like a brother to me." Taking out a tissue, she blew her nose and wiped it.

The urge to reach out and catch those falling tears from her eyes was nearly Reid's undoing. He *hated* to see a woman cry. It got to him faster than a bullet could and did more collateral damage. Tears tore him up every time. He supposed that was part of his Neanderthal makeup. Placing a steel clamp on his desire to reach out, frame her face with his hands and wipe her tears away with his thumbs, he sat there staring at her. Janet's words haunted him: *You're heartless, Reid. You can't reach out—ever—to someone who needs you. You're afraid. You're afraid because to reach out means you're vulnerable, too, and you can't stand the idea of being less than perfect. Heaven forbid that you'd be a fallible human being like the rest of us.*

Tucking the tissue into a side pocket, Casey placed the briefcase beneath her seat again. "We're all just reeling in shock over this," she managed to add.

"Sounds like a concussion grenade hit the OID over

this,'' he muttered uncomfortably. "I didn't realize the impact of their deaths on you."

Sniffling, Casey wiped her tears away with trembling fingers. "In our business, we're grateful for twenty-four hours of life at a time."

Reid began to understand her just a little. "So, going into the hot-zone lab a couple of times a week makes you a little more cogent about living? About life?"

She warmed at his understanding. Despite that marine-officer veneer, the man had some feelings and depth to him, after all.

Casey was pleasantly surprised, and she found herself wanting to throw herself into Reid's arms, to rest her head against his broad chest and to sob out a lot of feelings she hadn't expressed yet. It was a ridiculous urge, she realized, as she sat there staring at his hard, unyielding face. It was his warm gray eyes with those huge, black pupils that held her—and her heart—in their sway. Sniffing again, she whispered, "Life? In my business, it's one heartbeat at a time. One inhalation, one exhalation."

"I can see that...." And he could. One slip of a scalpel, one bone sticking out of a dead carcass filled with virulent Ebola could slit into the protective gloves she wore to do autopsies, and result in her death. Feeling suddenly suffocated by that possibility, because Casey Morrow was one of the most alive people he'd ever met, Reid fell silent.

The jumbo jet halted and the engines began to whine at a high pitch. Reid knew that in a few moments, the huge bird would launch skyward. He tried to relax as he sat back in preparation for takeoff. But when he heard Casey sniff and blow her nose again, the pain in him, like a huge fist pushing up from his heart into his chest and throat, forced him to do something he'd never done before. Seeing her left hand on the armrest, he reached out and covered it with his own.

Chapter Three

As the jumbo jet powered down the runway toward take-off speed, Reid kept his hand over Casey's. The fear of reaching out dissolved. The initial shock over what he'd just done was gone. Instead, new feelings—damn them—grew. A warmth filled his heart and then lapped outward, gently, wonderfully, and he held his breath, surprised by it all. The warmth moved downward and a new sensation replaced it. He ached to glide his fingertips across her soft skin. He found himself wanting to do many things with her. But Reid resisted. Since his debacle with Janet, he'd lost interest in women this past year—or so he'd thought. Until this red-haired hellion, who brooked no fools in her life, crashed into his unexpectedly.

Reid didn't look up to gauge Casey's reaction to his touch. He could no more explain to her his spontaneous reaction than he could to himself. Telling himself she was like a hurt animal that needed care, he let it go at that. Though he expected Casey to withdraw her hand, she didn't. Maybe Janet had been wrong. Maybe he did have feelings, after all. Maybe he wasn't the cold, unfeeling machine she'd accused him of being. A tiny thread of hope moved through his heavily walled heart.

As the jet became airborne, he released a breath caught deep inside his chest and allowed the pressure of gravity to press him against the seat. Closing his eyes, Hunter felt his awareness moving deep within himself, creating a volatile mix of feelings. An ache was centering in his lower body, a hunger that hadn't been fulfilled or fed for a long, long time. Simultaneously, the sense of need—for Casey— serrated him and unexpectedly opened up his guarded heart like a knife. It was a painful sensation for Reid; the need for a woman was something he didn't want to feel again. And not just any woman. He wondered how Casey felt about his hand over hers. Did she read it as sexual harassment? One human consoling another? What? How badly he wanted to ask. How scared he was of doing so. He'd never reached out like this before, so he had no experience, no way of knowing how she was responding to it. On another level, Hunter felt like he'd just stepped on a claymore mine in the middle of a field. If he stepped off it, the whole thing would blow up in his face. If he remained standing on it, he was still in danger. What was he to do?

Casey stopped sniffling as Reid's long, powerful fingers draped protectively over her own. She felt instant relief from her grief as his hand covered hers. She knew his gesture wasn't a sexual or provocative one. No, she sensed he was trying to comfort her even though he was painfully uncomfortable with her tears, with her easy display of emotions. Something good and healing flowed from his warm fingertips into hers. Casey knew more than most what it took to allow oneself to remain open and vulnerable. It was easy, very easy, to close up like a book or a fortress and not let people in, not feel the full array of emotions. Somehow, as the jet took off, the gravity pressing like invisible hands against her, she felt safe, if but for a moment.

Sensing tension in Reid's hand, she finally pulled hers free from beneath his as the jet continued to climb high into the deep blue, sunlit sky. Pretending to need another tissue, Casey busied herself momentarily. She felt Reid shift abruptly next to her. Blotting her eyes free of the last of her tears, she turned and studied his hard, chiseled profile. His face appeared carved from granite, there was no doubt. Yet for all his rocklike hardness, he had a heart and a soul of compassion, or else he would not have reached out as he had to comfort her. She saw the turmoil and confusion in his eyes, too. The hesitancy in his manner toward her. She sensed he felt as if he'd done something wrong. *No,* Casey wanted to tell him, *you've done everything right—despite yourself.* But she chose not to say anything. Hunter didn't appear ready for that kind of discussion right now. Instead, she turned to another topic to try and soothe the torment she saw in his eyes.

"Every summer I climb El Capitan, a huge granite cliff at Yosemite," she began softly, to catch his attention. When Reid barely turned his head, his gray eyes almost colorless now, the pupils dark and inquiring, Casey's breath hitched. She read desire in the depths of his intense, intelligent gaze. Maybe she was wrong. Probably was. Right now, the way she felt, she was interested in no one on that level. Grief over Vince's and Stan's death had hit her hard and she was still reeling from the shock of it all, the reminders of her earlier painful loss. With a weak wave of her hand, Casey whispered, "Anyone looking at that gray granite face would think it was hard and unyielding." She held up her palm. "When I place my hand against the rock, though, I feel the mountain's spirit. I feel its heart, a pulsing life within the stone I am climbing." She shook her head, one corner of her mouth lifting ruefully. "The stone is warm, like skin.... It has a heart. And as I climb higher and higher on the face, I feel my heart opening to it and I begin to feel an incredible oneness with the granite, with the spirit that lives captured within that stone.''

Reid stared at her hand. Beyond the clean and bluntly cut nails, he saw small, yellowed calluses sprinkled across her palm, indicating that she was an active rock climber. He saw old scars, too, garnered from such exercises against nature and death. She had long fingers—long and expressive—and he hotly wondered what it would be like if she trailed them languidly across his flesh. How would he react? Swallowing hard, he realized his thoughts were not at all appropriate as he held her warm, tearful gaze. But her lips were slightly parted and just begging to be touched, tamed and brought into union with his.

Disconcerted, Reid forced himself to listen to her on a deeper level. ''What has the mountain taught you, then?'' he asked, his voice gruff with more emotion than he wanted to hear in it.

''It has taught me that even stone has a heart, has feeling....'' She gazed at him thoughtfully. *You think you're made of stone, too, but you're not. I see inside you. I feel your heart, whether you want me to or not....* All those words remained deep within Casey even though she wanted to blurt them out to Reid. She was hoping he'd understand her analogy.

Turning her hand, she studied it momentarily and then allowed it to rest in her lap. The desire burning in his eyes was very real to Casey. She found herself a little breathless and more than a little needy. How could she feel all these things at a time like this? Steve had died a year ago. Her heart was still torn and bleeding from his horrible, unexpected death. But Reid Hunter's intense inspection made her feel vulnerable in a feminine way that she'd *never* felt before, with any man. What was going on?

"Climbing that rock face is like continuously taunting death. Is that what you like to do? Face death?"

He had remarkable insight. Much more than Casey would have originally given Reid credit for. "I do it daily, anyway. Does it matter if it's a virus that might infect me in the lab, or if I miss a handhold on the rock and fall to my death?"

Her words were visceral and he felt his gut tighten at the thought of Casey falling off that sheer rock face. Even though she had the looks of a college girl, she was a courageous woman warrior. A throwback, maybe, to that red-haired Celtic queen who had challenged the entire Roman Empire so long ago. Queen Boudicca and Casey had a lot in common.

Reid saw the challenge in her darkening green eyes as they met and held his gaze. There was an energy connection between them, too, he discovered. He was as physically aware of it as he was of her closeness, of that faint, spicy fragrance she wore on her skin.

Meeting her gaze, he said, "They say that from the moment we're born, we begin to die."

Her lips curved. "Just as I thought, Captain. You are a man of great depth and philosophy. Not to mention a die-hard pragmatist."

"Death always gets my attention."

"What about living?" She saw him scowl as he looked away.

"I don't know what you mean." His heart thumped hard to underscore the sudden panic he felt by her incisive question. She could see straight through him, just as Janet had—only Casey was far more insightful, and gentler in some ways. For that, Hunter, who tried to consciously tell himself to relax, was grateful.

"In your work, at least according to the file I was given on you, you're in the business of death and dying, too."

"So, what does that make us, good doctor?" he teased

abruptly. "Two people unable to live? Too scared to live? Too frightened to jump into that pot called life and take real chances and play emotional roulette? You tell me."

The parry—riposte with him was new to Casey. "You don't go for social talk, you go for the jugular, instead." She grinned a little. Casey knew she'd just scored a direct hit on his most vital area of contention. She saw his face flush—just like a young schoolboy's. So he was truly like a teenage boy with his emotions.

Reid liked the glow her smile brought to her freckled cheeks. It became her. Aching to reach out and glide his fingertips across them, to feel her soft, firm skin, was nearly Reid's undoing. "You're the one who likes honesty, remember? And no, I'm not very skilled at social graces. Maybe that's why I'm still a captain and not a major. I lack the ability to employ those social tools properly in order to climb through the ranks."

"Does it bother you, this lack of social graces?" Casey asked, intrigued. She was mesmerized by him. This was not the normal kind of man she usually encountered. He didn't play games. He was painfully honest even if it meant revealing his weak points. Reid had to have a very healthy ego in order to do that, and Casey had never met someone who had that kind of solid confidence. And yet he skittered around his emotional terrain as if allowing himself to truly feel would be his death.

"No. Maybe it was because I was raised in the wilds of the Rockies. I spent a lot of time fishing and hunting as a kid growing up. Probably more time watching wildlife than killing it. My dad taught me not to kill unless I was going to eat it. I spent a lot of time out in sunlit meadows watching life come and go without me interfering with it via a rifle."

"I haven't met many military men who were natural born killers."

Reid slanted a hard glance at her. "No," he said slowly, "I see us as protectors, not killers. We defend."

As the jumbo jet leveled off, the pressure of gravity against her eased. Casey had seen the flare of anger in his eyes when she made her statement. "You're very protective." *Of me.* But she didn't say that. She felt it to her core. To her bones. He gave her a brusque nod.

"To my detriment at times," he added sourly.

"Oh?"

He saw merriment in her green eyes, a gentle baiting. Reid was sure she knew who he was protective of. "Okay, I'll bite. Women and children. They need our protection."

"Hmm, Neanderthal to the core, aren't you?"

Her teasing was light and he took it in that vein. "I've been accused of it from time to time, Doctor. I'm sure on this little jaunt I'll hear it at least a couple times a day, aren't you?"

"Neanderthals have their place in our world. Not around me, however." She smiled a little and then sobered. "Better a protector than a hothead with a rifle in his hands," she commented dryly. "Because where we're going you aren't going to be carrying many weapons."

"I'll be carrying a 9 mm on my person all the time," he warned her in a low tone. "That's my job this time around. Being a Neanderthal guard dog—of sorts...."

Casey felt shaken by his sudden intensity. This man was a warrior. Just the clear look in his narrowed eyes sent a chill down her spine—for whomever his enemy might be. "Do you..." she hesitated, then licked her lower lip. "Do you really expect trouble?"

"From the moment we land."

Feeling cold, Casey rubbed her hands up and down her arms. "Do you feel it will be that dangerous that soon?"

Shrugging, Reid saw the seat belt sign come off. He unstrapped himself and got up to stretch. "We'd be fools to play it otherwise."

As he rose, Casey appreciated his powerful physique. He was built like a swimmer, not like some musclebound gym maniac who worked out for hours every day. There was athletic balance to the marine officer. As he took off his sport coat and hung it over his seat, she appreciated the sculpted muscling of his arms. Strong arms. And hands that could hold a deadly weapon to kill with, if necessary. Again a chill worked down her spine.

As he flexed his hands, she watched the muscles work in his forearms. He was heavily tanned, and she suspected that he wasn't an office paper pusher—rather, any chance he got, he was outdoors with his men. Out in nature once again, as he'd been as a boy growing up. Nature didn't demand emotions of him, either, she thought as she smiled to herself.

"Isn't it funny how our childhood follows us around like a good friend?" Casey whispered as she unsnapped her own seat belt and eased out of the chair. She wriggled her toes and dug them into the carpeting. There was something about texture that she enjoyed. Reid was walking around the cabin until she spoke. Then he stopped and devoted his full attention to her. Again that sense of protection, like a thick, warm blanket, fell around her shoulders and embraced her. Maybe it was the slate color of his eyes as he held her gaze. Or maybe it was the softening at the corners of his hard, thinned mouth as he studied her in the building silence.

"What do you mean?"

Casey smiled a little. "When I was a kid growing up in the Cascade Mountains of Oregon, I was always climbing. I have a younger sister and two older brothers, and I was forever being found on some cliff with my rope and climbing gear."

"Your parents were rock climbers?"

"No."

"What does your father do?"

Casey felt an old pain in her heart stir to life. She slowly walked around the cabin. "He was a medical doctor. He died of a rare strep infection when I was twelve years old. It came as a real shock. One day he was alive, the next, dead."

"Sorry," Reid offered gruffly. He saw the pain on her face. Every emotion she had registered there, he was discovering. "What about your mother? She a rock climber, then?"

Shaking her head, Casey forced a sad smile. For some unknown reason, she was allowing him into her personal life, her personal world. Why, she had no idea. "No, my mom had her hands full with the four of us. She had opted to stay home to raise us, since my dad made enough money to support us."

"Probably got tougher after he died?"

"Very. My mom had to take welfare for a while until she got on her feet. My brothers and I found odd jobs and helped pull in money so we were able to get off public assistance."

"Twelve years old and you were working?"

She put her hands behind her back and halted a few feet from him. "I got a part-time job with our veterinarian down the street. I cleaned animal cages and did odd jobs for him. Actually, I feel Dr. Channing took me on as an excuse to contribute money to our struggling family. He was best friends with my dad before he died."

"And yet," Reid noted, "you became a virologist. Maybe the years you spent in the vet's office helped you decide what you wanted to do with your life."

"In part, yes. I was angry for a long time over dad dying. I developed a hatred for germs. Dr. Channing used to set me up with slides and the microscope and teach me about lab testing procedures. Pretty soon, I got curious about all these bugs." She smiled a little. "By the time I was fourteen, I was taking college prep classes and I knew

I wanted to be a virologist.'' Her smile disappeared. ''I didn't want another family to lose a loved one like we did. I was bound and determined to find out about viruses and bacteria and understand them, so that they couldn't take the amount of lives they had in the past.''

''I think that your father would be proud of you.''

She arched at his gruffly spoken compliment. Releasing her hands, she clasped them in front of her. ''I hope so.'' Sighing, Casey lifted her hands and gently massaged the back of her neck. ''Sometimes I feel like I'm in a war and we're losing the battle. The more we know about viruses and bacteria, the less we know.'' She gazed at his somber face. ''At least on days when I don't get enough sleep, that's how I feel.''

''And days when you do?''

''I feel more hopeful.''

Reid went and sat down in his chair. He wished he had Casey's ease with herself so he could comfortably shed his new hiking boots, which weren't broken in yet. He'd like to stretch his feet a little, too. ''With the viruses and bacteria mutating every time we make an antibiotic, your work must keep you busy.''

''Ugh, that!'' Casey walked over and sat down next to him. ''The bugs are winning in that area. It's only a matter of time before the superbugs outdistance our latest antibiotics and we become really vulnerable.'' Her mouth twisted. ''And then I'll be back at square one, just like things were in the days when my dad got sick. The strep that killed him was lethal. There was nothing available to stop it.''

''Well,'' he murmured, feeling more and more relaxed around Casey, ''we're both up against a real-time killer— Ebola.''

She studied him in the semidarkness of the cabin. The light cut across his features and emphasized his strength and warriorlike hardness. The thinned set of his mouth told her a lot about his feelings about Ebola. "I saw in your file that you have a Bachelor of Science in microbiology. I was impressed. What I can't figure out is how you ended up in the Marine Corps."

He met her winsome smile with a hesitant grin. "As a kid, I used to put drops of water from streams and lakes under a microscope. I was mesmerized by how busy seemingly clear, clean water really was."

"No such thing as dead water," Casey agreed with a chuckle. "So, your love of nature got you that degree?"

Reid found himself wanting to share a lot with her. That wasn't prudent, he realized. If he didn't keep some distance from Casey, how could he protect her? She was far too easy to like, and to talk with. Maybe it was her nurturing qualities that reached out to him. He could tell by the interest in her eyes that she genuinely wanted to hear what he had to say or thought. Opening his hands, he said, "You could say that."

"And how did you make the quantum leap from microbiologist to Marine Corps?"

"Sounds a little crazy, doesn't it?" He watched as she flashed him a grin. When Casey threaded her fingers through her mussed hair, he saw gold, burgundy and crimson highlights dance beneath the lighting in the cabin.

"I learned a long time ago that crazy makes the world go 'round."

He didn't disagree. Rubbing his hands against his thighs, he said, "My dad is a professor of biology at Colorado State University. My mother is a medical doctor."

"So..." Casey raised her eyes "...you got the degree because your parents wanted you to?"

"Somewhat," he hedged. "I really wanted to be a doctor. I'd taken premed."

"How did the Marine Corps get your attention?"

"It promised me adventure. I was sick and tired of book learning, lab work and too many classrooms. I craved the fresh air, the heat on my skin and the rain against my face. They promised me Recons and let me be the paramedic on the team. They delivered.'' He looked up. ''And here I am, on an elite NBC warfare team flying halfway around the world hunting two types of enemies at once—one we can see and the other we can't.''

Sobering, Casey leaned back. ''It's the ones we can see that have me worried. No one has been able to confirm many of Black Dawn's terrorists by name or photograph.''

''The few we have are here, in my briefcase,'' he said, gesturing to the black briefcase beneath his seat. ''I'll need you to look at them and commit them to memory before we land at Kinshasa.''

Rubbing her eyes, she said, ''Let me catch some shut-eye first? I'm running low on reserves, with only two hours of sleep under my belt.''

Patting his shoulder, Reid said, ''If you need a pillow, here I am.'' Why had he said that? He saw the look of surprise mirrored on Casey's features. The laughter that followed embraced him like a familiar lover.

''An officer and a gentleman to the last.'' Casey reached out, her fingers itching to make contact with this hard, athletic officer. As her fingers slid across his broad, capable shoulder, heat arced up her hand and into her arm. Instantly, her heart beat a little harder. His eyes narrowed upon her like a predator's. Mouth a little dry, Casey removed her fingers. She had felt his flesh tighten briefly at her light contact. He was all muscle, bone and tension.

''I'm well known for tossing and turning a lot in my sleep,'' she warned him throatily as she settled back into her chair. ''So just ignore me if I do try to use you as a big, overstuffed pillow.''

Grinning belatedly, Reid relaxed more. ''There's worse things that could happen, good doctor.'' A lot worse, but he didn't say that. The possibility of her lying against his shoulder was inviting. He found himself wishing badly that it would occur. Looking down at the watch on his wrist, he murmured, "Go to sleep. We're got a long time in transit yet. I'll wake you when it's time to get down to business."

Closing her eyes, Casey nodded. "For a Neanderthal, you're pretty decent, Captain."

"Thank you, Doctor, I'll take that as a compliment, coming from you."

Casey felt the corners of her mouth curve upward. The feeling of protection embraced her once more. She felt safe with Reid. Very safe and cared for. *Cared for?* Where had that thought come from? Too exhausted and sleep deprived, she just didn't have the energy to pursue the question in her head, though her heart continued to sense his tender regard. Casey hadn't felt this tired in a long time, but she understood the reasons for it. Not only was she still in shock over the deaths of her good friends and scared about going back to Zaire, she was excited about being able to perform fieldwork again and possibly finding the Ebola reservoir once and for all. But as sleep spiraled her into a warm cocoon of darkness and rest, Reid's hard face appeared before her. It was his eyes, her heart whispered, that told her he liked her more than just a little. There was such magnetism pulsing and throbbing between them, so alive and palpable to her. The last thought Casey had was that she had to somehow curb herself and not let the marine officer know how much she honestly *did* like him. Neanderthal or not...

Reid sat very quietly. When the flight attendant came up to take their dinner order, he waved him away. Casey rested her head against his shoulder. She was sleeping deeply. Peacefully. And she had been right: she was a tosser and turner. Sometimes, during the last six hours of flight, she had turned the other way and he'd gotten up to stretch and walk around the cabin. The darkness outside the window was complete now as they flew toward Africa.

In those hours he'd had a chance to study her. Concerned with how he was reacting to Casey—as a woman, not as a mission or a priority in the military sense—Reid found his emotions unraveling faster than he could stuff them back inside himself. It was one helluva disconcerting feeling. Ordinarily, it was the easiest thing in the world for him to shove them aside. But with Casey, his emotions were like a can of worms that refused to stay in the can. He found himself constantly scrambling to avoid what he was feeling or what he wanted to do, which was reach out, touch, hold, feel her and comfort her. What a crazy day this was.

Once they landed at Kinshasa Airport in Zaire, their lives would be in constant jeopardy. He was sure the Black Dawn knew they were coming. He was sure they would have spies looking for them. Casey was a well-known individual in the world of biology—epidemiology and virology in particular. With her mop of red hair, she'd be an easy target to spot coming off a plane.

His thoughts veered from military tactics and strategy into more molten desires as she stretched her long, lean body, reminding him of a svelte racing greyhound. It made him go hot with longing. Even the way Casey's lips parted during sleep haunted him. Her lower lip was full, soft looking, and he wondered what it would be like to press his mouth against hers. What would she feel like? Taste like? Every woman had a different taste, a different texture. And the desire to simply skim his fingers over the lush expanse of her freckled face and tunnel his fingers into that mussed red hair of hers made him ache.

Easing himself out of his seat once more, he slowly walked around the expanse of the cabin. He wondered why Casey was engaging all of his senses like this. No woman ever had before. Was it just some latent reaction to Janet?

Something deep in him that was crying out for a woman's touch? A woman's embrace? Was it the nurturing that Casey effortlessly extended to him that had fanned something within him back to hot, burning life? Reid shook his head and rubbed his face. Tiredness was beginning to stalk him in earnest.

An hour ago, he had gently reclined Casey's chair so that it was fully laid out, much like a bed. He'd retrieved a couple of blankets and spread them across her to keep her warm, after which her tossing and turning had abated to a great extent. Walking over now, he reclined his own seat and pulled down some blankets for himself. Turning off the overhead lights on a side panel, Reid found himself stretching out, his feet hanging out over the end of the seat. Tall people sometimes suffered, and he grinned tiredly. Moving onto his side so he faced the sleeping Casey, he watched her in the constantly glowing bulkhead lights, which highlighted her peaceful, sleeping features.

Her red lashes were thick and lay against her freckled cheeks. The darkness he'd seen beneath her eyes was disappearing during her deep, uninterrupted sleep. Her hands were beneath her cheek. She looked like an angel, Reid decided as he felt his lids grow heavy. An angel in a warrior woman's body. What a combination. A chuckle emanated from his chest as he pictured her with angel wings and an armor breastplate, shield and sword in hand. What a vision. One always thought of angels as…well, gentle, peaceful beings. And then Reid reminded himself that the archangel Michael was known as the Destroyer. Nope, scratch that. Angels could be warriors, too. A warmth spread across his chest as his lids closed, a slight smile lingering across his mouth.

The only thing Reid wished was that the inches separating their chairs would disappear. Then he could reach out, extend his arm and draw that tall, lean body of Casey's toward him. Yes, she'd fit nicely beside him—curvy and soft in all the right places. How long had it been since he'd lain with a woman? Far too long, Reid told himself. And Casey, whether she knew it or not, was alluring. Even now, he could inhale the faint scent of the spicy perfume she wore. As he spiraled down into sleep, Reid knew that this was the last time he could sleep deeply and soundly. He knew that when they awoke, he'd have to be on guard until they stepped back on board a plane bound stateside. If they ever did… *If* they survived Black Dawn. *If* they weren't infected by Ebola. So many ifs…and their lives weren't guaranteed in any way, shape or form.…

Chapter Four

Casey felt strong, caring fingers close over her shoulder, firm and yet gentle. She wanted to continue to sleep, and gave a little moan of protest as the fingers moved in a light, circular massage across her skin. How long had it been since she'd felt a touch like this—light, yet somehow inviting? Even before she managed to drag her lashes upward, her body was responding to his touch. *Reid Hunter cares for you,* her heart whispered as she felt his fingers trace the outline of her blanketed shoulder. She heard him call her name. He was close. Very close. His tone was intimate. Deep. Somehow, he was teasing her awake and her suddenly vibrant senses clamored for more of his touch.

"Uhh…" Casey muttered as she forced her eyes open and lifted her head.

With scant inches separating them, Reid managed an awkward, pasted-on smile. She looked like a little girl, her hair a glorious, messy mop, her green eyes cloudy with sleep, her lips parted and vulnerable looking. ''Time to get up, sleepy head.'' Forcing himself to remove his hand from her shoulder, Reid remained in a crouched position. He didn't want to wake her, but eight hours of solid, uninterrupted sleep was all he could give her. In a couple of hours, they'd be landing at Kinshasa Airport, and he needed her fully awake and on guard. The country was in turmoil, and nothing and no one could be counted on or trusted.

Pulling herself up into a sitting position, Casey felt the blankets slip off her upper body and pool around her waist and hips. Rubbing her eyes, she moved slowly. The blankets dragged along with her as she placed her feet on the carpeted floor. She heard Reid chuckle indulgently as he rose fluidly to his full height from his kneeling position beside her seat.

''Who took care of you before I walked into your life, Doctor? There's a definite need for a Neanderthal man, from what I can see....'' He leaned over and carefully untangled the rumpled blankets from around her legs. Her silk skirt was badly crushed and crinkled. The smooth, firm curve of her calf was briefly visible until he tactfully pulled her skirt down so that it fell around her thin ankles once again.

Sitting there, her elbows planted on her thighs, her hands pressed against her face, Casey struggled to wake up. She heard Reid's teasing, deep voice with its delicious sense of care. She felt the blankets being pulled away. ''I need coffee,'' she croaked from behind her hands. ''Any kind of coffee. Could you...?''

Folding the blankets neatly, Reid placed them in the overhead bin. ''Coffee? I'll see what I can do. Stay put. I'll be back.''

Somehow, Casey felt bereft when Reid left the upper cabin and walked down to the lower area of the jumbo jet. She slowly lifted her head and removed her hands from

her face. Without his larger-than-life presence, she did feel
more than a little vulnerable. Shaking her head, she rubbed
her eyes.

"You are certifiably nuts, Casey Jean Morrow," she
muttered defiantly to herself. "This guy—this Neanderthal—crashed into your life, and you'd think you were
nothing more than a bowl full of gelatin when he's around.
Geeze oh whiz, girl, get ahold of yourself...."

Pushing herself to her feet, Casey stretched languidly
and felt each of her main muscle groups responding in
kind. The chair had been comfortable, far more so than
she'd anticipated. And Reid, bless him, had thoughtfully
covered her with blankets to keep her warm as her body
temperature dropped in sleep. Yes, he was a protector;
there was no doubt about that. In many, many ways.
Touching her rumpled, white silk blouse, Casey studied it
for a good minute before she realized she needed to change
into her field clothes, which were far more utilitarian. Africa demanded brutal practicality. Her olive green cotton,
one-piece suit, with official-looking OID patches identi-
fying her, would be the uniform of the day.

Hearing a sound, she turned. Reid was climbing back
up the stairs with a small tray in hand. On it was a large
decanter of hot coffee, two china cups, silverware, milk
and sugar. Her lips pulled into a welcoming smile.

"I don't believe this," she murmured huskily as she
followed him over to their chairs. Inhaling the fragrance
of the coffee, she sighed audibly. "Coffee..."

Reid poured her some. He tried to stop feeling proud
and pleased as she stroked him with that deliciously husky
voice of hers. He wondered how she could so easily show
her emotions to him like this. "How do you like it?"

"Black, strong and hot," she said, leaning forward, her
hand outstretched.

Reid placed the cup and saucer in her hand. Their fingers touched briefly. Momentary, pleasurable tingles arced

up through his hand. He studied her still-sleepy features. Her eyes were puffy looking, and there was some cloudiness in her half-open green eyes. "It's fresh. When I told the flight attendant in what bad shape you were, he took pity on you and made a fresh pot."

Sitting down, Casey gratefully tasted the aromatic coffee. "Mmm," she whispered gratefully, "don't ever let it be said that you aren't a lifesaver, Captain."

A pleasurable warmth stole through his heart again, lapping outward through his entire chest cavity. They were feelings of joy, he realized. Something he'd not felt in a long, long time and certainly never to this degree or intensity. Scrambling, he sat down next to her and poured himself some of the coffee. "I think that you need to drop my military title and call me Reid. Or maybe I should say it again after you've woken up more?"

A careless smile crossed her face. She sipped the coffee religiously. "You're right—I'm not in the OID, where titles abound, but in fieldwork again. Thank *you*, Reid. You are truly a guardian angel."

Chuckling shyly, Reid savored his own coffee. "Even Neanderthals have their place in your world, eh, Doctor?" He preened silently beneath her heartfelt compliment.

Casey met his smiling eyes. She wondered what his face would look like if he fully smiled or laughed. Did Reid laugh? He was so serious and conservative in appearance. Yet so sensitive to *her* needs. The two didn't quite equate. To laugh would mean he'd have to be in touch with his feelings, and that seemed to be the last option on his list. "You're an enigma, Cap—I mean, Reid."

"Why? Because I'm a caveman throwback in a modern world that doesn't need them anymore?"

"No," Casey said between sips, "it's more than that...but I need to know you for a longer time and be less sleepy than I am right now to figure out the angles on you."

"Uh-oh, this sounds serious." Reid saw her sleepy, tentative smile. His heart opened, and it felt good. He was discovering he liked to make Casey smile—even if it was at the expense of his starchy, conservative Marine Corps image and way of living. Opposites attract, he told himself. And Casey was the diametric opposite, in some ways, to Janet, who had left him standing at the altar on their wedding day. Total, complete opposites. The one thing the two women had in common was their emotional vulnerability. Casey was much more open with her emotions, however. Was that why his heart pounded a little quicker when Casey bestowed that playful, little-girl smile upon him? It was a child's smile of delight, of utter spontaneous joy in the moment.

"How soon before we land in Kinshasa?"

Reid glanced at his watch. "Two hours."

Wrinkling her nose, Casey whispered between mouthfuls of coffee, "Good. I need to change and get into my working gear."

Eyeing her outfit, he murmured, "I kind of like you in what you have on now."

"Silk doesn't cut it near the equator, Reid. Right now, we're entering the beginning of the rainy season up north in Zaire. Heat, humidity and on-and-off rain. Whatta combo. Not my favorite thing." She looked at her hand. "My fingers swell up like sausages on some days. I hate it."

"Does it affect your head, too?"

Chuckling, she slanted him a glance. One corner of his mouth was curved. "You're a kidder, Hunter."

"Takes one to know one, right?" He enjoyed her liveliness and repartee. Laughter shone in her eyes as she sat there, both hands around her coffee cup as if she were worshipping it. He understood her need for good coffee. He appreciated a strong brew himself.

"I'm glad you can tease and be teased." She lost a bit

of her smile and stared at the grayish colored bulkhead. "When things get tense, I really get cracking the one-liners. Just so you know ahead of time, okay?"

"No problem."

"According to the state department, things aren't too settled in Zaire right now."

"They haven't been for a long time," Reid answered dryly. "Why should it be any different for us?"

"It means we may have to punt. The last time I was in Zaire, for three months of fieldwork, the pilot of the C-130 that was supposed to fly us into Yambuku, on the Ebola River, refused to. He thought he'd get Ebola just by landing on the dirt airstrip outside that little village."

"So, how'd you persuade him?"

"Money. American dollars. One of ours is worth a hundred and ten thousand of theirs."

"That's an economy out of control."

"No kidding." She waved her hand. "Greenbacks talk over there. The pilot got a ten-dollar bill and flew us in. It took a twenty-dollar bill to get him to come back in three months to pick us up. By their standards, he was a very, very rich man after those two flights."

Reid grew thoughtful. "With the rainy season being in effect for a month, the only way we're going to get around is by plane. What few roads there are in Zaire, the dirt ones, aren't negotiable."

"No," Casey agreed unhappily, "it's nothing but pigs in a quagmire, frankly."

"Is that what you feel like?"

She chuckled and poured herself a second cup of coffee.

"I've been in Zaire so many times over the last five years, I've lost count. I've been there in the dry season and the rainy season. Where we're going is in the rain forest. Just on the edge of it. The Ebola River, which flows into the Congo River, drains the northernmost part of this incredible rain forest. North of it is rolling savanna."

Reid poured himself another cup, enjoying her company. "According to my info, we'll be going in to a small village located on the edge of the savanna, a huge grassy plain."

Nodding, Casey said, "Vince and Stan were staying at a local village with Chief Henri Movasankani. He's the hereditary Bantu chieftain of his tribe—one of the few remaining. It'll be good to see Grandfather Henri." She pronounced his name with a French accent.

"You know him?"

Casey twisted her head to look at Reid. She saw the intensity in his eyes, his powerful attention focused on her and what she had to say. She understood that as a marine, the more he knew, the more he could anticipate concerning their security. "Yes. For five years. Grandfather is around eighty-five now. He's a tough old buzzard, lean and starved lookin', but he's smart as a whip. No one can fool that old man in the least. He's partially blind now with cataracts, but that doesn't stop him from leading his village of around five hundred families."

"Do you think he'll know who killed Vince and Stan?"

Her brows fell. "I don't know. It's something I intend to ask him as soon as we arrive."

"Do you think he's involved with Black Dawn?"

Snorting, Casey straightened up. "Grandfather Henri is one of the most trusted people I know in Zaire. He's worked with the OID and other international scientific agencies for years. He wants Ebola found, too. It has killed fifty of his people over the years. No, he's completely trustworthy, Reid."

"Think he can identify any of the Black Dawn members who might have killed Vince and Stan, then?"

She shrugged. "I really don't know. I hope he can...or one of his people can. Terrorists aren't always easy to pick out of a crowd. You know more about that than most."

"They blend in," he agreed. "Still, if Chief Movasankani is on top of things, he'll know who looks familiar, who is a stranger to his territory.''

"That," Casey said grimly, "is what I'm counting on to help keep us safe while we do our job."

"Speaking of our job," Reid said, placing his cup on the tray and reaching for his briefcase, "are you awake enough to look at some photos and memorize some names? We've got a few Black Dawn individuals in custody. They aren't talking about their cohorts, but running through their bios might help you."

Nodding, Casey said, "Sure, let's look at these bastards."

Cutting her a glance as he reached for a file, he said, "Why, Doctor, I wouldn't think you'd use cuss words."

"Watch me. If things get hot and heavy out there, I revert back to my teenage rebellion years in one helluva hurry. My mother used to wash my mouth out with soap, too."

He saw the warrior in her eyes and grinned tightly. "Maybe you aren't going to be such a liability in the bush after all, Doctor."

"You'll *want* me at your back if things start happening, Captain. Believe me," Casey warned him throatily. "I may not be an expert on SKSs, but I can handle a 9 mm with the best of 'em."

Musing about her husky warning, Reid handed the file to her. "Well, if nothing else, you'll probably be an expert at throwing rocks at them."

With a howl, Casey bubbled into laughter. She *liked* this marine. Maybe too much. The laughter dancing in his slate-colored eyes was unmistakable. "I'm really glad you're with me on this little jaunt, Captain."

"Yeah?" he baited. Was he hearing things? Casey *wanted* him on this mission? What had changed about him? Or maybe it was the way she looked at him that had changed. Her perception, the fact that she could see straight through him, walls and all, was disconcerting and uncomfortable. Yet somehow Reid realized that Casey wasn't the threat that Janet had been to him…to his deeply guarded emotions. There was a gentleness to Casey that Janet had never had. Maybe that was the difference? Hunter wasn't sure at all. This stuff with emotions was too damn new to him, and he felt so unsure of himself.

"Yeah, roger that."

He was relieved that Casey had experience working with military individuals. She knew the lingo. She knew the behavior patterns, and that was important, especially if things got a little tense or dangerous. And where they were going, it was going to be dangerous—all the time. If not from the threat of Ebola, then because of the unstable government, the various tribal wars that were constantly flaring up across the land. Then there was the treat of the dreaded, fanatical Black Dawn terrorists. No, when they landed at Kinshasa, all bets were off. It was only a question of *when* they would be in danger, not *if.*

There was a pall of rain across the countryside when they disembarked from the jumbo jet and made their way down slippery, wet stairs toward customs at Kinshasa N'Djili Airport in the Democratic Republic of the Congo, formerly known as Zaire. Reid proffered an umbrella and held it high enough that he and Casey could take some cover from the pounding rain. The tarmac was shiny with wetness. Soldiers in jungle fatigues stood at the bottom of the staircase and motioned for them to hurry up. The temperature was warm, perhaps in the eighties, from what Reid could judge. Though it was midday, the clouds moving slowly above the capital city's airport gave the sky a dark and murky look.

At the bottom of the stairs, Reid automatically placed his arm around Casey's shoulders and drew her next to him as they walked. She gave him a startled look, but didn't withdraw from his protection, either. Reid could taste the tension in the humid air. The looks on the soldiers' faces reflected it as well. They wore SKSs, and he could see that the safeties were off. Their hands seemed a little too quick to touch the trigger guard as the passengers disembarked.

Everyone was speaking in French, the main language of the former Belgian Congo. Luckily, Reid knew French as well as he did English. And so did Casey, according to the profile he'd read on her. What did surprise him was when two soldiers who stood on guard began speaking in Bantu. He didn't know what they were saying.

Casey leaned up and whispered, "There's trouble, Reid."

He glanced down at her, his stride slowing momentarily. "What kind?"

"Apparently a rival force is attacking near the airport, from what those two guards were saying back there."

Looking around, he keyed his hearing for the sound of gunshots. Casey was looking around, too.

"Which direction?" he demanded.

"I don't know. They didn't say." She grimaced, her mouth thinning. "And I'm not about to give myself away by asking them in Bantu."

"No, don't," he warned heavily. Knowing the second language of Zaire was a big plus. "What're the chances of the guards knowing English?"

She shrugged as they hurried toward the terminal doors, which were guarded by four soldiers. "Dicey. They know just enough to be dangerous. Stick to French and play dumb, okay? Customs can be a son of a bitch to get through...."

Meeting her worried gaze, he grinned tightly. "Doctor, my mother used to wash my mouth out with soap when I said a cuss word, too."

"Better have plenty on hand then, with me around," she warned gruffly.

Reid chuckled, the sound coming from deep in his chest as they moved up the rain-slick concrete steps that led to customs. Once inside the linoleum-floored area, where a number of customs people stared darkly at them, Reid removed his passport and handed it to a tall, older official. Reid's cover was the OID. On paper he was Dr. Morrow's lab assistant. Trying to suppress his worry, Reid watched as Casey presented her own passport to an official sitting behind an impressive-looking desk of carved mahogany.

Another customs official grabbed at his briefcase before Reid could say anything. That was all right; anything having to do with Black Dawn had been left on board the jumbo jet, shredded so no one could read the information, and left in the rest room trash. Everything else in his briefcase was concerned with lab specimens, cultures and other instruments needed for fieldwork. There wasn't much there that the customs official, who was scowling heavily as he pawed through the contents, could be upset about.

As they cleared customs, Casey moved to Reid's side. They walked down another corridor, again lined with soldiers who were nervously shifting from one booted foot to another, their hands hovering over their SKSs. Casey purposely moved close to Reid, until their elbows were touching.

"We're supposed to have a C-130 at our disposal. A Colonel Nsonjui is supposed to be waiting for us down there," Casey said, pointing toward the other end of the terminal.

Reid nodded and swiveled his head around the area as they emerged from the narrow passageway. For an international airport, N'Djili was looking very deserted—except for a lot of nervous soldiers armed to the teeth with automatic weapons. "Wish to hell we had flak jackets right now," he muttered under his breath as he lengthened his stride. Casey automatically matched his pace. He reached out and brought her to his other side so that he was between her and the plate glass windows. If bullets started flying, he didn't want her hit by a stray one.

"Flak jackets? Give me a helmet, too." She nervously looked around. "One of the Customs people back there said there's a firefight going on south of the airport terminal."

"How close?"

"Dunno. Ain't gonna ask, either. If those glass windows start to shatter, we'll have an idea of how close they really are...."

Grunting, Reid kept his hand around her upper arm and guided her toward the end of the terminal. He saw an officer in a highly decorated uniform waiting for them. It had to be the colonel. Dividing his attention between the outer threat and the angry-looking colonel, Reid found himself admiring Casey more and more every minute. Ty was right: in a bad situation, she was no weak sister. He could tell by the fine tension running through her that she was very much aware of herself and him in relation to everything else that was going on around them. He'd almost swear she'd had terrorist or undercover operative training by the way she was behaving. It served to put him in a more relaxed mode, at least with regard to his concerns about how she would react to danger.

"Colonel Nsonjui?" Casey said sweetly, holding out her hand as they approached him. "I'm Dr. Morrow. Thank you for meeting us."

Nsonjui, over six feet tall, his cheekbones high and prominent, his dark brown eyes assessing, took her hand. *"Mademoiselle,"* he murmured, and leaned over and kissed the back of her hand.

Reid watched the man with narrowing eyes. The officer's French was smooth and impeccable, not giving away the agitation that was mirrored in his taut features.

"We have a situation presently," the Colonel said, releasing her hand. He then thrust his hand toward Reid.

Reid gripped it firmly. It was a solid handshake. Maybe Nsonjui was just uptight over the firefight going on. The colonel was supposed to give them firearms once they were on board the C-130. Reid wished he had them now. "Reid Hunter, at your service, Colonel."

"Of course," he said. "Your papers are in order. The minister of transportation has asked me to fly you to Yambuku. It will be my pleasure. Shall we?"

Casey nodded. The colonel did a smart, efficient about-face and moved quickly, almost with relief, down another hallway that led back toward the tarmac. She hurried to keep up with him, while giving Reid a glance across her shoulder. He followed grimly behind her. She was getting her first taste of his marine side—the protector, the warrior. There was an incredible sense of power emanating from him, and she could feel the tension in him. His eyes appeared colorless, the pupils small and tight, his mouth thinned and hard. Yet the moment their gazes met and touched briefly, she felt an overwhelming sense of care blanketing her.

Opening the umbrella as they trotted down the wet tarmac to the awaiting C-130 Hercules cargo aircraft, Reid kept his hearing keyed for gunfire in the distance. The south end of the runway was where this plane would have to take off. What would prevent the rebels from firing up at its belly as it passed over them? *Nothing. Absolutely nothing.* Reid hurried Casey up the steps into the cargo hold of the gray-painted C-130. Handing her the umbrella, he watched as the colonel snapped at the flight crewman to shut the door behind them.

"Colonel?"

"Yes?" he said, clearly irritated to be halted on his way to the cockpit.

"Is this bird taking off to the south?" Reid held his stare.

"The wind direction is such, Mr. Hunter, that I have no choice."

Reid felt Casey grip his arm. She moved up to where he stood in the semidark hold.

"We're just concerned about the firefight, Colonel," she said.

He raked his long fingers through his black hair. "I am, too, Dr. Morrow. I am, too. I suggest you strap in. Prayer is an option." He turned on his heel, snapped a string of orders to the two flight sergeants and then climbed up a ladder into the cockpit.

Casey compressed her lips. "Welcome to Zaire," she muttered, and released Reid's arm. Turning, she went to the nylon netting that served as a seat. Reid followed her. One of the sergeants handed each of them a 9 mm pistol and several canvas pouches filled with extra magazines. They were both issued black leather shoulder holsters as well.

Before long, the C-130 was shaking as the four turbo-prop engines began to whine to life, one at a time. Reid sat beside Casey. He noticed the two flight sergeants, who were strapped in near the cockpit area, had donned flak jackets and helmets. Looking around the dimly lit hold, he saw a lot of boxes but no more flak jackets or helmets.

During their last flight Casey had changed into an olive-colored one-piece outfit. It was darkened here and there with rain splatters. The web belt around her waist made her look more the like a soldier than a civilian. The web belt was a good idea, Reid thought as he watched her attach the canvas carriers containing the extra magazines to it.

"Done this a time or two, eh?"

She smiled tightly. "Yes, you could say that." She

glanced at him. He'd put on a lightweight, dark green jacket. "Where are you putting the extra ammo?"

Removing the magazines, he said, "In the pockets of my jacket." Reid saw that the pistol did not have a magazine in it. Taking a clip, he slammed it into the butt of the pistol and locked it. In case the plane was shot at and forced to land, he wanted to be ready—for anything.

The C-130 began to move slowly. The whine of the engines increased and the hulking cargo plane began to make its way to the north end of the runway.

"Helluva welcome to Zaire," Casey muttered nervously. She pulled on the shoulder holster and snapped it shut. Making sure she had a clip of ammunition in her own pistol, she also locked it and then put the safety on. Pushing the weapon down into the holster, she placed the leather strap across it.

"I've never been shot at from beneath a plane takin' off before."

"Welcome to war, Doctor."

"Not my idea of fun, Hunter. Not at all."

He reached out, his hand covering hers, which was balled into a tense fist on her thigh. "This colonel knows what he's doing. He knows there's trouble down at the takeoff point. My bet is he's gonna do a JATO assist, and about halfway down this runway, he'll yank the yoke back in protest, so this bird sails straight up in a vertical takeoff to avoid that area."

Casey's eyes rounded. "Really?"

"Yeah, so hang on, Doctor. This is gonna get a little testy, believe me...."

She trusted Reid with her life in that moment. It was clear he knew about these things. And she'd seen the hardness in the colonel's eyes as he'd marched determinedly to the cockpit. The man had flown quite a few hours, and she was sure he wouldn't have survived this long if he wasn't good at what he did.

At the end of the runway, the C-130 began to shake and shudder as the colonel, who was at the yoke, pushed all four throttles into full forward position. Casey was familiar with JATOs—jet-assisted takeoff rockets. They were placed on the sides of the aircraft's fuselage to give it a short-runway takeoff. The shorter the better, as far as she was concerned. The warmth and strength of Hunter's hand over hers felt very good right now.

Her heart was beginning to pound as the C-130 began to shake like a dog trying to get rid of fleas. The engines were screaming like four banshees. She wanted to cover her ears, the sound was so high pitched and serrating to her sensitive hearing. Suddenly, the brakes were released. Almost simultaneously, Casey heard the JATOs ignite. The roar in the hold of the cargo bay was like thunder careening through the dimly lit area.

Her lips opened. She felt like screaming. The plane lunged forward, no longer the slow, ugly-duckling cargo aircraft of before. Gravity shoved Casey against the bulkhead. Reid's hand tightened on hers. From where they sat, she could see both pilots, since the cockpit was open. The C-130 was shaking badly now. The roar of the rockets heightened.

The shrillness of the engines increased to ear-splitting levels. Her heart thudded hard in her chest. She felt the nose of the plane suddenly thrust upward. Straight up! Gasping, Casey clung to Reid, as she was thrown violently against the bulkhead. She felt his arm move around her shoulders to steady her. The aircraft groaned, its metal plates straining. The noise in the hold was overwhelming. The shuddering increased. Were they going to crash?

Hunter held Casey tightly in his arms as the bird made a wobbling lunge skyward. Graceful the C-130 was not. Reid felt every bolt and plate in the plane's skin stretch in protest over the terrific amount of gravity imposed on her old, aging frame. Would this bird hold together in such an evasive maneuver? His gaze was riveted to the colonel's and his copilot's hands as they arced across those four throttles. *Come on, come on, hold together...hold together...!*

The C-130 continued its steep climb. The engines strained; the shrieking continued. Reid's heart jammed into his throat. His mouth went dry. The bird could fall apart under this kind of demanding strain. Reid had flown enough in the Herk to know that it was a powerful, undervalued workhorse. His faith in this Lockheed aircraft was on the line. He'd never seen a vertical takeoff like this one. Yet the pilot had no choice. It was either risk stalling out and falling out of the sky because the ascent was too steep, or risk getting 20 mm, full-metal-jacket bullets ripping up the belly of this old cargo bird and sending them into a fiery hell.

Casey had pressed her face against Reid's chest. Her gesture, her sudden need for protection, took him by utter surprise. She seemed so worldly, so capable of taking care of herself, yet in this moment she was turning to *him* for protection. It was a delicious shock to Reid. And even more astounding, he found himself winding his arms around her as she sought haven against him. He held her tightly as her arms wrapped around him, squeezing the breath out of him. He felt sorry for her, inadequately prepared for this wartime maneuver. The soft dampness of her hair pressed against his chin. If he had to die, at least she was in his arms, where he'd wanted her all along. The thought was forbidden, but filled with a bright, blaring life of its own. Reid closed his eyes, his body braced against the force of gravity and the bucking, violent motion of the aircraft. He inhaled her sweet, spicy scent. She felt good against him. She fit him in all the right places. Wildly aware of her breasts pressed against him, he absorbed her as a woman. Yes, if he had to die, this was the way he wanted to go—with her in his arms.

Suddenly, the pilot banked hard to the left. The C-130 hung in the air for a split second. Then the plane turned, practically on the tip of its left wing. Reid gripped Casey hard. He heard her cry out as the plane plummeted. Had the colonel stalled out? Reid wasn't sure; he wasn't a pilot. But he did know that too high an angle and not enough air under the wings could create a deadly stall where the plane would plummet earthward as it was doing now.

Breath jammed in his chest. Reid's eyes widened. He felt the C-130 lurch sickeningly. *What the hell?* He almost mouthed the words. Then, just as suddenly, the plane leveled out. Shakily, Reid released his held breath. His arms eased from around Casey as she slowly lifted her head, her gaze moving from the cockpit up to him. Their faces were inches apart.

"My God," she croaked, "are we out of danger?"

Reid released her so she could sit up. The C-130 was now climbing much less steeply, the JATO rockets suddenly cutting out. The silence was a welcome relief. "Yeah, I think so," he rasped. Worriedly, he looked her over. "You okay?" He was still concerned about stray bullets finding the C-130's vulnerable underbelly.

Pushing her trembling fingers through her hair, Casey nodded. "I—I think so. Wow, whatta takeoff, huh?"

He nodded and saw the fear in her dark green eyes. Her hair was badly mussed and he reached out to tame a few locks back into place, away from her eyes.

Reid's touch was galvanizing. Casey felt his fingers easing her hair gently behind her ears. His touch was electric. Necessary. Gulping, she sat very still with her eyes closed, simply absorbing his touch. Her stomach was quivering and she tasted fear. They could have died. The plane could have crashed. As she opened her eyes and met his colorless ones, she realized how precious life really was—especially now, with him. As he withdrew his fingers from her hair, she took a deep, shaky breath.

"Thanks, I needed that...."

"Anytime," he rasped. What on earth had made him do that? Tuck that errant, dark red strand of hair behind her ear?

Hunter wondered if he was losing it completely. He blamed the situation for his undoing. Unbuckling his belt, he rose abruptly. "Stay here. I'm going forward to see what's going down."

Her knees felt weak, so she didn't mind obeying his order. Usually she was the one in charge of field missions, but this time, Casey was grateful that Reid Hunter was with her. The sensation of his steely embrace remained hotly imprinted upon her skin like a brand. In those moments when she'd thought they were going to die it had felt wonderful to press her face against his chest and just be held by him.

Casey watched as Reid moved carefully toward the cockpit. He was a man who was very knowledgeable about a lot of things, she realized. Grateful that the defense department had given her Reid as an assistant, Casey swore she wouldn't ever rail against the military again. Reid knew what was going down. He had the experience, and he'd helped her negotiate this near disaster. Touching her rain-soaked arm, Casey felt an incredible warmth suffusing her chest and encircling her heart. Reid was surprising. And she found herself wanting to know more, much more, about the man who hid from his emotions behind that wall he'd erected so firmly.

Looking around the dimly lit hold, she wondered if there was going to be time to get to know him. At first she'd seen him as a pain in the butt, someone she'd have to shepherd along as she tried to do field research. Now the shoe was on the other foot. Would she be a liability to him? Only time would tell. As she rolled up the cuffs on her shirtsleeves, Casey knew the danger around them would be so palpable that they probably wouldn't have time to get to know one another on a personal level.

No, Reid's job was to protect her. Of all the places, Casey groused to herself, to find a man she was genuinely interested in—in this country where life and death were one and the same with breathing in and out. What made her think, under the circumstances, that she would be able to know Reid at all?

Chapter Five

"Night and day difference," Reid said as they stepped off the ramp of the C-130, which had landed at Yambuku. The sun shone brightly through holes in the low-hanging, pregnant gray clouds. It had been raining like hell in Kinshasa, but the farther north they flew, the less it rained. Maybe it was a good sign. Here, surrounded by palm trees and other hardwoods, it had barely sprinkled. Because Yambuku sat on the northern edge of the rain forest, rainy and dry seasons were often sporadic.

As they stood outside the fuselage of the Hercules, Reid studied the airstrip, which, although made of concrete, badly needed maintenance. The colonel, who was one helluva pilot, in Reid's estimation, had dodged all the potholes and the major fissures in the concrete and had brought them in for a safe landing.

Casey looked around fondly. "Home," she murmured. The humidity was high, but not intolerable here. She was glad to be wearing her utilitarian cotton suit. Though it was nearly three p.m. local time, she felt groggy and lethargic. She hated jet lag more than anything else. Their situation demanded alertness, and she struggled to maintain a semblance of it as Reid helped the airmen unload a number of boxes bound for a beat-up red sports utility vehicle that was parked nearby. The truck would be their transportation to the village, back to Grandfather Henri and his warm, welcoming people. Casey looked forward to seeing the old chieftain, who had adopted her the first year she'd stayed with them at the village.

Colonel Nsonjui emerged from the ramp of the C-130 and approached Casey. "The terrorists destroyed the makeshift field lab completely," he told her in a low tone. "All of this is from our warehouse in Kinshasa."

"OID equipment?"

"Yes." Nsonjui smiled and scratched his head as he looked around the area. "It is material from the last epidemic when Ebola struck. I make sure there are guards posted around the clock to keep these items safe."

Casey was grateful for the colonel's care and understanding because not all military officials thought highly of the OID and foreign scientific agencies, despite the fact that those agencies were engaged at the Zairian government's request. She knew the colonel grasped the importance of it all. "Thank you for everything you've done, Colonel," she said, smiling up at the tall, lean officer. "You did quite a job of flying us out of Kinshasa, too."

"Emergency times require emergency procedures, don't they?"

"Yes," Casey said dryly, and then murmured, "I need to help my assistant. Thank you, again." She held out her hand to him.

Nisonjui picked up her hand, turned it over and pressed a quick kiss to the back of it. "A pleasure, *Mademoiselle*. I will be back here in two weeks with resupply. You have a comsat link. You know how to contact me if you need me."

He was a throwback to the old days of Zaire, Casey thought as she watched the proud colonel climb back into the aircraft after the last box was off-loaded. French manners, French speaking and very French about women. Still, he was a pearl among pebbles in this dangerous territory, and Casey thanked her lucky stars for him.

Sweat stood out on Reid's brow as he put the last box of equipment into the Land Rover. He wiped the beads of perspiration away with the back of his hand. Thanking the two airmen, who had helped make an arduous job easier, he shook their hands and waved goodbye to them as they hurried back to the C-130. As Casey joined him, he gestured toward the plane.

"Take a look at the bullet holes stitching up the side of the fuselage there," he said, pointing to them.

"Wow…" Casey murmured.

"We sat over there, maybe a foot away from the nearest hole." He studied her. There was shock as well as a resigned acceptance of a cold reality on her face. "We got lucky."

Gulping unsteadily, Casey tore her gaze from the bullet holes. "At least we have luck, Hunter." She opened the back door of the vehicle and dropped her briefcase in on the seat. "I'll drive. I know the road to Grandfather Henri's village."

Reid held up his hands and walked around to the passenger door. "No argument from me, Doctor." He looked up at the sun. "How many hours to the village?"

Climbing in, Casey grinned sourly. She promptly put on her seat belt and made sure it was snug. As Reid got in and shut the door, she said, "Well, if it was a paved road, an hour. But since this is backwoods Zaire, where roads wash out during the rainy season and new ones are made during the dry season, the answer is who knows? Depends upon how much traffic is on the road, how many donkeys, carts and folks, not to mention how many ruts and holes we have to negotiate around, too.'' She leaned over, the key already in the ignition. "This old truck has been around since the first time I was here, five years ago.''

"It's a little weather-beaten,'' Reid said, looking around.

The windows had been cleaned haphazardly, but there was mud and dust coating everything. He gazed through the dusty glass at the thick palm trees that bordered the makeshift runway. He heard the engine grind and then catch. The truck came alive, a shudder running through the vehicle. Moving his shoulder holster a little in order to get more comfortable, he glanced over at Casey, who had put the durable vehicle into Drive. He saw the shadows beneath her eyes and the strain at the corners of her mouth.

As they slowly moved away from the little airport and down a deeply rutted, muddy road, Reid opened the window and placed his arm on the sill. The wind was humid, but it felt good.

"Any air-conditioning in this thing?'' he asked.

Chortling, Casey shook her head. "Air-conditioning? Out here? You gotta be kidding!'' She drove with both hands firmly on the wheel. Ahead were a group of color-fully clothed women, some balancing on their heads huge handwoven baskets filled with vegetables and fruit bound for the Yambuku markets. The road was the main one between the small town and the outlying villages that peppered the savanna up ahead.

The thick groves of palm trees were slowly giving way to grassy plains. At this time of year, with the sporadic rain, the grass was a bright green and close to knee high. In the distance, Casey could see zebra, wildebeests and springing brown-and-white gazelles. They lived in herds of hundreds and thousands out on the wide-open, sprawling plain during the rainy season. It was a sight to behold, one that always awed her.

Reid noticed that most of the traffic on the dirt road was pedestrian or donkey. It was rare that they encountered another car, and when they did, it was either a military jeep or a sports utility vehicle like theirs. This was tough country, for tough vehicles only. He divided his attention between Casey, who drove carefully, avoiding the major ruts and huge craters in the road, and the people around them.

The sweet fragrance of recent rain on the parched earth, the scent of fresh grass and other less agreeable odors filled his nostrils. The breeze coming in the open windows lifted Casey's hair from time to time.

"Now I know why you have short hair," he said with a grin.

Casey glanced sideways at him for just a moment. It would be foolhardy not to pay attention to this disaster of a dirt road. One wrong move and their vehicle could break an axle or have its underside ripped out in one of the huge potholes. "Oh?"

"The humidity here is pretty overwhelming."

"Short hair is the order of the day. It's easy to wash in a rainstorm, easy for someone to look through for ticks and other vermin, and the less hair, the less sweat on the back of my neck." She flashed him an eager smile. "In this country, you don't know who to trust. Grandfather Henri is someone you can. He's a gentleman from the nineteenth century. You'll love him."

Reid wasn't sure about loving the old chieftain, but the glimmer of joy in Casey's eyes made him feel a twinge of jealousy. "How long have you known him?"

"Five years." She waved her hand out the window toward the savanna on both sides of the narrow road. "He adopted me as his daughter the first year I came here. So many of the villages are gone, but his stays. Coming from a hereditary line of chieftains, Henri has been able to adapt to the changing politicians and governments, yet keep his village and people intact. Believe me, that's a miracle in itself."

"I don't have a file on him," Reid said, frowning.

"Consider him a guardian angel," Casey advised. She gazed out across the savanna. The thousands of animals that grazed on its succulent green grass made her heart swell with happiness. "*This* is the Africa I love so much! Just getting to watch the wildlife, so free, unfettered…"

Hearing the longing in her husky voice, Reid enjoyed the changing landscape of animals even more. The zebras, their black-and-white hides looking like busy, ever-changing geometric patterns, were a contrast to the hulking, slow-moving elephant herd that lingered to eat choice morsels of leaves from the edge of the rain forest.

Above them, the sky was a burning, brilliant cobalt that almost hurt his eyes. Thunderheads lay to the west and south, and Reid wondered if they would be in for some nasty storms later this evening. He wasn't at all familiar with African weather so he had no idea. Maybe the threatening white, turbulent clouds would disappear when the sun went down, like they did in the States. He wasn't sure.

Just getting to steal a peek every now and then at Casey as she drove made him happy. Joy was palpable in her glowing expression, in the way her green eyes had begun to shine with eagerness, despite her jet lag.

"What do you think so far?" Casey asked, keeping her eyes on the road.

"Of what?"

"Of Africa. Doesn't she steal your heart? Invigorate your soul?"

It was impossible not to smile a little. "Doctor, I do believe that setting foot on African soil has turned you into a ten-year-old girl at heart."

Laughing gaily, Casey nodded. "Oh, yes! It's my home

away from home, maybe because Grandfather Henri made me feel a part of his huge family. He took the OID team in like we were a part of his village. He's so generous and wise. His wives do all the cooking, and every night, after a long, hard, sweaty day in the rain forest, we'd trudge back and our huts would be cleaned, there would be wonderful food cooking for us, and all his children and grandchildren would be there to help us, if we asked for help.''

"There's a lot of danger here, too," he said.

"Africa, for me," Casey told him, "is a dance between darkness and light. Life and death. One false step, one time you're not paying attention, and you could step on an adder or black mamba snake. The next, Thomson's gazelles come springing past you, stealing your breath and your heart with their incredibly graceful leaps."

"I think you like living close to the edge," he declared, unable to keep his smile from her.

Casey reacted powerfully to the smile lurking at the corners of his very strong male mouth. "Isn't that what living is all about? Not the social niceties all the time. Not the safe, secure world." She gestured with her hand. "The lions are sitting on the edge of the savanna right now. The zebras and wildebeests ignore them. Come sundown, they won't. They know when it's feeding time, and that one of them will be the meal."

"It's the same for you," he said in a deep voice. "You trap an insect, a reptile or whatever, and carefully open it up in hopes of finding Ebola in it. One slip of the scalpel in your fingers, and you could infect yourself."

Pursing her lips, she said, "Yes, that's living on the edge, too."

"Maybe this isn't any of my business, but you're a woman with adventure in her blood. Do you ever see yourself settling down? Having a family?" Reid knew he had absolutely no reason to get personal with Casey, but damn it, she *invited* that kind of exploration. As he studied her clean profile, her skin glistening from the high temperature and humidity, he saw her mouth tighten for a moment. It was nothing obvious, but he caught it. Or perhaps he sensed it.

Shrugging, Casey felt tension gathering in her shoulders. Gripping the wheel a little more firmly, she tried to sound airy and light in her retort to him. "I could ask the same of you, couldn't I?" Inwardly, she cringed. She knew she was being defensive, but she didn't want Reid inspecting her emotional scars. They were way too fresh and she was still burdened with so much grief she had yet to release. Still, Casey found herself *wanting* to divulge her awful past to him. There was a part of Hunter that she knew, on some gut level, was capable of not only understanding, but also of healing her heart. That realization was so shocking to Casey she nearly choked.

With a slight, derisive laugh, Reid muttered, "Let's just put it this way, good doctor—my personal plans were deep-sixed a long time ago. Besides, I was never cut out for home, family or being a father."

Casey wasn't so sure. She heard pain in Reid's strained tone even though he'd tried to gracefully dodge her query. When she gave him a quick glance out of the corner of her eye, she saw him frowning, the slashes in his cheeks deep and pronounced, as if he were holding back a lot of pain he hadn't worked through yet. But then again, she was no prize in that department either, she thought. How long had it taken her to attract a man? Not that she'd worked at it, but her mom was worried that Casey would end up single and old and alone—like her mother was ever since her father's untimely death.

Wiping her fingers quickly on the material across her thigh, Casey tried to sound flippant. "Let's face it, Hunter, some people aren't meant for marriage, much less a long-term relationship." Hers had lasted one year. The best year—the worst year—of her life. The anguish cutting

through her heart was nearly overwhelming to Casey
Compressing her lips, she pointed ahead to a group o
white, round buildings with thick, yellow thatched roofs.

"There! That's Grandfather Henri's village up ahead!
wonder if he knows we're coming? Trying to get word ou
here is impossible unless you have a comsat link o
hookup, and he refuses to own anything mechanical."

Up ahead, the village stretched for nearly half a mile
flowing out onto the edge of the thousand-mile-wide sa
vanna. The circular homes, made of dry, packed clay
gleamed whitely in the burning sunlight. The roofs wer
thatched with a combination of dried palm leaves and lon
savanna grass. They looked like messy hen's nests an
reminded Casey of heads with yellow hair. She smiled
filled with euphoria because she loved Africa and espe
cially this village and its people.

There were huge herds of cattle out on the savanna con
tentedly eating their fill of the green, succulent grass. The
were tended by nearly naked young boys, who waved a
Casey and Reid as they drove by. Reid wondered if th
lions got to the herds or if Grandfather Henri had som
kind of defense system to keep his cattle safe.

More and more people filled the dirt road—children car
rying wood, mothers with large woven baskets balance
delicately on their heads, all in a swirl of rainbow-colore
clothes.

The villagers moved to the edges of the dirt road o
thickly callused bare feet. As the truck slowed to nearly
crawl, Casey would lean out the window and call out
name and greeting in Bantu. The child or woman woul
turn, the suspicious look changing to one of utter deligh
followed by shrills and calls of excitement.

Several children ran up to their vehicle. Casey laughe
and reached out as one young girl, her head a mass of littl
pigtails all tied off in red yarn, gave her a yellow orchi
with a purple lip.

"Thank you!" Casey called out in Bantu. She carefully tucked the fragrant orchid into her shirt pocket and chuckled. A number of older children forged ahead of them, yelling and screaming as they moved into the village itself.

"The kids will make sure Grandpa Henri knows we're here." Casey pulled over and braked next to a small, thatched hut. She turned and unbuckled her seat belt. "We've arrived," she told Reid huskily.

"Home?"

Looking up, she met and held his warm gray gaze. "Yes, home…" The smoldering look he gave her made her nerves go hot with longing. There was no misjudging his expression. She was thirty years old, not some naive girl. Opening the door, she said breathlessly, "Just follow me. I know where Grandfather Henri's hut is located."

The number of people who swarmed around them surprised Reid. Children of all ages ran up, quickly touching his hand or arm and then dashing off, as if playing a game of imaginary tag with him. The adults watched from a distance. He saw welcome in their eyes as their gazes fell on red-haired Casey, marching quickly toward the center of the village. He saw suspicion and curiosity in their eyes as they looked at him. Reid didn't blame them. Theirs was a history of wars, changing politics and battles at every turn. Who was their friend? Who was their foe? These were the questions in their eyes as they assessed him.

The smell of wood fires under the black iron tripods set up here and there, the many different delicious odors coming from the hanging black kettles, encircled Casey as she walked. Laughing and calling out the names of many children she knew, she dug into her deep pockets and brought out the colorfully wrapped hard candy she'd brought for just this occasion. The shrieks, yelps and cries of delight as the children surged forward, their hands open wide, made her grin with pleasure. Within moments, the candy was gone. Just ahead, she saw a very thin, aged man bent over the gold-headed cane he always relied upon.

"Grandpa Henri!" Casey cried, waving wildly at him. She trotted up the slight incline to where the old gentleman stood, dressed in a white linen shirt and black trousers, barefoot yet regal.

Tears filled Casey's eyes as the old man lifted his terribly thin, branchlike arms and held them wide—for her. He was nearly ninety now, and very frail, so Casey slowed to a walk. As was protocol, because he was chieftain, she stopped and bowed her head to him.

"Come, come, child," Henri chided in flawless French. "Let these old, weak arms hold you once again...."

Casey never tired of looking up at the chieftain, who, in his prime, had stood nearly six foot seven inches tall. Age had bowed his once proud back and rounded his once broad shoulders. He'd carried many loads and responsibilities in his lifetime. The look in his dark, sparkling eyes told her of his love for her, of his unabashed welcome at her return to them. Stepping forward, she wrapped her arms around his narrow torso and squeezed him very gently.

"Grandpa," she whispered, suddenly choked with emotion, "it's so good to be home again."

"Ah, my child," he said with a sigh as he wrapped his arms about her, "it is we who rejoice in your return to us."

Reid stood at a respectable distance and patiently waited.

The entire village, it seemed, was encircling the hut where the aged chieftain stood with Casey in his embrace. The man's face was narrow with high, proud cheekbones, his skin ebony beneath the bright sunlight. Around his neck he wore a necklace of sharply pointed teeth and fangs that Reid guessed had come from a lion. The necklace was the only outer adornment that proclaimed him leader of this very large village.

As Casey eased out of his embrace and turned to face the villagers, she placed an arm around Henri's back to steady him. He planted his ivory cane with the gold lion's head into the red soil.

"My people, our wandering daughter has returned to us! Let there be celebration!"

A cry went up around Reid, enthusiastic and spontaneous. A number of people began to jump up and down. The children danced around, their arms thrust skyward. When he looked back, he saw tears tracking down Casey's flushed cheeks. How beautiful, how vulnerable she looked in that moment, standing next to that proud old man. Her hair moved softly in the humid breeze, and she self-consciously took a swipe at her eyes with the back of her hand as she looked up with adoration at Henri.

"Grandpa, I have someone you must meet," she said as the children continued to dance around them.

Henri stood there, narrowing his eyes. "That young lion over by my second wife's hut?" he demanded in his deep baritone voice.

Chuckling, Casey nodded. "He'd probably like that compliment, coming from you. Yes, that's Reid Hunter, my assistant for the next three months."

Cocking his head slightly in her direction, his gaze never leaving Hunter, he said, "A young lion for an assistant? My daughter, do you think I'm blind *and* deaf *and* dumb?"

Chortling, Casey squeezed him gently. "No, Grandpa, none of the above."

"Humph, then invite him into my hut. The way he stands on guard, he awaits an attack from a leopard, or worse, a jackal."

Urging Reid to follow them, Casey flashed him a reassuring smile. Grandpa Henri ordered one of his younger wives, Celestine, to bring coconut milk, as well as other foods for their impromptu visit. Casey kept her stride shortened for the old man's sake as he moved haltingly with his cane.

"Our medicine woman said you were returning to us sooner than expected," he told her, his nearly toothless smile broadening.

Casey saw two of his many grandchildren pull back the colorful red-yellow-and-blue fabric that served as a door. Henri hobbled in and she followed. Looking back, she saw Reid approaching. He was on guard and tense. Here he could relax, but he didn't know that yet. She smiled to herself. She was getting a real taste of his guard-dog side. And then, as she moved to the large, airy hut, she corrected herself: his lion side.

As Reid entered the dim hut, he saw it contained four large windows that were open, allowing a breeze to flow through the confines. He stood a little uncertainly, because at the opposite end of the room, Henri was sitting in a huge embossed mahogany chair that had a lion's skin hanging over it, and looking every inch the king of his domain. Around him were scattered black-and-white zebra hides over the hard packed dirt floor. Huge, comfortable pillows of many colors were situated on either side of his throne.

Casey saw Reid's hesitation and came forward, her hand extended. "Come," she coaxed, her fingers closing around his.

Reid allowed her to lead him up to the impressive dais where Henri sat. Reid followed Casey's lead by standing more or less at attention and then bowing his head toward the alert chieftain.

"Grandfather," Casey said huskily, still gripping Reid's larger hand, "this is Reid Hunter. He is my very able assistant and will help me out in the field. I hope you will embrace him as you have me. Reid, this is Grandfather

Henri.'' She released his hand and stepped to one side of the throne.

Reid met the old man's sharpened gaze and knew the chieftain missed nothing. Henri might be old, but that took nothing away from the glittering interest in his ebony eyes as he slowly assessed Reid from his feet up to his head and back down to his feet once again.

''So, this time they send a young lion to watch over my adopted daughter?'' he challenged Hunter. ''You have the posture of one hunting for his own stake, his own territory. Your eyes are that of the gods of lightning. You move like one who is awaiting an attack.''

Reid held the man's slicing gaze. ''I take what you say, Chief, as a compliment. Casey has told me of your bravery, of your being a great leader to your people. I honor any man who can do what you've done.''

Henri raised one brow and looked in Casey's direction. She stood attentively near his throne. ''And the tongue of a diplomat?''

''He tries, Grandpa,'' she said with a chuckle. ''Actually, Reid is honest to the bone. I told him about you. You're a great man and I wanted to share with him how I felt in my heart about you.''

''I see....'' Once again, Henri looked Reid up and down with that stripping gaze of his. ''You don't let many into your heart, daughter.''

Casey looked down at her booted feet, embarrassed. ''No, Grandpa, I don't,'' she whispered painfully.

''And this young lion replaces your loss?''

Her mouth went tight. Pain serrated her momentarily. ''Well...I...''

''You've chosen well,'' Henri continued, praising her. He held out his hand toward Hunter. ''Welcome, young lion. Sit here, next to me. My youngest wife, Celestine, will bring us coconut juice to quench our thirst and celebrate your being among us.''

Reid saw sudden tears in Casey's eyes. He wasn't privy to her past, so he didn't know what to make of what the old man had just said to her. Following the chieftain's orders, he sat down on a gold-brocaded pillow to the left of Henri's throne.

A young woman no more than twenty years old, dressed in a dark-blue and yellow skirt and white blouse, hurried in with a platter of freshly sliced fruit and a wooden pitcher of coconut milk, along with three amethyst-colored glasses. Bowing deeply, she murmured a greeting in Bantu to Henri. The old man, with a flourish of his hand, ordered her to serve their guests first.

Reid sat at enough of an angle to watch Casey, who sat crosslegged on a red pillow. She struggled to blink back her tears and regain her composure. He found himself wishing he was sitting next to her so he could slide his arm around her slumped shoulders and comfort her. She was obviously in great pain.

"Much has happened since we saw you six months ago," Henri said, lifting his glass to them. "Drink, and we shall talk more, my daughter."

The coconut milk was lukewarm, but sweet, and it quenched Casey's considerable thirst. Coconuts and palm oil were two major exports of the country and Henri had nearly a thousand acres of palm trees. The work kept his people employed, and the money, as little as it might be, was enough to keep them alive and their bellies full. Nowadays, that was a miracle in itself. She admired Henri's leadership and farsightedness despite the upheaval his country seemed to always endure.

Smacking his lips, Henri looked over at Hunter. "Ahh, you were thirsty. Celestine? Fill his cup once again."

Eagerly, the young wife pushed up from her kneeling position in the center of the hut and brought the pitcher back to Reid.

"Thank you," he murmured to the beautiful young girl.

He noticed she was pregnant and he smiled to himself. Henri might be an aging ruler, but he had an eye for beauty and was still able, at his advanced age, to father more children to ensure that his dynasty would live on. Reid raised his cup in toast to Henri, who nodded deferentially to him.

"What has happened since I left?" Casey asked the chieftain, her hands wrapped around the large glass. As Celestine passed the silver platter of sliced fruit, Casey picked up a piece of papaya. She didn't feel like eating but forced herself to do so. She did not want to disappoint Henri, who watched her every move like a doting relative.

Sadly, Henri shook his head and waved away the offer of fruit from the platter. "A witch has cursed our village, I'm afraid, my daughter. He has sent the devil to us. The devil hunts my people, day in and day out. I've hired many sorcerers to stop it from attacking, from killing, but they are useless!" He turned and looked at her worriedly. "And now, my heart must stay awake at night and worry for you, as well. This devil is here to murder my family, one at a time." He held out his hand and stroked her hair gently. "Because you are of my family, you are in danger as well...."

Chapter Six

"What," Reid demanded, "is the devil?" He saw Casey's expression grow guarded after he asked the question.

Grandfather Henri rubbed his chin with consternation. "You would call him a black mamba."

Reid shot another look in Casey's direction, and she responded to the question she saw in his eyes.

"Black mambas are the deadliest, most poisonous snakes on the face of the earth, Reid." She twisted her head to look up at Henri. "They live in eastern and southern Africa. Grandpa, how did they get up here?"

"Diamond runners," he growled unhappily. "In a village thirty miles from here, a family stole some diamonds from them. The thieves got even. They transported at least twenty black mambas up here and loosed them on the village in revenge. Thirty people have died so far. The mambas, as you know, are family oriented. They live in nests of five or six." He gestured unhappily toward the savanna.

"Three months ago, my little granddaughter was digging in an old, rotting log. She found fifteen white eggs. She thought they were from a bird and brought home as many as she could carry with her. Her mother, who was nearby, was walking back with her when this brown snake with a cream-colored underbelly came rushing up like the wind itself." He raised his hand. "My daughter swears the snake stood as tall as a man. It looked at my granddaughter, who had the eggs gathered in her apron. It was then that the mother realized they were snake eggs, not bird eggs."

Sighing, he said, "Wisely, my daughter told her to gently place the eggs on the ground. She had no idea that she was dealing with a black mamba. Aiyyee," he muttered, pausing as he struggled with his emotions. "As the granddaughter placed the eggs on the earth, the snake struck her." Henri wiped his watering eyes as he held Casey's gaze. "She died in a minute's time. A minute! My daughter came screaming home, carrying her dead child in her arms. Many of us saw the black mamba. It followed her. I swear, the snake is a wind god! He whipped around so quickly! We tried to chase it off with sticks, shovels and spears, but it outran us! It outran the fleetest warrior in my village...."

Casey gulped. "The black mamba, Grandpa, is the most dangerous and poisonous snake there is. Not only that, it's the fastest moving. It has been clocked at fifteen miles an hour." Gesturing with her hands, she said, "The mamba has been known to grow to thirteen feet in length, and when it moves through the grass, it will literally raise its head three feet upward."

Reid whistled softly. "Do you know how much muscle and strength that takes, to hold up that much of a snake's body?"

"Yes," Casey said seriously, "I do. I've seen black mambas up close. Too close. I was with an OID field unit over in east Africa and had two run-ins with them. We were out collecting insects on a savanna and I got a little too close, I think, to a family nesting site. I had this twelve-foot female come whipping up to me out of nowhere.''

Henri stared at her. ''So, you have met them....''

Grimly, Casey said, ''Yes. Enough to know that they are lethal, they are easily spooked and they strike very fast. You can't outrun them.'' She opened her hands in a help-less gesture. ''One of the men working with me, a scientist from Johannesburg, was struck and killed by a black mamba.''

''By any chance, was he collecting with you?'' Reid asked, his voice deepening.

''Yes,'' Casey said, ''he made a move, and the snake struck at him instead of me. I told him to remain absolutely motionless, that the mamba strikes something that is mov-ing, but he wouldn't listen to me.''

''And why did it not strike you?'' Henri demanded.

''I got off a shot and blew its head off.''

Reid studied her, a slight smile on his mouth. ''I'm im-pressed.''

''I *do* know how to use a pistol,'' Casey said. She re-turned her attention to the chieftain. ''The black mambas live around here, then?''

''Yes. Right now, four of my family have been stalked and bitten by them. No matter where we go out on the plain to hunt, the black mambas follow us.''

''Then they've got to have a nest nearby,'' Casey mut-tered. ''They don't go out of their way to attack. It's spring, time for them to lay their clutch of eggs.''

''Is there anything we can do?''

''Find the nest and destroy it,'' Casey said grimly.

''But to do that, you'd better have well-trained snake handlers, because mambas are very territorial and they do protect their own.''

Henri waved his long, arthritic finger at her. "You, my daughter, must be careful out there."

Reid sat there stewing internally. Great, now they had the world's most deadly and fastest snake in their backyard. He knew little about this venomous creature. One more thing to stay alert for.

"Is there antivenin available on the mamba?" he demanded.

Casey laughed. "On a mamba? A child dies in a minute. Three minutes max for an adult. No, there's nothing available because you're dead before it can ever be administered to you, Reid."

With a shake of his head, he glanced at his watch. "I need to make a comsat linkup." Morgan Trayhern wanted a check-in with them every twenty-four hours to ensure they were safe.

"Grandpa," Casey said as she reached over and squeezed his hand, "do you have some small huts we could use while we're here?"

"I have one, my child. Where you parked your car. My family has grown since you were last here. Two of my wives have had children." He smiled proudly. "I only have one small hut to give you."

Casey hid her disappointment. That meant she and Reid would have to live, eat and sleep there in close proximity to one another. Panic ate at her. It wasn't that she was scared of him, but the feelings he'd awakened in her were frightening.

"That's fine, Grandpa, I understand. With your permission, we'll leave and get settled in for the evening?"

"Yes, and then tomorrow we will officially celebrate your return to us. I will have one of my sons kill an antelope in your honor. We will feast on roast antelope and talk of what has happened to you since we last saw you."

Casey smiled and slowly rose. She released Henri's parchment-thin hand. His fragility was obvious, yet the depth of life in his sparkling dark eyes made her smile. "That would be an honor, Grandpa. We'll be there." She made a little bow in front of him and then turned to leave. She noticed Reid followed the protocol as well.

Once outside, Casey noted the sun was setting in the west, the shadows long and dark across the savanna outside the village perimeter. She waited for Reid to catch up with her. When he settled his hand on her arm, she caught her breath momentarily.

"If Black Dawn doesn't get us, the black mambas will," he growled so only she could hear him. He kept his hand firmly on her upper arm as he guided her through the village. "Helluva turn of events."

"This is a helluva place, Hunter. Welcome to Africa, where life and death dance moment to moment with one another." She knew she should pull free of his hand, but she craved his closeness, his touch.

Looking around, he saw the purple and apricot colors along the horizon. In the distance, he could hear monkeys hooting and howling back and forth to one another. Out on the savanna, the herds continued to mill ceaselessly, the clouds of dust rising here and there. It was a land of incredible beauty, yet it was a deadly place, too. Just the thought that Casey might be bitten by the feared black mamba and die within minutes made his stomach knot. As he glanced at her, he saw that her cheeks were flushed and her lips slightly parted, and his fears dissipated momentarily. He liked the fact that she allowed him to touch her, that she remained close to him.

"Diamond runners, huh?" he asked, attempting to rein in his straying thoughts.

"Yeah, terrorists of another sort, is all," Casey muttered. "They don't have any morals or values, either. Zaire is a hot spot for diamonds, and many times the gems are stolen and traded to these cartels. They won't waste any time seeking revenge if you screw with them, believe me. It's like signing your death warrant.''

"Them dropping a crate of black mambas on those poor bastards in that other village is enough for me to believe you on that,'' Hunter said.

She gave him a derisive look. "I'm not a drama queen when it comes to Africa, Hunter. But Africa *is* drama. High drama. All the time. If you like living on the edge, if you like danger every time you place your foot in front of you, then you'll love this place.''

"Reminds me of a war zone,'' he griped as he moved around a large thatched hut. "Only it's not land mines we have to worry about, it's black mambas. And we've got human enemies in Black Dawn possibly stalking us or watching our every move.''

"And,'' Casey said with a sigh as they approached their small, white-walled, thatched hut, "don't forget Ebola. It is present in many things around here.''

"Antelope meat, by any chance?'' Reid asked. As they reached the truck, he reluctantly dropped his hand from her arm.

There was no doubt that Casey was in top physical shape. The firmness of her arm attested to that. Then again, Africa demanded a person's best, he thought grimly as he unlocked the rear of the vehicle to locate their luggage. A number of children came to silently observe him. They stood off to the right, their hands in front of them, their faces curious.

Casey opened the front door of the truck. "Antelope isn't a carrier of Ebola, so you can eat it without worrying.'' She grinned as she pulled out her knapsack. "Instead you have to worry about food poisoning if the meat is out in the hot air too long, or parasites or worms that don't get destroyed if the meat's undercooked.''

"Rations sound a helluva lot safer.'' Reid chuckled as

he lifted the two black, nylon suitcases from the rear of the vehicle and followed Casey to the hut.

Casey pulled aside the colorful black-purple-and-red fabric that served as the door to their hut. Following Reid in, she noticed that the earthen floor was hard packed and there were handwoven grass mats over most of it. Opening each of the three square windows, she saw that wherever they slept, mosquito netting was going to be a must. Turning, she realized just how *small* the hut was. Swallowing hard, Casey felt her face go hot as she envisioned them lying down for the night on that hard earth floor.

"This hut is *really* tiny," she muttered, heading out to the vehicle once again.

Reid crouched by his luggage and pulled out a small radio. The light was fading, the inner hut dim and he had a hard time seeing. Rising to his full height, he went outside to punch in the numbers that would link him with a satellite wheeling overhead. Several of the children followed him as he walked a little ways from the hut. He heard Casey calling them back in Bantu. Like frightened gazelles, they all scattered and raced back around the hut to where she was. He wondered what she'd said to them and grinned a little. Casey obviously adored children, and they, her.

Casey was busy setting up "house" in the hut when Reid silently entered behind her a few minutes later. She was on her hands and knees, anchoring the thick, protective mosquito netting to the floor. It wasn't so much that she *heard* him enter as she *felt* his considerably charismatic presence as he filled the confines of their hut. Twisting her head, she saw him standing there looking down at her. Instantly, her heart thudded with feminine awareness of the banked heat smoldering in his darkened gray eyes. Her mouth went dry. Momentarily frozen, she quickly shook off the reaction and went back to what she was doing.

"You get that comsat link to Morgan?" she asked huskily.

Reid placed the radio on a small wooden table that stood near a wall of the circular hut. A well-used hurricane lamp sitting on the table would provide light against the coming darkness. "Yeah, I did. All's well." He came over and bent down to help her anchor the rest of the very necessary protective netting. "Need help?" His fingers brushed hers.

Casey quivered. Reid was so damn strong, confident and unflappable. Well, wasn't that why he'd been chosen to guard her? Flames licked up her hand where he'd brushed it. "Uh, no, I can get the rest of this...."

Reid straightened as he watched her fumble with the material. "I'll get the kerosene lamp going. Darkness falls pretty rapidly around here, doesn't it?"

"Yes," Casey whispered a little breathlessly. She stood up and brushed her hands nervously against one another. Their "beds" would be at one end of the hut. The netting was tacked to the walls and hung like a tent above the blankets she'd put down for each of them on the grass pallets. No matter how she moved them around, a mere two feet at the most separated their beds. Uneasy, she sighed and put her hands on her hips.

"I don't bite."

She whirled around, startled. Reid was watching her with that predatory intentness of his. A warm sensation lingered in her lower body, a purely feminine reaction to his look. "Uhh..." She gestured nervously to their beds. "It was the best I could do. That netting only stretches so far, and believe me, you don't want to try and sleep without it. The mosquitoes will drive you crazy."

Reid grinned slightly. "Right now, it looks like you'd rather have the mosquitoes feeding on you than sleep that close to me."

Heat suffused her face. Without realizing it, Casey

touched her flaming cheek. "Well," she muttered, "it's just that I'm a rambler and rover when I sleep."

"We'll work it out," he soothed, seeing how genuinely distressed she was about his sleeping so near to her. Swallowing his smile, because he was actually anticipating sleeping close to Casey, Reid turned and left the hut. At the truck, he tried to tell himself that he shouldn't enjoy Casey's discomfort so much. Most men would read her response to mean that she wasn't interested in them. But he saw the interest in her direct green gaze.

As he dug through one of the OID boxes at the rear of the truck, lightning flashed warningly in the distance. The returning rumble of thunder told him he'd better hurry, because the storm looked like it was racing across the savanna directly toward the village. Locating a flashlight and a small tin of kerosene, he locked the car and moved back to the hut.

He nearly ran into Casey at the doorway. She had a towel over her shoulder and a washcloth and soap in her hands.

"Where are you going?" he demanded, stepping aside.

"To the stream nearby," she said, pointing down a well-used trail that disappeared into the forest.

"Hold on, I'll come with you."

Giving him a pained look, Casey said, "I'll be safe enough, Reid. I'm not going to have you watch me strip naked and wash up in that stream."

He set the can of kerosene down on the table. "My orders are not to let you out of my sight." He turned and met her defiant gaze. "So don't give me that look. It won't do any good."

"Hunter, this is ridiculous!" Casey heard her voice go off key. "I've bathed in that stream hundreds of times! Nothing has ever happened to me. It won't now."

"Do black mambas range around at dusk?"

"No, they don't. They're cold-blooded and need the

heat of the sun to get them up to speed. Right now, they're all tucked up for the night in their various burrows." She sounded childish even to herself. "Look, I'll be okay!"

He smiled gently and led her out of the hut. "It's going to be pouring rain in the next hour or so if that storm drifts our way. I could use a bath myself. Got enough soap for two?"

Panic set in. Her eyes narrowed on his darkened, dangerous-looking features. If Casey didn't know any better, she'd think he was *enjoying* her discomfort. "Hunter—"

"Doctor, I'm coming with you. So let's not waste any more time arguing about this, shall we? I'll turn my back at the appropriate time, fair enough?"

Her mouth snapped shut as she was propelled forward by Reid. His hand was steadying on her left arm as he walked her down the path that led into the forest.

"This is ridiculous! We're safe here at the village."

"No," Reid whispered, his mouth very close to her ear, "we're not safe anywhere, so get used to it. You didn't have Black Dawn crawling around before. This village is a target because you're here, and you know that." He straightened and scanned the darkening forest that enclosed them as they walked quickly down the path. "Wasn't it you who called me a guard dog?" he teased, trying to get her to relax.

"I guess," Casey muttered defiantly. She wrested her arm from his hand. "I can walk on my own, Hunter. You act like a broody old mother hen!"

"Now I'm a chicken."

Giving him a dark look of warning, Casey growled, "You are *dangerous*."

Reid chuckled indulgently and kept up with her lengthening stride. "A dangerous chicken?" The trail led to a small pool of dark but clear water. Opposite them was a waterfall about five feet high. The pleasant sound of water tumbling and falling into the oval pool was nice and could easily lull them into a sense of security. However, Reid knew better. Scanning the area once more, his hand under his jacket where the pistol rested, he said, "How am I dangerous, good doctor?"

Sitting down on a flat, smooth stone near the pond, Casey began to unlace her hiking boots. She flung them to one side and yanked off her socks. "You just *are!* Now, will you turn around?"

Chuckling, Reid spotted a huge, smooth red boulder nearby. He found a place to sit with his back toward the pond. From between the branches of the surrounding forest, he could see flashes of lightning now and then.

"How am I dangerous?" he called over his shoulder.

As Casey stripped out of her one-piece cotton suit, her heart pounded in her breast. "Just take my word for it, you are, okay?" She moved quickly into the waist-deep water. It was cooling and welcoming to her hot, perspiring flesh. Taking the washcloth, she dipped it into the water and quickly washed her face. How wonderful the water felt! With a little moan of pleasure, she crouched down, the water flowing over her head and wetting her hair. She was fatigued and the water revived her once more. Standing up, sputtering, Casey scrubbed herself. Stealing a look over her shoulder, she saw that Hunter sat with his back to her. She could tell by his posture that he was alert and on constant guard.

"I've never had a woman tell me I was dangerous before," Reid called out, grinning.

"No?" Casey said archly. Lathering soap on the washcloth, she cleaned her neck, shoulders and arms.

"No. Should I take that as a compliment?"

Casey choked on her laughter.

"Why not?"

"Your kind would," Casey retorted as she quickly rinsed off and moved out of the pool. "You're all so damn overconfident. Male testosterone at its finest—or some such thing...." she muttered. Finding the towel, which she'd hung on a nearby branch, Casey dried herself off. She'd brought a sleeveless cotton shift, socks and a pair of leather loafers to wear on the way back.

Sitting down, she quickly slipped into the white cotton socks and pushed her feet into the loafers. Standing, she said, "It's your turn...and I'm not staying here and playing guard dog for you. Okay?"

Reid slid off the rock and turned around. His grin widened into a smile. "You look like Raggedy Ann."

The warmth burning in his eyes, the sense that he was embracing her with his gaze, caught Casey off guard—again. She nervously ran her fingers through her red hair and tried to tame it into some kind of order. "My hair is always messy looking," she said lamely, "no matter what I try to do with it. It's naturally curly. It has a mind of its own...."

"Like you," Reid said with a quiet laugh. "I know a lot of women who would kill to have naturally curly hair like you have," he said as he approached her, his gaze moving over her. The red-pink-and-white shift hung to her knees and revealed her fine, thin collarbone and hinted at the swell of her breasts before it fell loosely to her knees.

Casey stepped to the side. Reid was too close. Way too close. Thrusting the towel into his hand, she muttered, "Here. The washcloth and soap are over there on the rock. I'll see you when you get back. All I want to do is go to sleep and get rid of this jet lag."

Chuckling, Reid watched her take off down the path. Now that he'd had a chance to survey the area, he decided not to push the guard dog thing too much with her. When there was danger around, the hairs on the back of his neck always stood up in silent warning. Right now, he sensed nothing but a sleepy village preparing for nightfall. The illumination of lightning skittered across the sky to the west of them. Not long afterward, thunder growled.

Turning, he began to strip off his clothes. A quick dip in this refreshing pool was just what he needed to wash away some of the jet lag lapping at his senses. As he waded in, the thought of lying down to sleep with Casey no more than a foot or two away snagged his attention. Could he keep his hands to himself? Reid wasn't sure, but he knew what he had to do. No matter how badly he wanted to touch Casey, taste her and feel her pressed up against his hard male body, it couldn't happen. One woman had stood him up at the altar. He was damned if he was going to be hurt by a woman again. To make sure that wouldn't happen, he had to remain immune to Casey. On all levels...

The next morning they drove across the emerald savanna, which was covered with thousands of animals grazing eagerly on the rich, green offering. Casey took the wheel because she knew where the last scientific site had been set up. Hunter was on guard, his gaze constantly shifting. If he was honest, he'd admit he wanted to center his attention on her. She wore that comfortable, one-piece, olive green suit and sensible shoes, and her mop of red hair was a glorious crown to her drab outfit.

Still, he saw the strain and tension in her. They were going back to where her two friends had just been murdered weeks before, and as a result Casey wasn't herself. As beautiful as Africa was on this sunlit morning, Reid knew she didn't see beauty; she saw only death. Her full mouth was pursed, and as much as he fought against it, the suffering in her green eyes reached out and seared his heart. How could he handle all the emotions he saw in her? She was too raw, always leaving herself wide-open to more pain and suffering.

The jungle loomed before them as they approached the old scientific site. Casey parked the truck at the edge of the savanna. A red flag nearby indicated the start of the trail to the site itself. She moved jerkily as they transferred necessary items into large backpacks. Her usual camaraderie was nowhere to be found, and Hunter felt pressed to say something to relieve the tension that hung around them.

As he helped her into her backpack and then shrugged into his own, he turned to her and said, "Let me lead."

Casey opened her mouth to disagree, then compressed her lips once again. "Fine. Go ahead." Her heart was throbbing with pain. She was trying to prepare herself to walk into that clearing where the temporary lab had been set up.

"Not even a fight to take the lead?" Reid teased. He lifted one corner of his mouth.

Casey knew what he was trying to do. "I'm not good at hiding anything," she muttered by way of an apology.

He wanted to reach out, to tell her it was all right, but he resisted. Standing less than a foot away from her, he nodded and forced himself to keep his hands at his sides. "Yeah, I understand. When you lose good friends in combat, it hurts."

Casey studied him. "Have you lost friends that way?"

"In the Gulf War? Yes, I did."

"Did you have to return to the site where they died and continue your work?"

He saw her point. Clearly. Looking down at the damp grass between them, he rasped, "No, I didn't have to do that…not like you have to now.…"

Damn. There was no getting around Casey. Around her pain and grief. Hunter turned on his heel, at a loss for what else to say or do. He felt ill equipped to deal with this whole situation. And it was only going to get worse.

They moved into the jungle. Large-leafed bushes swatted at them as he followed a small, well-trodden path back into the gloomy depths. Many sounds and smells surrounded them as they walked in the fragrance of orchids hanging from trees or growing on rotting logs they crossed, the screech of monkeys, the calls of birds. His senses were awake and ready for Black Dawn. Almost unthinking, he touched the holster at his left side, where the pistol rested, unstrapped, locked and loaded.

Casey followed, lost in a fog of grief. Her friends' faces danced before her. She didn't see the beauty of sunlight cascading in golden sheets through the trees and palms. Normally, the melody of the birds enthralled her, but it didn't today. The loss of Stan and Vince blanketed her until her vision blurred. When Casey realized she was going to start crying, she fought back the tears. She knew Hunter didn't like to see women cry. Besides, she had a job to do. The camp needed to be reclaimed, set back up, and the work had to begin, regardless. Girding herself, she did her best to shove down her morass of grief and doggedly follow Reid up the gentle incline leading to the clearing.

It took nearly twenty minutes for them to reach the site. Casey halted when Reid stopped and held out his arm in warning. She didn't want to look up, but forced herself to anyway. In front of them was an oblong clearing about the size of a football field. It was here that Stan and Vince had been working for nearly three months, sifting through the remains of animals and reptiles in an effort to find the Ebola reservoir. Her stomach clenched painfully as she gazed across the clearing. The folding tables were still there, the worse for wear, all of them tipped over, their aluminum legs aimed at the sky. There was evidence of where Stan and Vince had maintained a campfire, and Casey knew from long experience that near the charred hole in the ground there had also been two tents. The grass had grown a lot in the last few weeks and she knew it was because of all the rain.

Once Reid was satisfied there was no danger, he slowly moved forward, and Casey forced herself to do the same.

As her boot touched the green of the dewy grass, she flinched. From the black-and-white photos she'd seen of the place, she knew exactly where Vince and Stan had been shot and had fallen to their deaths. Her throat closed up. Breathing became an effort. Hunter was already in the center of the clearing and had shed his backpack. He'd drawn out the pistol, and the intensity on his face left no question that he was in his guard dog mode, making sure they weren't in jeopardy.

Hunter moved rapidly around the perimeter of the clearing. It took nearly twenty minutes for him to do his job and do it thoroughly. First, he listened for sounds in the jungle that surrounded the area. Then he looked for evidence of fresh footprints, freshly broken branches or any possible indication that Black Dawn could be hiding, or may have been lurking. When he found nothing, relief thrummed through him and he put the pistol into his shoulder holster and turned around.

His heart clenched painfully in his chest. His breathing hitched momentarily. There in the center of the clearing was Casey, kneeling on the ground. One hand was pressed to the green earth, the other to her face, her head bowed. Off to the left was her backpack. Releasing an explosive breath, Reid wavered. He saw her shoulders shaking. She was crying—hard. But there was no sound. In an instant, he realized she wanted to sob out loud, but wouldn't. Instead, he saw the racking motions working up her back, saw her shoulders tremble. She was weeping for the loss of two very dear friends.

His mouth went dry. His feet wanted to hurry forward toward Casey, but panic seized him. Should he? Should he reach out as he had in the jet and touch her, try to comfort her? At what cost to himself? It had nearly unstrung him to touch her in the aircraft. He'd been so scared, but something had driven him to it. That same obsession captured

him again. How badly he wanted to hurry to Casey, lean
down and—*oh, to hell with it.*

Hunter strode toward her. He couldn't help himself. Approaching her from the rear, he knew Casey wasn't aware
of his presence. Recalling the photos of the site, he knew
that where she had placed her hand was where Stan had
fallen and bled to death.

Reid's heart was pounding hard in his chest. He jerked
to a halt, mere inches from where she knelt, her head
bowed, her face hidden. From this distance, he could hear
soft sobs being torn from her. He saw her fingers dig convulsively into the dark, rich soil.

Touch her. Help her.

Reid cursed himself. Like a robot, he moved his hand
out toward her shaking shoulder. His movements were
jerky and uncoordinated. A part of him wanted to rear
back, as if burned. Another part screamed at him to make
contact with Casey. *Damn it, man, she needs your help!
Comfort her. You can at least do that much for her.*

Reid stood over her, his shadow falling across her, his
fingers stretched outward, a bare inch separating them.
Fear ate at him. He couldn't do it. He just didn't have
what it took to reach out, fold Casey in his arms and hold
her, simply hold her. That was what she needed. Why
couldn't he give her that? Why? He was such a coward.
A coward about living life. About risking his own worthless hide to help another person who was hurting so terribly.

Turning away, Hunter felt bitterness assail him. He
hated himself. He hated the fact that he had no heart. No
ability to feel, just as Janet had declared that day a year
ago. Damn it. Damn his inability to be human. A cry like
that of a wounded animal rose violently within him. It hit
his throat and he swallowed convulsively as he moved
morosely toward his backpack. He had to do something—
anything—to not feel this pain of hers. The soft sobs from

Casey tore at him. Each sob was like someone placing a red-hot meat hook into his heart and jerking it, as if trying to tear the organ out of his chest. He hurt with anguish. Her anguish. It felt as if someone had slammed a scalding brand across the flesh of his massive chest. Reid could barely breathe, barely move. Leaning down, he jerked at the buckles on the backpack. He didn't see the pack. All he could hear and feel were Casey's sobs of grief, her goodbye to her very close friends who'd been murdered for no reason at all.

At times such as this, Hunter didn't like himself. The ugliness in him, the shortcomings, were all too visible right now. Any decent human being, any other man, would have gone over to her, knelt by her and put his arms around her to assuage the terrible anguish she was going through. Janet was right: he was only half-human. The other half of him was dead. Numb to the world and to the people who needed him. Kneeling down, he continued to pull angrily at the release buckles on the backpack. Someone had to set up camp. Someone had to be a guard dog. Well, those were two things he *could* do right and do well. Yanking the pack upright, Reid began to take pieces of equipment out of it one at a time and put them in neat rows for use later.

Let Casey cry. He was no good at comforting others. He never had been. A huge part of him wanted to comfort her, but he didn't know how. He was sure he'd bumble it, embarrass himself and screw it up for her. And in the end, he told himself with dark, seething anger, all he would do was make Casey feel worse, not better. At least let her have this cry, this final goodbye, without his messing it up, as he had every other intimate relationship he'd ever started in the past.

In those serrating minutes that followed, with Casey's soft sobs filling the clearing, Reid moved in a haze of self-loathing. Janet was right: he was worthless.

Chapter Seven

Casey's skin tingled as Reid made himself comfortable beneath the protective mosquito netting over their beds. Without it, they'd be eaten alive by insects. Right now, Casey seriously considered that option. Last night sharing the small sleeping area hadn't turned out to be an issue. Both of them were so exhausted from traveling they'd fallen fast asleep. But tonight Casey felt gutted. Her weeping in the clearing today for Stan and Vince had been unexpected. But Casey couldn't help how she felt. Hunter had acted like she was a leper for baring her emotions at all, but that was too bad. Then later, after he'd set up the tables and gotten out the equipment they needed to begin their research, he'd been solicitous. Even at the dinner feast Henri had prepared that evening in her honor, he'd acted strangely.

But Casey couldn't be angry with him. She understood that Hunter had a problem with showing his feelings. He was afraid to expose how he felt. Most men were. Reid, however, seemed to have more walls to surmount than most, she realized, feeling exhausted. He'd tried to make up for his lack of humanity in many ways during the rest of that day, and Casey had absorbed each little nuance greedily. She'd cried so hard out there that her stomach still felt tied in knots, and she unconsciously rubbed the area. More than anything, she'd craved a little care from Hunter, but he'd been unable to provide it. He'd busied himself instead with setting up their base camp. She tried very hard not to expect anything of this hardened warrior, but her heart kept crying out for him, reaching for him.

So many times today Casey had wanted to find an excuse to have her hand touch his. Or to pretend to bump into him by accident. Casey couldn't bring herself to do that. She was an honest person, not a manipulative one, and she knew it was grief that was making her consider such an action. A part of her understood that despite Hunter's toughness, he was far more fragile in an emotional sense than she was presently, and that was why Casey didn't chew herself out about how she'd felt with Reid today.

As he shifted in his bed beside her, she sighed. Why did he have to look so damn appealing in his light blue pajama bottoms? Why couldn't he have worn the top instead of revealing his massive, dark-haired chest, which begged her to slide her fingers across it and enjoy? The air was hot in the hut, almost stifling. Casey wished one of the thunderstorms rolling across the savanna would lift the oppressive heat and humidity from the village. Anything to take her mind off the fact that she needed his touch, craved his embrace and simply wanted to sink against him and be held for just a little while.

Her pale pink cotton nightie seemed little protection against his powerful sexual appeal. The lace bordering the deep V-neck accentuated her femininity, suggesting a hint of her breasts beneath the lightweight material. Casey lamely realized that the normal nightly attire she'd thrown into her suitcase, while practical in this humidity, wasn't suited to sleeping in a hut with a man next to her. It was too late to do anything about it. Tugging in frustration on the hem, she wished it fell far below her knees.

She lay on her side, her back to Hunter and her arm beneath her head. Even the cotton nightie clung to her. She had to adjust to Africa's sweltering humidity again. Until then, she'd perspire just as Reid was doing. The windows in the hut were open, but the air was sluggish at best. She felt trapped by Reid's closeness. Casey swore she could feel his masculine heat rolling off him like bright sunlight. She itched to move. But where? They had anchored down the netting so insects couldn't crawl beneath it. She was as close as she could get to the barrier and yet her heart palpitated wildly in her breast.

"Good night," Reid rumbled.

"Sweet dreams," Casey replied unhappily. He sounded like he was already half-asleep. And why not? They were both still drunk with jet lag and travel fatigue. So why wasn't she sleepy? Scrunching her eyes shut, Casey forced herself to stop thinking, but she couldn't help being aware of Reid's closeness. His obvious male aura beckoned her and she fought it with panic.

I'm afraid of him, she realized, while another voice taunted her: *You wimp, Morrow! Come on, you're made of sterner stuff than this! You're like a teenage girl with a crush on the first boy you loved. What gives? He hasn't touched you and you're acting like a drama queen!* Sighing loudly, Casey flattened her lips, very unhappy with herself and her reaction to Reid. It was those damnable heated, smoldering looks he gave her from time to time that were stimulating her, whether she wanted the stimulation or not. Her body certainly entertained the thought of his hands moving across her. And she couldn't deny that her feelings were growing by the second for this...Neanderthal man. Of all men to be drawn to! A caveman throwback! Casey snorted at the ridiculousness of the situation.

Hunter snored.

Well, at least he was getting some sleep! Casey was disgruntled with herself and her jumbled feelings. Reid was obviously not interested in her or he wouldn't have fallen asleep so quickly, logic told her. Casey heard thunder rumbling again in the distance. If only it would rain! Then maybe she could go to sleep. She needed to rest up before they returned to the site. She didn't want to feel her need for Reid's touch to heal her broken, torn heart again. Just being out in that clearing today and knowing her friends had met their death there had nearly sapped the last of Casey's strength. Could she go out there tomorrow and work? Her heart whispered that Hunter *could* give her the necessary, sustaining strength she needed, but he wasn't about to touch her in any way, shape or form. Casey fell asleep wondering what it would be like to kiss that strong mouth of his. She found herself smiling faintly as she dropped off into the spiraling darkness, finding temporary relief in dreams that comforted her just a little after the brutal reality of her day.

Casey's dream of a pleasant, heated response to Reid's mouth pressed hotly against her lips changed. Soon a nightmare stalked her and darkness overtook her. As she plunged downward at a dizzying rate, she heard her own screams, her own cries of anguish. Pain replaced the too brief pleasure of Reid's mouth upon her own. She saw dark, crawling worms coming toward her. She heard harsh breathing. The stench of death cloaked her. A crashing sound ripped through her grief and pain. Casey fought to run away from it. The worms caught up with her, slithered around her and began squeezing her. She felt hot blood pouring out of her nose and mouth. *No! Oh, God, no!*

Reid snapped upright as Casey screamed. Sleep was torn from him as her cry echoed rawly through the darkened hut. *What? Where?* He instantly went into action, thrusting his hand toward the revolver that lay next to his pillow. *An intruder? Where?* He was on his knees instantly, hands on the pistol. As he aimed it toward the door, lightning flashed and thunder caromed right above them. The hut shook violently. Rain was slashing through the open windows. Gusts of wind funneled through the hut.

Once Reid was assured there were no intruders, Casey's sob distracted him. Breathing harshly, he twisted toward her. The lightning illuminated her huddled form. She was sitting up, sobbing wildly, her hands pressed to her face. Reid threw the netting aside. Closing the windows so the rain would stop pouring in, he yanked the rest of the netting away from Casey. Breathing hard, he hunkered above her, inches separating them. What should he do? Her cries were tearing him apart. He shut his eyes as his world tilted out of control. Heat burst across his chest. How badly he wanted to help her! If only…if only he could…if only he wouldn't screw it up and hurt her more… What should he do?

His hand ached to reach out for her tousled hair, illuminated by the lightning once again. A thunderous crash caromed above them and he winced. She was crying like a frightened child. A child, not a woman. He remembered all too well how scared he'd been as a child. As a four-year-old, he'd hidden in the broom closet to get away from a violent storm that had frightened him. No one had been there for him. His mother had been at work, and so had his father. The baby-sitter was somewhere else—where, he didn't know. He'd been alone. Alone in the dark, hurting badly and crying so hard for Mama and Papa.

Cursing softly, Reid threw caution aside. If Casey was feeling half of what he'd felt as that little four-year-old kid, then anything was better than nothing. All he could do was reach out to her and try. Driven by memories from his past, Reid moved forward.

"Hey…" he soothed as he knelt down beside her. His reactions were purely instinctual. He was still fatigued, his senses spinning, his adrenaline high from the attack that hadn't materialized. Blindly reaching out, Hunter brought her into the shelter of his arms and used his body to protect her as he nestled her between his thighs. "Come here, it's all right, sweetheart…it's all right," he whispered roughly. To his utter surprise, Casey collapsed against him. Without hesitation, she pressed her cheek against his damp chest and her arms went around his naked torso. The sobs tearing from her stripped away his grogginess. As he sat there holding her, feeling each shaky sob work its way through her, Reid pressed his hand against her hair and tried to simply soothe her. She must have had one helluva bad dream, he decided distractedly. Probably about Stan and Vince. He knew that this morning Casey had worked valiantly to stifle her sobs and hide her grief from him. Guiltily, he knew she was more than aware of his discomfort over her crying. She'd tried so hard all day to keep her feelings from him. Now her sorrow was stalking her again, and this time he hoped he could be of help in allowing her the time she needed to cry, to heal the wounds deep within her heart over the loss of her two friends.

But his other senses were registering the feel of her soft hair against his jaw. The scent of her as a woman filled his flaring nostrils. He placed his mouth against her head and kissed her hair. It felt vibrant and soft—like she did. Gently rubbing his hand in a slow up and down motion across her back, he felt the accumulated tension in her.

"It's okay," he rasped, "let it go, just let it go…. I'm here, I'll take care of you…." And he would. Reid knew he was only a guard dog, a protector. Right now, that's what Casey needed: his help. His care. Nothing had ever seemed so right or so good to him as when he began to rock her gently in his arms. She was like a hurt child whose sadness wouldn't be assuaged.

Driven by her grief-filled sobs, by the way she clung to him as if releasing him would mean drowning in a sea of virulent pain, Reid kept murmuring her name and tenderly stroking her hair, shoulders and back as he held her tightly with his other arm. She felt so damn good against him, the willowy length of her against his chest and torso, and trapped between his thighs. Heat and hardness began to gather in his lower body to a painful degree. He felt the firm softness of her breasts against his chest. Felt the heat of her tears as they dribbled down through the thick hair there. With trembling fingers, he awkwardly tried to remove the tears from her cheek. She only cried harder.

Another bolt of lightning flashed across the village. The hut trembled violently, as if mirroring the throes of agony that Casey was caught up in. He kissed her hair again, mesmerized by her sweet, womanly fragrance. He felt her arms tighten as he sought and found her damp cheek. Without meaning to, because he was no longer thinking, just instinctively reacting to her needs, he pressed his mouth against the soft curve of her cheekbone. She tasted sweet and salty. He felt her release him, her fingers dragging across his chest, as if asking for more of what he was giving her.

It was so easy to give Casey solace in this form. Reid surrendered to the explosive moment as her fingers trailed shyly across his shoulder and then encircled the back of his neck. She wanted him to kiss her. The realization was galvanizing. Necessary. Life-giving. His whole self, his normal reactions, were in chaos. In those seconds, Reid surrendered to the craziness of the situation and followed the cry of his heart. Leaning down those scant inches that still separated them, he sought and found her parted lips, bathed in tears. He took his tongue and gently ran it across her full lower lip. The salt mingled with her taste as a woman. The texture of her mouth met his. She trembled violently. He hesitated as he heard a sob catch in her throat. Driven by the need to help her, Reid slid his hand beneath her jaw and guided her face upward to meet his descending mouth.

As his lips closed over hers, he felt her suddenly tense, and then, just as quickly, she melted as his mouth took hers. He sensed what she needed and pushed beyond his normal guard, taking her mouth fully, deeply, and moving his tongue inside to explore her. The sweetness of the fruit she'd eaten earlier, the taste that was only her, filled his senses. Fire arced through his lower body and he groaned as she sought, matched and met him on equal ground. Her breath was shallow and swift. He could feel her heart pounding against his chest.

Moving his hands to her face, he imprisoned her and tilted her head to a better angle to kiss her, to take her more deeply, to brand her and make her his in all ways. She was hungry. As hungry as he was for her, he discovered in those molten, pounding moments. He was barely aware of the thunder around them. The white-hot flash of lightning scored him internally and he ached to bury himself within her yielding, soft form. Her mouth was pliant, giving and taking, teasing and testing. Her hands moved restlessly across his chest and shoulders. Wildfires of need burned in the wake of her fingertips as they caressed his taut, screaming flesh.

Rain pounded down upon the hut. The sound drowned out their own heavy breathing, the clamoring of his heart. Reid swam in the heat and light of her response to him. She was a strong, confident woman and he'd never met someone with quite her boldness before, much less had the enjoyment of kissing her, exploring her as he was doing right now. As he gently nibbled her lower lip, he felt her sink against him, as if begging him to continue teasing her, tasting her. Reid knew he had to stop, but he didn't want to. Casey was one of the most alive women he'd ever met in his life. She was one of a kind. And even though they were diametric opposites in many ways, she fit him like sunlight fit darkness. His ache to take her all the way, to bring her down on top of him, to arch and sink himself into her hot, melting depths, nearly overpowered him.

But right now, he was the one who had to take control of the situation. Though it was the last thing he wanted to acknowledge, he knew right from wrong. His instincts screamed at him that she was in pain and he was helping to heal her. To go too far, however, would be to take advantage of the situation—and Casey. In the long run, Hunter knew that if he didn't stop kissing her now, he would ruin any possible future with her. And more than anything, that's what he wanted: a future with her. The thought sent fear sizzling through him. How could he want that? Hadn't he learned from Janet? Hadn't she taught him he was half a man, not a whole one? A woman like Casey would never settle for someone like him. Never. And Reid could never withstand another confrontation like he'd had with Janet. No, it was his stupid, blind heart that wanted this pipe dream.

As he dragged his mouth from Casey's soft, well-kissed lips, Reid was breathing hard and fast. He held her gently in his arms afterward. She trusted him. Completely. That realization staggered him as he gazed down at her tear-dampened face, her closed eyes and those delicious, begging, glistening lips of hers. The driving ache to claim her mouth again was nearly his undoing. Groaning softly, Reid shifted Casey to his right side so that she could rest against him, her head on his shoulder. Lifting his other hand, he tried his best to remove the dampness of the spent tears from her now very flushed cheeks. Each time he stroked her flesh, she trembled a little. The last of her sobs eased as the thunderstorm passed beyond the village, and soon Casey quieted in his arms.

Reid lay with his back against the wall of the hut in the consuming darkness and realized he had never felt so alive. So raw. So scared. Somehow, he hadn't screwed it up this time. Somehow, through some miracle unknown to him, Casey—warm, firm and sensuous in his embrace—was content to just be held in the aftermath of her own internal storm. A soft sigh of relief escaped from him and Reid closed his eyes and rested his jaw against her hair. He could feel her heart slowing down a bit now. Her breathing was becoming normalized. Taking in a deep, broken breath, Reid smiled a little.

"You're going to be okay now...." The words came out low and deep and strained. Yes, he was exhausted. It had taken every ounce of inner strength to not take Casey all the way with him. Reid knew it would have been the greatest thing to happen to him in his entire life. His mouth tingled with the memory of her lips against his. She had such courage. Such fire within her, which she'd shared so bravely and fully with him in those stormy moments when her grief had taken charge of her. With awkward movements, he stroked her hair, her shoulder and arm. And without meaning to, he began rocking her again as if she were a scared child. Wasn't she? That was what had galvanized him into action—his sharp remembrance of his own four-year-old response to being terrified and alone. He had connected with Casey on that level and had been able to reach out and comfort her.

Reid opened his eyes and lifted his chin. His gaze narrowed on the rain-streaked window opposite them. The lightning was less and less frequent now, the storm leaving the village far behind. Cool air breathed in and out of the hut and relieved the stifling humidity within. He took a deep, halting breath of his own. Tonight, in this moment, his whole world had changed. Just having this wonderfully alive woman in his arms, sharing her tears, her pain with him, had forever changed him.

Reid was scared as never before, holding this woman who met and matched him fearlessly at every breath, every heartbeat. As he moved his fingers through her silky hair, he closed his eyes and savored their unspoken intimacy. Casey kept her arms around his torso and continued to rest her head wearily against his shoulder. How good it felt to be needed! Old pain came back along with old memories of the day that Janet had called off their wedding. She hadn't needed him, not like this; not like one human being needs another to feel safe, to feel cared for and loved when all hell breaks loose. Janet had been so sure he was heartless that she'd never given him a chance to see if he really was. Now, with Casey in his arms, he had living proof that maybe—just maybe—he wasn't as unfeeling as he thought.

What did he feel for Casey? Love? Reid's eyes snapped open. His hand hovered over her head. *Love?* Trying to push the word out of his mind and out of his heart, he allowed his hand to come to rest on her slumped shoulder. Her skin was cool now and not damp as before. The softly rumpled cotton of her gown contrasted with the supple smoothness of her flesh. His brow wrinkled as he tested the word again—carefully this time.

Reid thought he knew what love was all about; after all, he'd fallen in love with Janet. Hadn't he? Then why were all these emotions, like bright, scintillating lights, going off in his chest, in his heart? Janet had never made him feel like this—strong, needed and desired. And she'd repeatedly pointed out his shortcomings, his inability to love her the way she needed to be loved. She'd claimed she needed a whole man, not half a man.

Reid's attention was snagged as Casey sighed audibly. Shifting his weight, he looked down at her. He felt her sadness even though her eyes remained closed. He heard it in her sigh. Smiling softly to himself, he rested his jaw against her hair.

"Just sleep, sweetheart. You'll feel better in the morning. Daylight always makes things look better, believe me...." He began to lightly stroke her shoulder and arm as he might soothe a fractious, frightened four-year-old who was wild-eyed with fear. When she took in a deep breath, Reid breathed in with her. And when she released it, he did as well. How easy it was to meet and become a part of Casey. How exhilaratingly easily.

As Reid sat there with her in his arms, her long body stretched out between his thighs, her lower legs across his own, he'd never felt so happy. So complete. And with that thought, he allowed his hand to come to rest on her arm, and closed his eyes. The spicy fragrance of her perfume combined with her womanly softness conspired to lull him asleep. As a marine, he'd slept in much more uncomfortable positions than this. He knew the healing value of sleep and, within moments, dropped off into it. Only this time, his heart whispered as he spiraled into the warm darkness, he held the woman who could fulfill him in every conceivable way.

Bright sunlight lanced into the hut's window, waking Reid. He felt the warmth on his face and groaned, lifting his hand to rub his eyes. Almost instantly, he missed Casey being in his arms. Tearing himself from sleep, Reid sat up. Where was she?

He blinked, trying to rid himself of the grogginess that still blanketed his senses. Looking around the sunlit hut, he realized she was not here. Outside the hut, he heard the pleasant Bantu language drifting into earshot. Several dogs were barking somewhere in the distance, and he heard a number of children screaming and playing nearby. The odor of food made his stomach growl. Rubbing his belly, Reid forced himself to his feet. Looking around, he saw that Casey's feminine nightgown was neatly folded on the table.

Had last night really happened? He touched his mouth, the taste, the feel of Casey still there, still resonating and making him tingle with longing. Yes, it had happened. His body remembered it well. His heart felt wide-open, like someone had put a hot brand on it. Rubbing his chest, he slowly turned around and pulled aside the fabric that covered the door. The sunlight was strong and he blinked several times before he realized the truck was gone. Casey was gone! Suddenly, all his warrior senses sprang to life.

With a curse, Reid moved back into the hut. He shed his pajama bottoms and quickly pulled on a pair of dark green marine utilities and a white cotton shirt. After he laced up his hiking boots, he slipped on the shoulder holster and pulled a lightweight jacket over it. Hurrying outside, he noticed the rainstorm of the night before had left the land washed clean, and the red soil a muddy mire.

Children played around some of the campfires where food was cooking in kettles. He saw a number of older women tending the fires and food. Shading his eyes, he made a sweep around the village. The truck was nowhere to be seen. And neither was Casey.

"The morning is old."

Reid whirled around, his eyes widening. A man in his mid-forties judging by his salt-and-pepper hair, and wearing jeans, boots and a white linen shirt, smiled at him.

"I am Paul, oldest son of Henri," he said, extending his hand.

Reid grasped it, noting the man's resemblance to Henri. Paul had his father's thin frame, broad brow and high cheekbones. Reid immediately felt he could trust him. "Reid Hunter. Have you seen Casey?"

"Yes, I did. She left several hours ago. I assume you want to help her out at the site?"

Reid nodded. "I do. How can I get there?"

"By horseback." He smiled again.

"I see...."

"Follow me. I will take you by horseback to the cave area. We have no cars here, other than those brought by visitors. My father has some fine Thoroughbred horses given to him several years ago. When I come home from Kinshasa for a visit, he allows me to ride them. My father is too old to ride, but my children, as well as Henri's other grandchildren like them."

Reid nodded, noticing how good Paul's English was. It was obvious he was well educated. "Okay, I can stay on board a horse." Lucky for him, he'd been raised around horses in Colorado. He used to own a quarter horse, which he'd shown as a kid.

"It is an hour by horseback to Casey's site. I like to gallop across the plains among all the wild animals. Doubtless, you will enjoy it, too."

Paul's eyes gleamed playfully, then danced with laughter. Reid liked him instantly and would have enjoyed his easy comaraderie under other circumstances. Right now, his mind was centered on Casey. Why had she left him behind? In one way, he was relieved. He didn't know what to say or how to apologize for his awkward attempts to comfort her last night. He hadn't meant to kiss her. He was sure she had left this morning embarrassed and properly shocked by his behavior, and wanted to be left alone. Did she see him as taking advantage of her? Of their situation last night?

"I hope you like English saddles," Paul warned as they left the central area of the village. "No western saddles in Africa, I'm afraid."

Reid kept pace with the man's long stride. Outside the village, in a huge stockade of fifteen-foot-high poles that had been assembled vertically into a huge holding pen, he saw ten horses of various colors and sizes. "Where I come from, western saddles are the only type we know."

Chuckling, Paul rubbed his long, artistic hands together. "If you fall off, then, I will stop and pick you up."

Reid didn't think there was much chance of that. All he wanted to do was get to Casey. A number of Henri's grandchildren tagged along, and at the corral gate, Paul asked them to catch a big, gray Thoroughbred gelding and a black mare of equal height. They were the tallest animals in the stockade. Within minutes, the horses were saddled and bridled.

"Take the black mare," Paul instructed as he mounted the restive gray. "She is swift and surefooted and tolerate riders who may not know what they're doing." He laughed deeply.

There wasn't much to the English saddle, in Reid's opinion— a mere postage stamp of leather on the mare' broad, shining back. She, too, was anxious to get moving tossing her head and snorting in anticipation of getting to stretch out her long, fine legs across the savanna. Mounting, Reid automatically wrapped his legs around the horse's barrel, heels down, toes up and pointed toward her refined head. Gathering up the braided leather reins, he kept light contact with her soft mouth. These horses were not only well cared for, but obviously well trained. That surprised him a little as they moved out at a ground-eating trot and circled the outside of the corral.

"They want to run!" Paul shouted over his shoulder as they quickly left the village behind.

Ahead of them lay the rolling green savanna. Reid estimated there were at least a thousand zebras and wildebeests in front of them, strung out over many miles of the seemingly endless grasslands. He kept the fractious black mare in check as she danced and sidled, wanting much more than a sedate trot. Then Paul gestured for them to gallop. Reid swallowed hard and hoped like hell there weren't many holes in the earth, or else they could end up breaking a horse's leg and flying off their mounts.

The gray moved like a streak of lightning as Paul gave the horse his head and leaned low in the saddle. Reid' black mare bucked and lunged against the tightness of her snaffle bit. He talked soothingly to her as he planned where he wanted the horse to gallop. He could feel her quivering with pent-up energy. Of all the things he'd expected from Africa, riding at a furious gallop through chest-deep green grass was not one of them. Leaning low, the horse's black mane whipping in his face, he kept the mare steady between his legs as he guided her around the scattering black-and-white zebras. The wind gusted past him and his eyes watered as the mare lunged powerfully forward, her long legs eating up the distance between them and the fleeing gray gelding.

Laughter tunneled out of Reid spontaneously. Memories of his childhood, of riding his dun quarter horse across the open valley bracketed by the Rocky Mountains, came flooding back to him. He'd missed the feel of a good horse under him. And now this black mare, who snorted with each stride, her small ears laid back against her head, was carrying him closer and closer to Casey. To the confrontation to come. His hands were damp against the braided leather reins. Would Casey confront him? Be angry? Give him the silent treatment? Fear stalked Reid as he rode the speeding horse closer and closer to the edge of the savanna toward a line of hardwood trees and palms in the distance. Fear that he wouldn't say the right thing. Fear that Casey would reject him.

But beyond his fears, Reid felt his heart bursting with desire for Casey. He thirsted for more of what they'd shared last night. Never had he wanted anything in his life as much as he wanted another chance to hold her in his arms. Would she ever give him that chance again? Reid knew he didn't deserve one. At all. Further, he didn't know if he'd have the guts to walk down that path with her if she offered herself to him. He'd done it once with Janet and his whole world had been turned upside down. It was something he couldn't conceive of ever risking again.

Chapter Eight

Casey's hands froze above the specimen that she was dissecting at the sound of horses approaching. Clothed in a makeshift paper lab coat, protective goggles and several layers of gloves, she stood at the table, her microscope and slides nearby. Her heart bounded violently in her breast as she heard the sound of Reid's laughter, along with another man's. Glancing around, she saw Paul on a gray mare and Reid dismounting from a black horse. How handsome Reid looked!

Gulping, Casey forced herself to pay attention to her work, to where she placed the scalpel in the dead bat in order to carefully dissect it. She was looking for Ebola. One wrong slip with the deadly blade and she could slice through her gloves, cut into her skin and infect herself. Whether this species of bat had Ebola in it or not, she didn't know. The stains on the slides would be sent to the OID in Atlanta, Georgia, for verification.

She heard Paul's voice. He and Reid were talking like

old friends. Brothers. That rankled Casey. She wondered how much Reid knew. Had Grandpa Henri talked to him? Did he know the truth? That she had planned on leaving this morning, catching a flight out of Yambuku and returning to Kinshasa? What a coward she was! In that moment, Casey didn't like herself very much. One kiss! One heated, heart-melting kiss and she was running like a frightened animal. Her hands trembled. She stopped, took a deep, steadying breath before continuing to work.

The sound of the horses leaving caught her attention. When she glanced up again, she saw Reid had been left alone. Tension crawled through her as she anticipated his approach. She felt his eyes on her back. Her heart skittered. Her fingers hovered over the dissected creature on the table before her. She caught the sound of Reid's boots moving through the damp vegetation of the jungle floor. He was coming slowly but surely toward her. What was she going to say? She was scared. So scared.

Out of the corner of her eye as she leaned over to place a slide inside the bat, Casey saw Reid come around one side of the table. Forcing herself to concentrate on the task at hand, she retrieved the sample from the bat. As she reached for a clean slide to put over it, Reid handed one to her.

Mouth dry, she carefully took the slide, afraid that she might contaminate him with her bloody glove. "Thanks," she whispered hoarsely. He was so close. And so damnably, pulverizingly male. She ached for his touch, his protective embrace once again. How could she? Placing the slide into a paper container, she straightened up. Well, now she had to face the music. Reid didn't deserve her cowardice, but her honesty, instead.

Stepping away from the table, Casey lifted her head and met his slate gray gaze. "What took you so long?"

Reid smiled tentatively as he cautiously gauged her reaction to him. "I overslept this morning." And then he added teasingly, "Had a busy night last night, but I'm no complaining." He saw the tension on Casey's very read able features. He was more than a little aware of the fea banked in her eyes. She was standing as if trying to prepar herself against a physical blow. Why? With the paper hoo over her head, the goggles in place to protect her eyes from any splattering while dissecting and her paper lab coat on she looked alien. But the goggles couldn't hide how sh felt. Her green eyes were in absolute turmoil, her gaz skittering and never quite meeting his. Then his own gaz moved down to her soft, lush lips, which were now com pressed tightly, and he realized she was holding back a lo of feelings.

"Do you need some help getting out of that space sui of yours?" he asked, hoping to put her at ease.

Casey knew Reid deserved an answer for her reaction to him. Instead, she focused on the task at hand "Yes...could you? Put on a clean pair of gloves though before you touch this stuff." She pointed to a biohazard box, where all the paraphernalia would be placed and then burned. Viruses died in sunlight, bleach and extreme heat She turned around so that Reid could untie her paper lat coat. Taking a shaky breath as she felt his fingers brush her back, Casey tried to capture all her escaping feelings His touch last night...it had been excruciatingly tender and oh, so healing to her. How badly she wanted his touch again! It was crazy. Crazy!

Reid helped Casey disrobe from her biohazard gear. Af ter putting the items in the box, they stepped away from it. Carefully placing the goggles in a bucket of bleach, he straightened. The tension was palpable as he went and dropped his gloves into the box for later burning. Turning he saw Casey running her fingers nervously through her flattened hair.

"How's the dissecting going?" he asked as he moved over to the table. Reid wanted to give her the space she needed. He had no desire to make this confrontation any more torturous for Casey than it obviously already was. He saw relief sheet through her as he moved away from where she was standing.

"Oh, that… I paid the warriors to go out and catch four different species of bats and I dissected them and took slides from them." Clearing her throat, Casey pointed to the table. "I identified the species and marked each set of slides for the OID."

"So, all we have to do is collect them and then take them to Yambuku in two weeks so the colonel can fly them out?"

Casey tried to keep her mind on the conversation, but what she really wanted was to cry. To laugh. The storm of feelings vaulting through her made her voice tremble. "Yes…yes, we'll go to Yambuku and meet the colonel there in two weeks."

Gazing at her, Reid said softly, "We need to talk, Casey." Fear vomited through him. Now that he spoken the words, he wondered how she would respond. Would she lash out at him like Janet had? Scream at him? Call him half a man? Heartless? Selfish? He tried to prepare himself.

She closed her eyes and took in a deep, shaky breath. As she released it, she opened her eyes and met his warm gray gaze. "Yes…we do.…"

Opening his hands, and keeping the table between them, Reid said, "Paul told me you were here. He offered me a horse to ride over on."

One corner of her mouth hitched upward. "He must be home from the university in Kinshasa for a visit. He's a professor of English there."

With a shrug, Reid said, "It was a pretty rough time for you last night.…"

Looking around the small clearing, at the tropical palm trees and the orchids twined here and there along their trunks, Casey whispered, "I didn't realize just how much of a coward I really was until now. I thought..." she slowly turned and held his sympathetic gaze "...I thought I had everything under control...but last night...those nightmares...the Ebola coming after me...Steve's breathing just before he died..." She shut her eyes and felt hot tears pressing against her lids. Unable to speak, she choked on a sob.

Steve? The word nearly leaped from his mouth. Frowning, Reid realized that whatever her reactions had been last night, they weren't for Stan or Vince. Who was Steve? Reid started to move around the table toward her.

Casey's eyes snapped open and she threw out her hand. "No!" she said in a choked voice. "No, don't...hold me...don't touch me, Reid. I can't handle it... you...please...."

Chastened, he halted at least six feet away from her. The suffering on her face, the pain in her voice nearly unstrung him. Tears glimmered in Casey's eyes and she refused to meet his gaze. She wrapped her arms tightly around herself and stood rigidly, obviously trying to get a handle on her feelings.

His mind whirled with a hundred questions. His heart was suffused with anguish over her suffering. Something terrible had happened to Casey. Something far worse than he'd ever endured, he guessed. Opening his hand, Reid slowly extended it toward her. "Listen to me," he rasped, "I'm here for you, Casey. What happened last night...it wasn't intentional...not like you might think. When you screamed, I bolted awake. I thought there was an intruder, a terrorist. I came up with pistol in hand. You didn't see me because you were curled up in a ball, your face covered with your hands, sobbing."

Casey winced. Valiantly, she fought back her tears. How soothing and calming Reid's voice was to her. Even her heart, which had been pounding ferociously in her breast, began to quiet beneath his deep voice. Did he know how healing an effect he had on her? Casey wasn't sure. She closed her eyes. Her arms tightened against her chest.

Reid intuitively trusted his gut and went on speaking. He saw the instant effect his quiet tone had on Casey. "I was pretty tired. I wasn't thinking clearly, just reacting out of blind instinct. When I realized we weren't dealing with an intruder, I guess I knew you'd had a bad dream or something. I put the pistol aside and all I wanted to do was to help you in some way, Casey." He stopped, his voice laced with frustration. "I know you find this hard to believe, but my holding you wasn't sexual. It was to help you get through whatever pain you were holding on to...." He saw her lift her chin, her dark green eyes upon him.

"I didn't mean to...kiss you. It—I—it just happened," he rasped. "I take full responsibility for it, for my actions. You were in so much pain I could feel it, Casey." He touched his chest where his heart lay. "I can't stand to see a woman or kid cry. It just rips the hell out of me. Right or wrong, it just does. I was torn up by your sobbing, by all that pain I heard coming out of you. I thought you were still crying over Stan and Vince, and coming here to this clearing where they'd been killed." Helplessly, he dug deeply with his gaze into her wounded-looking eyes. "I didn't know what else to do. So I started by giving you a few kisses, like kissing a kid on the head after she bumps it. That was all it was meant to be...." Reid breathed raggedly. "If you thought I was taking advantage of you and the situation, I can see why you'd want to leave the village and go home. But I swear, it wasn't like that. You're going to have to trust me on this, Casey. And if you can't, well, I don't know what to do or say to fix it between us.... If it can be fixed...."

Rubbing her eyes, Casey muttered, "You deserve the truth, Reid."

Reid stood there feeling helpless, like he should be holding her. But he didn't dare try to do it though he saw the punishing agony clearly etched in every feature of Casey's pale face. His fingers and arms itched to move out, to embrace her, to drag her into the safe haven of his arms. Reid *knew* he could help her to heal. He'd felt their synergy last night, and that wonderful connection, whatever it was, was still throbbing palpably between them right now, like an invisible umbilical cord. Swallowing hard, he gave her a brisk nod. "Okay, the truth." Again he tried to prepare himself to be dressed down by Casey for all the things he'd done wrong with her last night.

Casey closed her eyes, her voice sounding broken. "I was engaged to be married to Steve Bower. He…he was a scientist at the OID. I'd known him for years. We'd been to Africa together, off and on, and the last two years trying to locate the Ebola's reservoir. Over time, I just sort of fell for the guy.…" She smiled sadly. Opening her eyes, she saw Reid's forehead wrinkle and a penetrating darkness enter his eyes. "Steve and I were in the hot zone lab at the OID a year ago with some monkeys that we suspected were infected with Ebola. Ebola tai, the latest mutated version they'd found originally on the Ivory Coast. Steve went to catch one in a cage and it attacked him and ripped a hole in his bio suit. The monkey's claws went through it and scratched him on his arm."

Casey grimaced. "I got so scared. I knew. I just knew…" Her voice went lower. "Steve instantly got out of the hot zone and performed all the procedures for Ebola infection. I went ahead and caught that monkey, dissected it, and the autopsy showed he had Ebola tai. By the time I got out of the lab, they had Steve in that special room where they take Ebola patients." Casey sniffed. "I didn't even get to say goodbye to him—not like I wanted to. I couldn't touch him or go in the room without being in our level-four space suit. In forty-eight hours, he showed the first signs of Ebola infection. Everyone—" her voice cracked "—everyone did everything they could to save Steve…but…he died.… He bled out.…''

Casey pressed her hands to her face and choked back a sob. "Yesterday was hell for me, coming to this clearing. All I could see were those black-and-white photos showing Stan and Vince dead here. I cried for them. Last night…maybe from being here in Africa again, facing Ebola again…I had a horrible nightmare about the Ebola worms, and it was mixed in with the last breaths Steve took before he died. I was in that sterile room with him, sitting at his bedside, holding his hand with my gloved one. I saw the Ebola virus wrap itself around me, and I felt myself dying.…'' Casey removed her hands from her face and looked at Reid, whose own face was alive with anguish—for her, for what she'd lost. "That's when I screamed, I guess. I remember my voice echoing like it was in a sound chamber. Last night's thunder…I don't know, really. All I remember is my panic. And I felt so much grief over losing Steve coming up through me that all I could do was cry like a little kid. Sob and shake.…'' She gave a rueful shake of her head as her voice trailed off into silence.

Casey couldn't continue. She couldn't share with Reid how much his presence, his care, his embrace, meant to her. He had stirred her womanly longings to life in the process, and he'd opened her heart when she thought it would never open to another man again as long as she lived. The fear of loving Reid, the fear of losing someone she loved again, was too much for Casey to endure or even contemplate right now. All these things wanted to tumble out of her mouth, but she choked them back. It was beyond her as to why she was so inexorably attracted to Reid Hunter after all she'd been through.

As gently as he could, Reid whispered, "I'm sorry, Casey. For you…for your loss of Stan and Vince. I didn't know about Steve. He must have been a very special man

to have captured your heart...." And he meant it. Casey
didn't suffer fools gladly. She was a proud, intelligent and
courageous woman who would make most men run in terror of her. It would take a man who was immensely comfortable with his own masculinity—not too full of testosterone, as Casey would dryly point out—to get her interest,
much less hold her heart in his hands like the treasure it
was. The misery and grief Reid saw in her eyes as she
studied him in the gathering quiet, struck him deeply. He
had no doubt that she'd loved this man with all her heart.
For a moment, Reid wished she could love him with that
same kind of singular fierceness. What would it be like for
her to open her heart to him? The kiss they'd shared last
night had opened him up as never before. It had left him
vulnerable, hungry and wanting more of Casey in every
possible way. And on its heels came the absolute fear of
rejection by her because he could never measure up to a
man like Steve. Obviously Steve wasn't half a man, like
Reid was.

Reality dampened his hungry desire for her. It was clear
she was still in mourning from her loss of Steve. Reid
understood about grief, about how it took its own time
with a person. Not everyone healed at the same rate of
speed from such a devastating loss. Janet leaving him at
the altar had certainly stained his life, the way he saw
women in general, he admitted sourly. Yet the kiss he'd
shared with Casey last night had felt like someone had
wiped the slate clean for him once and for all. He'd felt
buoyant when he'd awakened this morning. Happier than
he could ever recall. And today hope had thrummed
through him so strongly that he'd felt like laughing just
for the sheer joy of feeling that energy tunnel through his
chest and up and out of his mouth.

Glumly, Reid realized it was sharing the kiss with Casey
that had made this all possible, this healing that he'd re-
ceived from their mouths clinging hotly to one another.

Studying her in the silence, he felt his hope dissolving. Casey was still in mourning. How would he feel if he loved someone and then watched her die such a horrible, horrible death? More than likely, the same as she did, he admitted. A woman like Casey would need a man like Steve, not a man like Reid—a heartless warrior without human compassion.

"Maybe you just needed to release some of your grief. Maybe you'd held on to it too long," he murmured.

With a half smile filled with pain, Casey lifted her chin and gazed skyward. "You're right. I sort of buried myself in my work after Steve died. It hurt to feel." Casey pressed her hand to her heart. "Every time I felt or thought of him, I'd burst into tears. It got to be embarrassing around the OID. I'd be having lunch in the cafeteria, and out of nowhere, I'd start crying." She met his somber gaze and tried to smile, but it didn't work. "It got so no one wanted to eat with me. Not that I blamed them..."

"If I'd been there, I'd have put my arms around you, held you and just let you get it out of your system." Now where had *that* comment come from? Stunned, Reid searched himself in panic. It was his heart speaking. His foolish, blind heart.

His deep voice blanketed her with such warmth and care that Casey almost stepped forward—into his waiting arms. The burning light in his eyes, that smoldering look of protection, embraced her. She felt awkward. She felt lonely. Reid could offer her so much—so much if she'd let him. Fear shot through Casey. Clearing her throat, she said brokenly, "Yes, you would have."

His smile was tentative, unsure. "I guess it's another side of my Neanderthal nature, maybe?"

Casey managed a strained, short laugh. "I think it is...but it's a nice part of you, Hunter." One she desperately needed and wanted right now. Lifting her hand, she added, "I'm sorry I scared the hell out of you last night.

Normally I don't get nightmares like that. I think it was just jet lag, overwork and the stress we endured at the Kinshasa airport...."

"That was probably it," Reid agreed quietly.

Nervously, she ran her fingers through her hair. "Uh...I think it would be best if we don't stay together in that tiny little hut...."

He looked at her sharply. He felt his chest go cold with new terror. She couldn't do this to him!

Casey felt his gaze go straight through her. Panic ate at her. "Look, I obviously have some stuff to work through. Being in Africa is dragging it all back up to the surface. I can't keep you awake, or scare the hell out of you by waking up at night and screaming again..."

His heart contracted. The last thing Reid wanted was to be away from Casey. Yes, it was purely selfish on his part. He hadn't expected her to make this suggestion. He hadn't anticipated her asking that they separate. "I'll take my chances with you, Casey. I'd rather be there than not be there for you." That was the truth. Reid didn't look too closely at the other reasons he wanted to be sleeping near her. If he couldn't have her, at least he could absorb her nearness. It was better than nothing now that he understood the circumstances about her behavior toward him.

Casey felt her nerves tighten. Anxiety swept through her. She moved suddenly, almost robotically, toward the table. "No! You don't understand. I don't want you sleeping in there with me. You can't."

Reid stood in front of her. She halted abruptly, her eyes widening. The fear in them cut at him. She feared *him*. The realization made his mouth taste bitter. "I can try to understand if you'll let me, Casey."

Breathing hard, she spun around him. *"No!"* She grabbed the microscope. Her hands were shaking so badly that she nearly dropped it. If not for her quick reflexes, she would have.

He watched as she walked quickly to the truck. The back was open and he watched grimly as she placed the microscope safely into a wooden case. Nostrils flaring, Reid turned and walked slowly toward her. He saw her breasts rising and falling rapidly beneath her olive coveralls. Her red hair was in disarray. She looked like a disheveled doll in that heartbreaking moment. Her face was so pale, her eyes dark with fear and grief. It hurt to know that she didn't want to be near him. That was worse than anything for Reid to bear. Besides, how could he protect her when he couldn't be near her?

"We don't have a choice in this, Casey," he said wearily. "I was sent here to *guard* you twenty-four hours a day. If I sleep in another hut, how can I protect you? We don't know who might be Black Dawn members. For all I know, they're in Henri's village just waiting for a chance to kidnap or kill you." He met her startled look as she turned toward him. "I'm sorry, but I'm not going anywhere. We'll stay in the hut together. And from now on, if you get the urge to run, we'll do it together." Somberly, Reid looked around the clearing in the jungle where they stood. "If Henri hadn't sent four trusted warriors with you this morning, Black Dawn might have made a bid to capture you. Had you thought of that?"

Anger sizzled through Casey. It squelched her momentary fear. "I can take care of myself, Reid!" She brushed past him, walking quickly back to the table to retrieve the other items that needed to be packed for the return trip to the village.

"We don't know who our friends or enemies are."

Glaring up at him, she snapped, "I sure as hell do! Henri is our friend. He'd know if there was a terrorist living in or near his village. You can damn well bet he would!"

She was gripping a box as if her life depended upon it.

Reid tried to steady his own stunned emotions. Casey didn't desire him at all. Not like he desired her. In an emotional sense, she saw him as a threat, not a protector. With a huge effort, he worked over those gut-wrenching realizations and tried to keep focused on the issue at hand. He was here to protect her, and he never backed away from a mission. "Terrorists hit and run. They could come roaring into that village in a couple of vehicles and tear the place apart with their SKSs. No," he rasped grimly, "we're staying together whether you like it or not."

Her hands shook. She instantly grabbed a reference book lying nearby and held it against her stomach. "I can't take it!"

Startled by her cry, Reid's mouth tightened. "You mean take me."

"Yes! No! Oh, hell, I don't know!" She pushed past him again and walked quickly to the makeshift camp.

Reid watched her as she gathered up several other items and brought them back to the truck. Holding on to his patience, he said, "Casey, let's just stop this merry-go-round we're on, and sit down and talk it out."

His voice was cooling to the fire consuming her. Fear mixed with adrenaline and made her perspire. She felt like a trapped animal. She remembered how his hot, melting kiss had brought out so much pain and grief from deep within her. Dumping the items into the vehicle, she placed her hands flat against the floor. The metal felt cool and steadying against the power of the storm roiling within her. Trying to control her ragged breathing, her adrenaline pumping overtime, Casey closed her eyes.

"What happened last night was an accident," Reid declared, almost pleading with her. "I promise I won't reach out for you again, even if you wake up screaming. Okay? I can't let you be alone, Casey. Not with Black Dawn lurking around somewhere. Our lives are in enough peril hunting the Ebola virus. And then we have that black mamba colony somewhere out there on the savanna, roving around looking for people to kill. I don't need you looking at me like I'm an enemy, too. I'm not.''

Her fingers curled against the metal. Head drooping, she tried to force herself to speak. She felt Reid's overpowering nearness. Did he have any idea how much he affected her? Casey couldn't believe he didn't know. When she twisted her head to look in his direction, she swallowed hard. Guilt washed through her. Reid looked absolutely vulnerable standing there. The naked pain on his features, the agony she saw in his eyes, told her much more than she wanted to know. He didn't have a clue how she felt about him.

"Last night when you held me—" Her voice cracked. Casey slowly straightened up, her nails biting deeply into the palms of her sweaty hands. "I've never felt so protected as when you held me, Reid." There, it was out. She saw utter surprise flare in his eyes. And then his gaze narrowed ruthlessly upon her. She felt like a quarry. Her heart thudded with pain, with longing—for him. The shock of that revelation stunned Casey for a moment. Floundering, her voice ragged and wispy, she said, "I don't know how it happened...or why. I'm too raw to ask right now. I hurt too much from the past. I'm too afraid to look for answers." She forced herself to hold his dark gray gaze, his pupils huge and black. Her mouth went dry. "I—just can't take any more. I had no idea that was going to happen...I didn't...."

Reid knew she was talking about the heart-shattering kiss they'd shared. He saw her cheeks flush brightly and saw the shame in her eyes. "Neither did I," he admitted with a growl, "but I'm not apologizing for it, either." *Liar. You saw that kiss coming from the moment you laid eyes on her,* he admitted to himself. He quelled his real feelings and knew he was a first-class hypocrite. If he told Casey anything else at this delicate moment, she'd bolt and run.

Too much was at stake. He disliked himself for not being completely honest with her, but he had no choice.

Casey tried to smile but failed. ''Neanderthal to the end, aren't you?''

Appreciating her attempt to lighten the tension sizzling between them, he forced a smile he didn't feel at all. ''Yeah, I guess I am.''

Shrugging helplessly, she whispered, ''I know you held me to help me. I could feel your care for me....''

Now it was his turn to avoid her soft, haunting green gaze. Looking down at his muddy boots, he could only nod, a lump in his throat. ''It won't happen again, Casey. I can tell you that.''

Inwardly, Casey cried. His kiss had been the cleanest, most beautiful one she'd ever savored, ever shared. Afraid to admit it, she laughed brokenly. ''We're adults. We'll handle this.''

Looking up, he caught and held her vulnerable gaze. ''Sometimes adults feel like frightened little children inside, too. They deserve to be held when they feel like that.'' The image of himself as a four-year-old scared out of his wits by the thunderstorm as he hid in the broom closet loomed before him.

Casey rubbed her brow, embarrassed. He saw through her like glass. Was she *that* obvious? Or did Reid just have a special kind of knowing? Caught off guard, she pressed her hand to her wrinkled brow. ''Please...can you sleep elsewhere?'' *Anywhere else, but not with me. I'm afraid I'll reach out for you when I'm hurting. I'm afraid I'll crawl into your arms and want to be held again. I'm so afraid....*

Reid felt like a real bastard. He heard the crack in her husky voice. She was begging him. Taking in a deep breath, he placed his hands on his hips and looked down at her. ''I'm sorry, Casey. No. You and I are staying together.''

* * *

Reid thought the tension in the hut that night was so thick he could feel it. Casey lay against the mosquito netting, turned away from him and lying as far as she could get from him, which wasn't very far. He lay on his back, his hands behind his head as he stared up into the darkness. Replaying their conversation earlier in the day, he sighed heavily. Casey had been jumpy all evening, as if dreading going into the hut and being alone with him. *Damn!* Pursing his lips, he slanted a glance in her direction. All he could see on this moonless night was the vague outline of her darkened form.

To hell with it. He had to do *something* to ease the tension between them, even if it was at his own miserable expense. "I have a story to tell you," he began quietly. "A true one."

Casey tensed instantly. She lay very still. As tired as she was, she couldn't sleep. Reid was too close. Too masculine. Too inviting to her raw, shredded emotional state. "My mom used to tell me stories and that would put me to sleep," she whispered thickly.

"Well," he murmured, "close your eyes and maybe this one will put you to sleep." Heartened by her soft response, Reid took in a deep, ragged breath and began. "Once upon a time, there was a marine officer. He had made good on his education and he was well thought of by his commanding officer and his men. He'd been to the Gulf War, got a silver star and come home to a parade where he was praised. To anyone on the outside looking at his life, he had it made. Except for one thing. The marine was lonely. His job couldn't replace that feeling in his heart. The men he worked with and was proud of couldn't fill that spot in his heart, either.

"One summer evening he sat on a hill at Camp Reed, out in the middle of that rocky, cactus-strewn desert, and wondered what was wrong with him. Why couldn't he attract a woman who liked him just the way he was? Was it because he was honest? That he didn't play games? That he valued truth, honor and integrity above the societal games and manipulation he saw going on all around him? The marine acknowledged that one of the reasons he hadn't made major yet was because he wouldn't play the political games expected of him within the officer corps to get the higher rank. That didn't bother him as much as being without the right woman, however.

"Giving this a lot of thought, he decided that maybe he'd have to initiate a search for this woman. He wasn't the type to go to the Officer's Club and get drunk or party very much. No, he valued quiet walks in nature and he liked to walk along the beach and watch the Pacific Ocean roll in, instead. He went to the O Club to have dinner. He didn't like the odor of cigarettes, the loud music or the drunkenness he saw there. It wasn't that he was a prude, it just wasn't his idea of having a good time.

"On the way out of the club after dinner, he met this beautiful blond woman named Janet. She was just going into the club. She was dressed in a short red dress and it made her blond hair look like a gold crown. The marine was smitten by her dancing blue eyes, her easy laughter and the way she looked at him. He invited her to go to the beach for a walk. Janet liked the idea and went with him. They spent half the night talking around a small campfire that the officer had made.

"The marine was happy. All his loneliness disappeared that magical night. Here he'd been wishing with all his might, and almost miraculously, this woman materializes before him. Well, his happiness took off like an eagle for the next four months. Janet seemed happy to take walks along the beach with him, have a picnic up in the mountains or go hiking in Yosemite when they could get away from their respective jobs.

"His happiness was complete when he gave Janet a diamond engagement ring one night on the beach. She promised her undying love to him through her surprise and tears. He promised his love in equal measure to her. They sat there on a driftwood log, watching the moon rise over the Pacific, in one another's arms, talking of the future…of children…and how many they wanted. What they might look like twenty years from now, and what they hoped for in their future together.…

"The marine set the wedding date with Janet's approval. She was an orphan, without birth relatives, but her adoptive family, who lived in California, were eager to attend the coming wedding. The ceremony would take place at the chapel on Camp Reed. All the marine's best friends, his Recon team members and their families, were in attendance. The marine was so happy. At last he no longer felt lonely. He felt that space in his heart being filled in a way he'd never dreamed possible. Standing at the front of the chapel in his dress blue uniform, with his honor guard of six fellow officers and six bridesmaids, he waited for his love, Janet.

"Time went by. And then more time. The officer became worried. Where was Janet? The maid of honor came out of a side door of the chapel, the bride's room. She was crying. In front of the whole group, she said that Janet wanted to talk with him privately. The marine was suddenly scared, but he went back to meet with her. Janet said she didn't want to marry him after all. She gripped the marine's hand and apologized profusely for her last-minute decision. She felt terrible.

"The reason why Janet couldn't marry this marine was because he had no heart. They had had many discussions about this officer's inability to feel, to deal with emotional issues. Janet was afraid he would never open up and share how he felt with anyone. The marine pleaded with her to marry him. He promised to try and change, but Janet tearfully said no. Eventually, the marine agreed. He went back and told everyone to go home, that there wasn't going to be a wedding. He apologized to all of them.

"That evening, the marine went to the beach alone. He was a heartless being. A robot who could not feel. Janet had said he was only half a man, not a whole one, and she could never settle for what little he offered her. He stood there, watching the waves rolling in from the Pacific Ocean and felt so very alone. The marine was very confused and hurt. He didn't know what to do. The next day, he phoned Janet's apartment, but there was no answer. He then went over to her adoptive parents' home and they said that she'd moved away. Janet had left the state. Thanking them, he left.

"So the marine went back to what he knew and did best, being a soldier. He tried to put Janet out of his thoughts. He tried not to blame himself for what had happened. Over time, he came to realize that even though he was only half a man, a man without heart, he could still be a good officer and leader." Reid closed his eyes, a sad smile tipping the corners of his mouth. "Sorry, some fairy tales don't have a happy ending."

Casey lay there, her eyes wide. "My God," she whispered. "That was awful." She sat up, wrapping her arms around her drawn-up knees. Looking over at Reid, who appeared incredibly masculine in only the thin blue cotton pajama bottoms, his chest broad and darkly haired, Casey met his pained gaze. "This happened to you."

He nodded. "You're supposed to have gone to sleep. I told you a story."

Her heart bled for him. He was trying to be so nonchalant about it all. Casey could see the devastation it had cost him to tell her the story. There was anguish in his dark, slate-colored eyes. Whatever it was about Reid, she found herself wanting to roll over, stretch out beside him, wrap her arms around him and simply draw him against her and hold him. The urge was very real. Casey felt her fear dissolving as she held his gaze. How powerful he was, and yet it was power in balance. The promise not to touch her or kiss her echoed in her memory. Her gaze dropped to his strong, well-shaped mouth. It was twisted with pain.

"I'm sorry...." Casey whispered. "You didn't deserve that. You're a good man, Reid. And you aren't heartless." *You're too good for me.* And he was. He had such integrity and morals. How hard it must have been on him to be embarrassed in front of all his superiors, his friends and the men who worked under him. How painful to stand there in that chapel, alone and deserted. She rested her brow against her drawn-up knees. "We're a lot alike, you and I," she murmured tiredly.

Reid ached to sit up and reach out for Casey. He didn't dare. Keeping his hands behind his head, he chuckled softly. "No, I'm the Neanderthal, remember? You aren't."

Pain moved through Casey. Reid's pain. She felt deeply for him. His attempt at teasing made her tremble inwardly. For her sake he was trying so hard to put on a brave front over his own anguish. "Sometimes life sucks," she muttered defiantly, lifting her head and looking down at him. "It just sucks."

Reid saw the fire, the life, back in Casey's narrowed gaze. "Yeah, doesn't it?" He patted the blankets that lay across her pallet. "Come on, lie back down. You need to sleep. You've had your story told to you, now hit the sack."

He was irresistible in that moment. Reid had given her a gift, she realized. Two gifts, in fact. Following his bidding, she eased down on her pallet and lay on her right side, her back toward him. All the fear of him was gone. The tension had bled out of her with his sharing of his own miserable story of love and loss. Closing her eyes, Casey felt a small ray of hope in her heart. Hope for what, she didn't know. She was too fatigued and worn-out to follow that thread within her. More than anything, she now felt safe with Reid. And she hadn't before.

Sleepily, she whispered, "Will you tell me another story tomorrow night?"

He chuckled softly. "Sure, if you want."

Her lips parted as sleep began to claim her. "Yes," Casey said in a slurred voice, "you're a good storyteller, but next time, can it have a happy ending?"

Reid smiled up at the ceiling of the hut as he heard Casey's voice dissolve into sleep. "For you, anything," he promised her softly. Positive that Casey had not heard him, Reid turned on his side, facing her relaxed form. Something healing had happened between them. He didn't know exactly what, but he was grateful for the tension being dissolved. Yes, telling her true stories about himself, his career as a marine and his life as a boy growing up, would be very easy to do. Maybe the next three months in Africa wouldn't be a continuous hell, after all....

Chapter Nine

The cooling air of a thunderstorm moved languidly through the darkness of their hut. Casey lay on her back, her hands behind her head, contented. A month had passed and it barely seemed like a week to her. Reid's nightly stories were the highlight of her day. She'd never told him that, but they—and he—were.

Tonight she was restless. The last remnants of lightning flashed at the windows and she saw Reid lying on his back, his hands behind his head as well. His upper body had a sheen to it; the hut was humid and warm. The breeze lifted the curtain at the front door and Casey sighed. "Feels wonderful, doesn't it?"

"Anything cool feels good," Reid said dryly. "What I'd do for a glass of iced tea with real ice cubes in it."

Giggling softly, Casey closed her eyes. She was less than two feet from Reid, but she absorbed his nearness, the intimacy he always gave her so effortlessly. The past month had eased the tension between them, she realized.

They were turning into good friends. For so long Casey had wanted to talk to him about his statements about being heartless. She felt good tonight, and solid emotionally. The ups and downs of grief over Steve and her friends had slowly dissolved, too. For her healing process, she owed more than a little thanks to Reid and his own hesitant brand of warmth and attention.

Turning on her side, she rested her hand on her head and looked at him. She saw him cut a look at her and then slowly ease onto his side, assuming the same posture as she. Softly, she said, "How anyone could call you heartless is beyond me."

Instantly, Reid's good feelings were deluged in icy panic. It was as if he were waiting for chastisement from Casey, a report card on what he lacked emotionally as a man. Now that time was here, he realized with a horrible, sinking feeling.

Reaching out, Casey allowed her fingers to rest on his darkly haired hand. "No, you don't. Don't you dare crawl back into your cave, Neanderthal Man."

Her teasing steadied him momentarily. The unexpected warmth, the touch of Casey's hand convinced him that she wasn't going to cut him to pieces like Janet had. When her fingers closed confidently over his, his mouth curved ruefully.

"What brought on that statement? Was I acting like one of late? More than usual? Or is this the thirty-day report card on the cad I am?"

Her heart bled as she saw the pain banked in his dark, troubled eyes. Casey began to realize the extent of damage Janet had caused in Reid. He was hurting and vulnerable. As gently as she knew how, Casey whispered, "In my heart, you get an A, Captain Hunter. You've been wonderful. No one could have asked more of you than you've given."

"Oh? The proverbial servant doing bwana's bidding?"

Laughing, Casey said, "No, you don't, Hunter. I'm not letting you wriggle out of this one."

"Was I wriggling?" He met her warm, drowsy green eyes with a tentative smile. It was so easy to open up to Casey. How often he'd wanted to, but Reid was always cautious about it. Maybe his nightly stories of his years growing up in Colorado made Casey feel more relaxed with him. He enjoyed her freedom to express herself with him, her childlike innocence. Never had he seen anyone enjoy life more than she did. When a butterfly would wing its way through their science camp, she'd shout, point and get so excited about it. Her enthusiasm was infectious in the best of ways for Reid. Living with Casey was like living with an effervescent sunbeam in love with life to the fullest every possible moment.

"You know you were!" she chortled. Taking a bold risk, Casey eased her fingers up Reid's arm to his elbow and allowed them to slide back down to his hand. He caught her fingers and squeezed them very gently. She saw the panic recede from his eyes. In some ways, he reminded her of a child who had been terribly traumatized by one single event and was looking for it to be repeated again and again, no matter how old he was. Her intuition told her it had to do with the trauma of Janet standing him up at the altar.

"About this idea you're heartless?" she said firmly.

Frowning, Reid couldn't hold her bold look. "Yes?"

She heard the frisson of fear in his deep tone. "It's for the birds, Reid."

He digested her statement.

"Did you hear me?"

Looking up into her deeply shadowed face, he clung to her warm, vulnerable gaze. "Yeah, I heard...."

Her brows drew down. "You don't believe me? You think I'm lying to you?"

"One thing I'd never accuse you of is lying to me," he

told her seriously as he laced his fingers through hers. This was the first time she'd ever reached out to him. The moment was shocking and beautiful to him, a dream come true. A dream he'd never thought would ever leave the realm of his imagination, and yet here it was. Casey had reached out to him, touched him, and was touching him on a much deeper level, grazing his hurting heart, which longed so much for her.

Matching his seriousness, Casey whispered, "No one should have ever accused you of being heartless, Reid. I've seen you with the children. They love you. You play tag with them. You laugh with them. They laugh with you. A man without a heart wouldn't do that. When you're with the children…" She sighed and closed her eyes while absorbing the strength of his fingers. "I love to watch you together. You turn into a kid before my very eyes, Reid. Gone is the marine. Enter the little boy. You become one with them and they know it. And you can never fool a child, you know?" She opened her eyes and stared straight into his hooded ones. "A child always knows if an adult likes them or not. If you were truly heartless, these kids would avoid you like the proverbial plague."

"That's a good pun."

"Oh, suffer through it, will you? And don't avoid what I'm saying. You *know* what I mean, Reid, so admit it! Go on. Admit it. You're not heartless."

If he didn't release Casey's hand, he was going to do the unthinkable: follow the urge of his blind and foolish heart. Hating himself, Reid released her hand. He rolled over on his back and laced his fingers together, placing them behind his head once more. He stared up at the mosquito netting, the silence pleasant between them.

"Okay, I'm not heartless. Not totally, at least…"

"You're a tough customer when you want to be," Casey growled. She sat up, crossed her legs and arranged the nightgown over her knees. Folding her hands in her lap, she stared at him. How virile and strong Reid looked to her. He was like a sensual male lion at rest, and yet the threat of his power, his danger as a male, beckoned her. For once she had to stop this and think clearly. When she was around Reid, that was difficult to do, because her feminine side had other feelings and desires she would rather follow up on.

Chortling, he aimed a look up at her petulant expression. "I'm not being evasive, good doctor."

"Yeah, right." She wagged her finger at him. "You're into avoidance patterns, Hunter. Let me put it more bluntly."

"Oh," he drawled, "here we go. Bluntness as in honesty, right?"

"What do you know? Neanderthal Man is fighting back. Well, too little too late. Suffer my consequences with good grace, will you?"

His grin widened considerably. With her hair tousled, he ached to reach out, slide his fingers up the clean line of her jaw and take that silky red mass in his hands and kiss her senseless. That would take away that know-it-all smile lurking on her full lips once and for all. The thought was hot. Melting. Reid gently tabled it, however. He tapped the mat beneath them. "I get the feeling that strat and tack is needed here."

"Ha!" Casey cried out. "See!"

"See what?" he demanded darkly. She looked absolutely triumphant.

"My point exactly, Hunter!"

He scowl deepened. "I missed the hell out of it. Want to point it out to me?"

She preened.

"Don't gloat so much. Just explain to me what I just missed."

Casey sighed and sank her elbows into her thighs, leaning forward. "You just proved what I was saying beyond a shadow of a doubt."

Reid had a tough time keeping his eyes level with hers. In his peripheral vision he could see the shadowed cleft of her breasts beneath the delicate pink lace of her nightgown as she leaned forward. He was sure she wasn't aware of what she'd done, caught up in the fervor of another of their verbal sparring matches. Swallowing against the dryness in his mouth, he rasped, "Be kind to this dumb Neanderthal, will you? Spell it out for him and his kind?"

"You said *feeling* a moment ago, Reid," she said fiercely. Again she jabbed her finger toward him. "If you didn't have a heart, if you were truly cut off from yourself emotionally, you'd *never* have used that word. Don't you see?" Casey sat up, supremely pleased with herself and her insight into him.

Reid sighed. "Dumb as a brick."

"Well, you're not a total loss for a Neanderthal," she added more gently. "In my eyes, you have a heart and a soul. And more than anything, you show it here with me, with the kids, all the time. I see it and so do they. Why don't you?"

Glumly, he shrugged and stared back up at the netting. "I think it's you. I think you've infected me with a new strain of virus called feeling."

"What?" Casey's voice rose in stridency. "Hunter, what on earth are you muttering about now? What do you mean, I've 'infected' you? Are you accusing me of making you feel? Or that because we have to work together, I'm making you feel more?"

It was his turn to grin like a wolf salivating over its prey. "Yes."

"Pshaw."

"Pshaw?"

"Yes, that's a word."

"Is that anything like 'go to hell' in disguise?"

Laughing softly, Casey wanted badly to simply lean forward and press her long body against Reid's. He was like a little boy in that moment, open, vulnerable and trusting. The moment was molten. Charged with possibility. "Well, something like that. Remember, my mother washed my mouth out with soap every time I used a cuss word, so I learned to develop another vocabulary that avoided the soap but still got my point across. You know, you're pretty good at translation."

"For a Neanderthal?"

Her smile became dazzling. "Especially because you *are* a Neanderthal."

Raising his eyes, he said dramatically, "Goodness gracious, you mean there's hope for us hopeless caveman types, after all?"

Reaching out, Casey touched the side of his cheek. As she drew her fingertips down across his darkly shadowed face, which looked so dangerous and alluring to her, she felt the sandpapery stubble of his beard beneath her sensitive fingertips. The sudden, surprised look in his eyes stunned her. She froze momentarily, and then she jerked her fingers away. The contact had been casual, as if she were his lover. But she wasn't. And more and more, she wanted to be. The heated look in his suddenly hooded expression made her go shaky and warm inside.

"I—yes, there's always hope," she said raggedly, her voice sounding wispy and terribly soft even to her ears. Trying to gather her strewn thoughts, Casey added, "And you have a heart. Please believe me if you believe nothing else I ever say, Reid. You are *not* heartless."

He lay there for a long time afterward, replaying their conversation, recalling her tender, fervent expression as she'd said those words that had changed his life in every way. It was a gift even though Casey didn't realize it. A beautiful, wonderful gift that she'd bestowed unknowingly upon him. Closing his eyes, Reid wondered what the second month would bring. And he worried, too. For one thing had not changed about Africa—danger was everywhere.

"She has gone, young lion."

Reid whirled around at the commanding baritone voice. His eyes widened as he saw Henri leaning heavily on his cane, gauging him steadily. The chieftain's mouth curved faintly.

"Your lioness left early this morning," he said, gesturing toward the savanna.

Hunter's heart pounded hard in his chest. "Where did she go?" He demanded, his voice dark and tinged with worry. He had to protect her! Casey should have awakened him. She knew better. Black Dawn was still probably sniffing around for their whereabouts, watching their activities. Reid was about to remind Henri of the danger Casey might be in, but he stopped at the last second.

Chuckling indulgently, Henri said, "Yesterday, I told her of several small caves on the northern edge of the savanna, just inside the jungle. She said she was going to capture and look at bats there to see if they carry Ebola."

Relief sheeted through Reid. "Then…she didn't really leave?" For some crazy reason, Reid thought Casey had run away. Hadn't Janet? Why not Casey, too? He tried to get ahold of his unraveling emotions. His reaction wasn't warranted, he realized. Last night had been wonderful, heady and incredibly tender. Casey had reached out and touched him of her own accord. The moment was stamped like a brand in his heart.

Henri was studying him intently, and Reid felt as if the old chieftain could look straight through him and know what lay in his heart and mind. It was a disconcerting sensation, for Reid wasn't used to such incisiveness on another person's part. Somehow, he felt Henri would understand, because he saw compassion in the old man's eyes after he'd blurted out the question.

"You know," Henri said in a rumbling tone, "when a young lion finds his mate, he worries that she won't accept him." He motioned toward the rolling green plain near the village. "I see it all the time. A young lion claims his territory. The next thing he looks for is a mate with whom he will live out his lifetime. And lionesses have minds of their own, you know? They don't just passively accept anyone. No, they are equally as strong, smart and wise as that young male." His mouth puckered. "Some lionesses are scarred from their past. Sometimes they run because they are in pain. It is not the fault of the young lion, but he must understand that and be patient." Pointing his finger at Reid, Henri added, "In my years of living, and having ten wives, I can tell you that they have taught me patience. Great patience. This morning, my adopted daughter was very scared." He tapped his chest. "And if I didn't know better, I would say that her heart is open and bleeding."

Reid nodded. "Yes, it is...." But he had no idea over what. He knew it wasn't him. Or maybe it was. Could their growing intimacy, their sharing with one another, have made her feel such pain? The thought was pulverizing to Reid, because the last thing he wanted to do was hurt Casey. He'd suffered enough from Janet's words to him on their wedding day. He had no desire to ever inflict that kind of pain on anyone else, much less courageous Casey Morrow.

Henri limped forward and reached out, wrapping his thin, arthritic fingers around Reid's upper arm. "Come, my youngest wife has just gotten eggs from our hens. There is fresh, warm goat's milk. You will eat with me and we will talk further. Do not worry about your lioness, my friend. She is fine—and safe."

Reid almost resisted. But something in the chieftain's

demanding stare told him to acquiesce. "I'm just worried for her safety."

"Yes, yes, I know, but I sent three of my best warriors with her this morning. They are showing her where these caves are located. These men have all stalked and killed lions with their spears—and lived to tell about it. They guard her right now." Chuckling as he slowly turned around, Henri said, "You have time to dine with me, no?"

Graciousness was not to be denied, Reid thought. He managed a curt nod of his head. "I do. Thank you."

"Good, good," Henri murmured, pleased. He limped slowly toward the center of the village, his hand on Reid's arm to help his balance. "We shall talk more of your lioness as we enjoy the hens' eggs and the goat's milk, eh?"

Reid hadn't been prepared for scrambled eggs, fried goat steak and warm goat's milk for breakfast. As he sat near the cooking tripod in front of Henri's hut, a number of the old man's wives attending them along with their babies and older children, he began to relax a little. The babies climbed into Henri's lap as he sat on a chair. His deep chuckles of pleasure as he played with his children made Reid smile. A number of the children also climbed eagerly into Reid's lap. He found it very easy to hold them, squeeze them and rock them in his arms.

There was incredible love everywhere Reid looked around here. The village was alive with people, animals, comings and goings. It throbbed with life, with a joy that seemed almost palpable. As he sipped the bowl of goat's milk, a little two-year-old boy in the crook of his left arm, Reid began to understand on a much deeper level why Casey loved being here and why she had looked forward to returning to this magical place out of time.

Henri called his wives to take the children away, saying that the men must talk in private. Within moments, the women had gathered up all the children and left Reid with Henri. The fire beneath the blackened iron kettle was mere coals, a wisp of white smoke twisting languidly in the cool morning air. Placing the empty bowl aside, Reid wiped his mouth with the back of his hand.

"Thank you," he told Henri. "I never expected this." And he hadn't.

"Because you love my adopted daughter, you are accorded our family generosity," Henri rumbled. He took his lion-headed cane, placed it between his feet and draped his hands upon it.

Reid's heart pounded once, hard, in his chest, to underscore Henri's gently spoken words. He slitted a glance at the old chieftain. The glimmer in Henri's eyes told him the old man knew the deepest desire that lay in his heart. Opening his hands, Reid remained silent, since he didn't know what to say. In America, men didn't talk of such things—at least, not in casual conversation like this. He could taste the fear that Casey wouldn't or couldn't love him like he did her.

"The young lion is frightened, no?"

Reid studied his clasped hands in his lap. "There's a lot in life to be afraid of," he muttered quietly.

With a sigh, Henri nodded as he gazed proudly across his village. "I remember all the times, as a young boy growing up here and the son of a mighty and powerful chieftain, when I was fearful, too. I worried that I would not be a good leader for my people when my father died. I worried that I would not find a woman who would love me as all my father's wives loved him. I worried that other tribes would slaughter our people and kill me." Henri's eyes crinkled. "All my worry was put to an end when I met my first wife, Desiree. She was like your young lioness— proud, capable, brave and strong. My father chose her from among all the young women of our many villages. He told me that the dowry had been set, and that I, sixteen, would marry this beautiful, beautiful child-woman who scared me to death!"

Henri chuckled indulgently. "Oh, yes, I was far mo[re] frightened of Desiree than of anything else before that! Sh[e] was tall and supple like a palm tree. She had the heart [of] a lioness. When she danced, it was as if the wind wa[s] moving through and with her. And when she laughed, [it] was rain falling upon the parched land that I was, feedin[g] me, giving me life. And most of all, she was a fighter fo[r] the rights of the women and children. How fierce she wa[s!] The look in her eyes made my knees quake. She chal[-] lenged me, my manhood, on every level of my bein[g.] Why, I would rather have faced a lion without a spear tha[n] marry her! I told my father, finally, and he laughed so har[d] he fell off his throne while he held his belly. When he g[ot] up, wiping the tears from his eyes, he told me that facin[g] a lion with a spear is nothing compared to facing a youn[g] lioness in a woman's body. There, he told me, was a man'[s] greatest fear and desire come to life.

"A strong woman makes a man feel weak in man[y] ways," Henri continued with laughter in his voice. "Me[n] such as we are, used to the company of other men. W[e] know how to gauge another man's strengths and weak[-] nesses. But a woman's? Aiyee! A woman will lift her chi[n,] jut it out, and her eyes will flash like the lightning throw[n] by the gods from the sky. She will stand tall and prou[d.] She challenges us on our softer side, that side of us w[e] don't know at all. She will pull our heart from our ches[t] and play with it. She knows the power of how to get t[o] us and control us. Of course, men see this as somethin[g] terrible." Henri laughed heartily and slapped his kne[e.] "Men are brave and courageous, but they are stupid whe[n] it comes to matters of the heart. That is a woman's terri[-] tory. That is what she knows best—feelings and instincts[,] like those of any lioness."

Henri wiped his watering eyes with his trembling hand[.] He regarded Reid somberly. "Last night, your lioness gav[e] her heart to you. I saw it in her face, her eyes, this morn[-]

ng. I urged her to go to the caves alone, to feel her way
through this fear of hers. Time alone helps us think clearly.
I shared with her that sometimes things happen that make
us scared. Even good things make us frightened at times,
eh?''

Uncomfortably, Reid rasped, ''She was scared?''

Henri shrugged very slowly. ''When I saw my adopted
daughter six months ago, she was wearing darkness around
her.'' He made a motion toward his shoulders. ''I asked
her about the tears in her eyes. She said that someone she
loved had died suddenly. Unexpectedly. The three months
she spent with us were very sad times for all of us here,
because she would not speak of her grief. It is very bad
not to cry out or scream out your grief, eh? Perhaps it is
the country she comes from, but here we wail, we tear our
hair, we cry together, we hold one another through our
grief and sadness. We pray together for those spirits who
have departed. But grief such as this is not buried as my
adopted daughter has tried to bury it.'' Henri lifted his eyes
toward the deep blue sky. ''Something tells me that the
storm that came over our village last night was symbolic
of what is alive and hurting within her. No?''

''I don't know,'' Reid muttered. ''But I can try and find
out.''

Pleased, Henri smiled and leaned over and patted his
shoulder. ''Yes, I feel in my heart that my daughter could
begin to heal if you continue to open your heart to her. I
feel that last night the process truly began for her. And
you are not a stupid young lion. I see your generosity of
spirit. You hide your heart. You hide from her how you
feel toward her. Perhaps it is time you walk past the fear
in your heart and reach out to her, eh? With two very
scared young lions, one of them must be courageous
enough to move beyond their fear to offer a hand—or a
touch, perhaps? Kind words spoken from the heart may be
frightening to you, but can be freeing for the other, yes?''

Slowly rising to his feel, Reid dusted off the seat of his pants. ''In our country, too few people listen to our elders. I'm not one of them.'' He smiled slightly. ''What's the best way to get to these caves?''

When Henri smiled his toothless smile, his laughter rolling like thunder across the village, Reid felt some of his fear melt away.

Chapter Ten

No one was more surprised than Casey when Reid showed up on horseback near noon. The three warriors who had been sent by Grandfather Henri to help her as well as protect her sat outside the cave, talking in low voices and roasting over a fire a gazelle they had brought down earlier. Casey was standing at the fourth cave when she saw Reid on the black Thoroughbred mare. Her heart pounded briefly to underscore the sudden panic and joy she felt.

Watching him dismount, she was once again reminded of his incredible athletic grace. As he tied the mare to a nearby bush and turned, Casey met and held his clear gray gaze. Smiling a little tentatively, she removed the latex gloves from her hands and went forward to meet him.

"Hi, stranger," she called.

Reid nodded to the three warriors near the first cave. They lifted their hands and shouted a greeting in Bantu to him. He returned it. His Bantu was not as smooth as

Casey's, but it got his meaning across. Turning his atten
tion to her, he saw that she was decked out in her pape.
garb. It was obvious she'd been exploring the caves.

Coming to a halt less than three feet from her, he restec
his hands on his hips. The paper hood hid her gloriou:
mass of red hair except for a few tendrils peeking out here
and there in defiance of the rules of scientific study. Reic
grinned a little—her hair was like her.

"Having fun this morning, are we?"

Relief sheeted through Casey as she dropped the latex
gloves in a biohazard bucket. "Caves. You know, I can'
resist them. When Grandfather Henri told me about them
this morning, I gotta 'fess up and tell you, I was all ears.'

"Hmm," Reid said, gazing around at the four caves
which sat in a semicircle around them. "Bats, right? The
lure of finding a new species of bat to dissect to see if i'
is the reservoir?"

"Yep." She sighed. "The warriors have been helping
me. We've found three new species so far." She turnec
and pointed to the fourth cave. "This cave is tricky anc
small. It's less that four feet high and winds back like a
wind tunnel. The farther you go into it, the smaller it becomes." She looked at the front of her paper suit. It was
smudged with dirt and debris. Wrinkling her nose, she
said, "I crawled back on my belly as far as I could, took
a lot of photos, and I just got out when you arrived."

Frowning, Reid studied the area. He was more than a
little aware of the warriors benignly watching them from
a distance. "Did they scout the area for possible Black
Dawn operatives?"

"Oh, yes," Casey assured him. She liked his presence.
that sense of safety Reid always gave her. Pointing to her
table, where all the items she needed for dissecting were
located, she said, "I want to get rid of this paper suit and
put on a new one for dissection. Help me?"

Any chance to touch her was always high on Reid's lis

of secret, unbidden desires. "Sure." He walked over to the folding table, leaned down and retrieved two new pairs of latex gloves. Handing one set to Casey, he put the other pair on. The goggles she wore were angled up on her brow. She took them off and handed them to him. He placed them in a bucket of water and bleach. Bleach would effectively kill any bacteria or virus she might have picked up while in the caves.

After Casey got into a clean set of protective gear—and three sets of gloves, just in case—they worked in companionable silence, side by side. She worked slowly and carefully at the table, a scalpel in one hand. Reid's job was to hold the opened cavity of the bat so that she could take a sample and place it on a glass slide. Once the liquid was smeared across the glass, Reid carefully put a clean slide over it to protect it. Then he labeled the slide with the bat species, numbered and dated. The slide was then taped and carefully put in an awaiting box to be sent to the OID, where a high-powered electron microscope would be used to see if it contained the deadly Ebola virus or not. The noon heat was palpable and sweat trickled down the sides of Reid's face as they worked on the third and final specimen. There was such a precision to Casey's work. She knew what she was doing and was completely focused on it. He liked to watch her graceful hand movements. He liked the fact that their elbows and hands touched many times. Each time, a frisson of heat would fly through him, reminding Reid how much he enjoyed her nearness.

Just as he opened the chest cavity on the last bat, he heard one of the warriors shout. Instantly, Reid jerked his hands away from the bat, thinking that the warrior had spotted a terrorist. As he whirled to the left, he heard a gasp from Casey. At once Reid jerked his attention back to her. Her eyes were huge; her lips were parted in a soundless cry. Following her gaze, his heart grew icy with fear.

"Oh no...." Casey whispered. She stared down at her hand—and a slit that had appeared in the layers of her latex covering her index finger. When Reid had jerked his hands away in reaction to the warrior's shout, the chest cavity on the bat had snapped shut, jamming the scalpel into her left index finger.

Her heart pounded hard in her chest.

"Damn it!" Hunter rasped. He turned to look at the warrior. The young man had leaped to his feet from his crouched position near the fire and was madly brushing the front of his loincloth. Apparently, from what Reid could make out, a spark from the fire had landed on the warrior's clothing.

Icy fear threaded through Reid as he devoted all his attention to Casey. Her face went pale as she stared down at her gloved left hand. When he saw the slit in the light green latex, he wanted to cry. *No!* Had the scalpel gone through all three sets of gloves and sliced into her finger?

"Get the gloves off," he told her tersely. "Now, Casey. Hurry." He was already reaching for the bucket of bleach and the strong disinfectant soap that sat nearby. What if she had been cut? What if this bat had Ebola in it? His gaze shot to her. She was standing there, petrified, her left hand held upward. He saw the blood from the bat smeared on her fingertips. Or was it *her* blood? It was impossible to tell. Why was she standing there? She knew the procedures.

"Casey?"

Just the way he snapped her name made her jump. Mouth dry, Casey shot a look over at his hard, sweaty features. She saw terror in Reid's eyes, and her memory of the day she and Steve had been in the hot zone came flashing back to her. Was this how she had looked when Steve had been bitten by the monkey? The expression on Reid's face mirrored terror, concern and...love? Too frightened, Casey didn't have time to take in all the feelings that were so alive in his almost colorless eyes. His pupils were huge and black and focused—on her.

"Step away," he growled. Reaching out, he wrapped his hand around her arm and pulled her back from the table. She was behaving as if in shock. And why wouldn't she be? Reid felt a scream working its way up through his throat. Breathing hard, he removed her goggles and threw them on the ground. Very quickly, he ripped the paper suit off her. How pale Casey had become. He wondered if she was going to faint. Wouldn't he if he had been cut?

Never in his life had he felt like crying more than in this moment as he guided her to a stump and made her sit down. All she could do was stare at her cut glove. Reid understood only too well what was going on in her mind—and heart. Steve had been bitten by a monkey and had been infected with Ebola. Now it could be happening to her. Wanting to cry out at the unfairness of it all, Hunter gripped her lower arm and peeled off the first glove that had been sliced through.

Please, please don't let her be cut. He prayed the litany over and over as he gripped the edge of the second glove, a hot pink color. They both stared at it; it, too, had been sliced through. The likelihood of the third one being cut was very real now. He heard Casey groan.

Grimly, breathing hard, Reid began to peel the second glove off her hand. There was blood on it; that wasn't a good sign. His fingers were trembling badly now as he tried to pull the cuff of the glove forward to expose the fingers of the white glove beneath it.

Casey's eyes bulged. Her heart was pounding heavily in her breast. Was she going to die like Steve had? The thought careened through her. At the same time, a cry of disbelief choked her throat. She didn't want to die! She was in love with Reid. She wanted a chance to tell him that. She wanted a chance to live once more, to reach out and love once more. Was Ebola going to cheat her of it in its macabre way? Tears stung Casey's eyes and she held her breath as Reid pulled the pink glove free. Instantly, her gaze shot to her index finger.

Hunter gasped. He gripped her hand hard and knelt down. *"Look! Look!"* His cry was choked off as he forced Casey to look at the white glove.

"Oh, God...thank you...." she whispered unsteadily. Fierce relief sheeted through her.

They stared at her white glove, the last defense between her and death. The index finger was intact. It had not been sliced through by the scalpel. Shakily, Casey pulled the latex glove off her hand. They studied her index finger carefully just to make sure.

"The skin's not broken," Hunter rasped as he held her hand between his. "It's not broken...not broken...."

Casey leaned forward, her brow pressed against Hunter's broad shoulder. She felt his care of her, heard the raw terror in his voice and saw his love for her in his narrowed, intense eyes. "Hold me...." she quavered. "Just...hold me? I need you...."

Her words were so sweet, so unbidden, that without thinking, Reid leaned forward and eased her off the stump so that he could fold her into his embrace. Suddenly it was so easy, so natural between them. He heard her moan softly as his arms encased her and he drew her hard against him and held her. Simply held her.

"It's okay," he breathed harshly against her ear. Closing his eyes, Reid could do nothing but gently rock Casey back and forth in his arms. She clung silently to him, her face pressed against his neck and jaw. He felt the skittering of her wild heartbeat. Her sobs of relief. The hotness of her tears as they coursed down the thick column of his neck.

Groaning, Reid turned that scant inch and pressed a shaky kiss to her cheek. "I need you," he rasped. And he did. In these last few seconds, her life could have been snatched unfairly from him. Grandfather Henri's words floated back to him as he raised his hand and traced the clean line of Casey's jaw. His heart swelled, opened, and he was helpless to do anything but follow his feelings, his need of her.

Without thinking, he guided her mouth to his. He felt her tremble violently in his arms, felt the soft rush of moistness as she broke the kiss momentarily. Blindly, he molded his mouth against hers once again. He wasn't going to let Casey escape. He was going to love her the only way he knew how, to let her know that he celebrated her living.

This time, she arched against him. Her breasts pressed against his chest. Her arms went around his shoulders. The world came to a speeding halt for Reid. He felt the strength of her mouth returning his unbridled, hungry kiss. Threading his fingers through her fiery, silky hair, he claimed her in no uncertain terms and refused to allow her to escape the power, the volcanic flow of feelings he'd held at bay for so long. It felt good to slide his mouth against hers, to feel her returning fervor. Her mouth opened wider, asking him to explore her, take her more deeply and to share in this chaotic moment where life and death had hung precariously in the balance.

Hunter felt as if they were dancing on the edge of a deadly saber blade. Now, as he traced her lower lip with his tongue and she moaned softly for more, he smiled to himself. He'd had the strength to overcome his own fear of Casey, his terror of her rejecting him, and she was here, in his arms, as she should be. As she was meant to be. As quickly as a flash of lightning, everything had changed between them. They were both stunned by the event, and yet they found solace and healing in each other's hungry, clinging mouths their hands ranging hungrily across each other in bold exploration.

Tearing his mouth from hers, Reid studied her, her face

mere inches from his own. He saw the turbulence in her sultry green eyes, saw the desire in them for him alone. The observation made him giddy with joy. Reaching out, he caressed her unruly red hair and gave her a trembling smile.

"You're going to be all right now," he rasped.

Casey closed her eyes. She surrendered to Reid's strength and care in that moment. Surrendered utterly. How good it felt! Casey absorbed him, his rasping comment, and simply felt how good it could be to be touched, cherished and worshipped by a man who loved her. Who she believed loved her anyway. Nestling her head against his neck, she sighed raggedly, unable to sort out her reeling and explosive emotions. Later, she would try to figure all this out. Too much was happening too fast. Moments ago, she'd thought she was going to die of Ebola, as Steve had. Now she was celebrating life, celebrating love, in Reid's protective arms.

In two short months, so much had changed. Casey could barely think. All she could do was feel the power of Reid's heart against her ear, feel his powerful arms around her and the tender way he continued to graze her cheek, her hair and shoulders. Life was being turned upside down for her. In two weeks they would be taking the slides to Yambuku, to be sent to the OID. Time was hurrying by so fast. Casey clung to Reid, filled in every possible way with her need for him.

"Hey, you ready to have these driven to Yambuku?" Reid called to Casey from the truck.

Casey looked up from the makeshift table in front of their hut. The early August sun boiled overhead. Perspiration dotted her furrowed brow as she scooped up the shipment containing the latest slides to be sent to the OID.

"Yeah! Hold on just a sec!" She leaned over and grabbed her journal, which would go along with the specimens. Trotting toward the truck, Casey knew that Reid had to hurry or he would miss the colonel, who wanted to make a punctual landing at the Yambuku airport. He didn't like waiting around and Reid knew it.

As she halted at the driver's-side door, she smiled at Reid. His returning smile was easy and filled with warmth. She felt blanketed, as always, by his attention. As she handed him the carefully prepared box, Casey wondered where the last months had flown. She was amazed at how much more she knew about Reid because he'd opened up to her by telling her a story each night. She marveled at his storytelling skills. But it was more than that, she acknowledged. The incident two weeks ago, when they'd thought the scalpel had sliced into her finger, had been a crucial turning point in their relationship. From then on, they were more intimate with one another. She looked forward to those times when Reid would reach out and shyly touch her hand, her arm. Or sometimes...rarely...he would slide his arm around her shoulders, give her a quick embrace and then release her.

How Casey loved those moments! They were too infrequent, but under the circumstances, the pace that Reid had set for them was the right one. He knew of her past with Steve. But her grief seemed to have been permanently laid to rest within her. Perhaps her mourning had reached closure, as it should. Now a new door in her heart was opening up—to Reid Hunter.

"Sure you don't want to come along?" Reid asked as he placed the package on the seat next to him.

Shaking her head, she said, "Positive. Henri wants me to be with him this afternoon." She shrugged and grinned. "You'll be back by dusk. I'll be okay."

Reid lost his smile as he put the vehicle into gear. "Dinner waiting for me? Right?"

Chuckling, Casey ran her fingers through her untameable mop of hair. "Right. Champagne, candlelight, the whole nine yards, Hunter. You bet."

Enjoying the ease that came naturally between them now, Reid grinned. He reached out and touched her blazing red hair, which was shot through with gold and burgundy. He watched the pleasure cross Casey's face as he caressed her curls. In the past month, he'd had the joy of seeing Casey blossom into an incredibly alluring woman, though she was still more child than adult at times. Oh, she was an adult when needed, but at night, in the hut, when he'd tell her a funny story from his growing up years, they'd lie there giggling like two teenagers at a pajama party. Easing his hand from her locks, he said, "I think, the day I come home and see a candlelight dinner on the table is the day you stop being yourself."

"What you see is it, Hunter. You know that better than most by now."

Sobering slightly, he said, "Listen, be careful while I'm gone, okay? Just stay alert."

The intimacy in his voice shook her, as it always did. He rarely used that deep, vibrating tone with her, but when he did, Casey felt her heart squeeze with an intense longing to simply fall into his arms and kiss him until she was senseless with the taste, smell and feel of him. Leaning forward, she pressed a swift kiss to the hard line of his mouth. It was one of the few times she'd done it in broad daylight in front of the villagers. Breaking the molten kiss, she saw his eyes grow thundercloud dark with desire—for her. Reid did not hide how he felt about her, and it made her feel strong as a woman in one way, and yet frightened in another. "Yeah...sure I will." She stepped away from the truck and lifted her hand. "*You* be careful."

"Black Dawn isn't interested in me," he drawled as he saw real fear banked in Casey's green eyes. "I'm a nobody compared to you, good doctor." He smiled, his mouth still tingling with sensation from having her sweet lips against it. He even tasted the papaya she'd eaten just minutes before as he gave her one last look before shifting the vehicle into gear.

Sticking her hands in her pockets, Casey watched Reid slowly drive off down the deeply rutted dirt road. Eight other villagers were hitching a ride with him into Yambuku. The truck looked like a bus and she smiled a little. Turning, Casey couldn't shake the sudden fear she felt. This was the first time she and Reid were parting from one another. Usually she drove to Yambuku with him. It gave them time together, and they usually did their limited shopping at the nun's mission, which was always filled with fun and laughter. Ruefully, she rubbed the back of her neck and turned around to walk to Grandpa Henri's hut.

It was crazy that she should feel this way. Why did she? The hot sunlight poured down on her head and shoulders as she walked slowly through the busy village. Children ran up to her and grabbed her hands, begging her to come and play tag with them once again. She laughed and resisted—but barely. Casey had often come out of the jungle campsite to go for a swim in the pool at dusk, and the children loved to go with her and get into water fights with her. All the while, Reid was there, perched on his rock, ever alert, his back turned so he wouldn't see her nakedness as she bathed after the children left.

She tried to shrug off her worry for Reid's safety, but it was difficult nowadays. Shortly after the scalpel incident, an Italian professor and a troop of men had driven into the village. They'd asked for Casey by name. Grandpa Henri had refused to verify one way or another if she was at their village. Reid had warned Henri about Black Dawn and the old man knew two OID people were already dead. Henri wanted to protect her at all costs. He'd given them no information and they'd disappeared. But who knew where? Reid had been concerned, too. Casey had reassured both of them that many foreign countries were sending their best scientists over to Africa to help discover the Ebola virus's reservoir. It was probably just a science group wanting to formally connect with her, trade information and then go their way.

She saw Grandpa Henri waiting for her so she hurried her step. Smiling, she reached out and touched the old man's extended hand. "Hi, sorry I'm late," she said breathlessly. "I had trouble wrapping up that OID package for Reid."

Henri gestured for her to follow him into his airy, sunlit hut, and Casey ducked in through the doorway behind him. The odor of roasted antelope tantalized her. She saw it on a platter being held by one of the younger wives, who smiled at her in welcome. Waiting until Henri sat down on his throne, Casey sat cross-legged next to him. As the succulent, freshly killed antelope was served on wooden plates, Henri turned his attention to her.

"Of late, we have not had much time together. That young lion of yours keeps you well entertained, eh?"

Coloring fiercely, Casey took the plate of meat handed to her. She thanked the young wife in Bantu. "Well...he makes me laugh a lot, Grandpa. Does it keep you or others awake at night?" she asked, genuinely concerned.

Chuckling indulgently, Henri whispered, "Child, your laughter is music to us! I have never heard you so happy before. No, we like your shared laughter. It is healing. It is good for one's soul and heart, you know."

Casey couldn't disagree as she chewed on the antelope. "Some nights, Grandpa, my stomach hurts and I'm in tears from laughing so hard. Reid's a funny man. He's a great storyteller, believe me. The best I've ever heard, anyway."

"We have a saying that the one who gives you the gift of laughter will steal your heart away." Henri looked at her sagely, expecting an answer as he slowly chewed on a small piece of antelope. He didn't have many teeth left and it was always a challenge to chew meat.

Feeling heat steal into her face once more, Casey avoided his glittering gaze. She took a drink of warm goat's milk. Wiping her mouth with the back of her hand, she said, "Sometimes he's like a dream come true, Grandpa...but don't tell him that."

"What we say is always kept between us, my daughter."

Casey felt her heart swell in her chest as she thought of Reid. "He's so good to me.... He tells me a story every night to help me go to sleep. And I do. My mind quits spinning. I just listen to his deep, low voice, and he uses words so well that I can close my eyes and picture exactly what he's painting with those words. And then...I just fall asleep."

"And do you tell him stories in return?"

"Er, no..."

"Why not?"

She frowned. "I don't know.... I guess it's a one-way street, isn't it?"

"He has opened his heart to you, no?"

"Yes. I know a lot about him now."

"And what does he know of you?"

"Not much, I'm afraid."

"That is right," Henri chided gently. He waved his finger at her. "The young lion has honor. He is a true warrior. He works hard. He cares for our old ones. He loves the children, for they flock to him upon his return from your jungle camp. If he were of my village, I would betroth you to him, daughter."

Casey choked on the meat. She coughed violently. Tears came to her eyes as she forced herself to swallow. "What?"

"You heard me," Henri said archly. "This man's heart is yours to hold. Surely you know that. I see how he feels about you every time you are not aware of him gazing upon you. There is nothing he has not done for you. And yet you do not honor the gift he has offered you. I wonder why not?"

Setting the meat aside, Casey frowned and rubbed her hands on her thighs. "Reid hasn't said anything like that to me."

Guffawing loudly, Henri shook his head. "This man must be made of stuff stronger than I have ever known, then. He feels much for you, and yet he does not speak of what he carries in his heart?"

Uncomfortable, Casey nervously rubbed her hands once more on the thighs of the coveralls she wore. "I'm afraid, Grandpa. I lost one man I loved…. I can't afford to love another and lose him, too. I—I just couldn't live through it again."

"So because you fear loss, you spurn his love for you, eh?"

Casey met his gentle look. "I'm a coward."

"No, just fearful. It takes courage to live, no? Courage to reach out to him? To tell him of what lies in your heart toward him? Yes?"

In a broken whisper, her head hanging, Casey said, "Yes…."

"Ah, my child, you are a lioness. Be one. Lost love can be replaced in time…with the right man. My heart aches for both of you." He patted her slumped shoulder. "I know he worries for you, for these Black Dawn terrorists. Each day is precious to us. Do not waste them. Do not throw happiness away…."

It was past midnight when Reid finally drove back into the village and parked at their hut. Casey, still fully clothed, rushed out at once. By the light of the full moon climbing into the sky, she could see the fatigue in his face as he unbuckled the seat belt and opened the door.

"You're a sight for sore eyes," Casey said, greeting him huskily as she caught and held the door open. "Is everything all right? You're really coming back late. I was worried sick."

Reid sat there simply absorbing Casey's presence. "Everything's fine," he reassured her tiredly. "The colonel was late getting into Yambuku. They had another firefight near the Kinshasa airport and they shut it down for half a day. Don't worry, he got there and I gave him the OID package and journal." He jabbed his thumb behind him. "More supplies from OID in the back. Slides and such. A more powerful microscope, too—the one you were asking for. I also got some dry goods for us from the Belgian nuns at the mission."

Maybe it was Grandpa Henri's gentle chiding that prompted her, or maybe it was her worry over him, but Casey stepped forward and lightly rested her hand on his strong shoulder. Reid instantly snapped his head to the left, his eyes narrowing upon hers. Her breath caught. She felt his hunger for her. She felt her own need for him. Every muscle beneath his taut skin trembled with awareness under her fingertips. Before she grew cowardly once again, Casey's breath rushed out and she blurted, "I'm glad you're back. I was so worried...."

Reid's heart soared with joy as their gazes met and locked. Her green eyes were shadowed and he saw the genuine fear for him in their depths. The soft parting of her lips made him groan internally and her hand felt like a burning brand on his damp cotton shirt. Reid violently checked his impulse to reach out to her. Recalling hotly how her mouth tasted beneath his, the texture of her, the taste of her, was nearly his undoing.

Busying himself, he muttered, "Well, I think I've solved the problem of keeping communications open between us so you won't worry over me if it happens again." He reached down and brought out an extra comsat phone.

"Compliments of Perseus. Next time I get stuck somewhere, I can call you and vice versa." He forced a smile he didn't feel as she jerked her hand away from him as if she were burned. What had possessed her to reach out and touch him? Reid wasn't sure. He hoped the gesture was out of care. Maybe a growing love for him? And then he shook his head. *Dreams. Stupid, unrealistic dreams,* he warned himself harshly as he climbed out of the truck.

Just the way Casey looked at him as she stood back, gripping the new comsat phone in her hands made him wonder sharply about the meaning of her new intimacy with him over the last two weeks. Up until then, there had been little touching shared between them. Only laughter. Good times. Wonderful times. The best times he could ever recall. Casey was fun to be with. Her glib wit, her dry sense of humor, her appreciation of his country life made him eagerly look forward to their nights together. But why had she touched him so much since the scalpel incident? What signal was she sending? What did she want him to know? The questions begged to be spoken, but Reid was too afraid of the possible answers.

Moving to the rear of the truck, he opened the back and gathered up several sacks of canned food. Casey moved in right behind him and brought in her share of sacks. They set them on the table in the dim light of the kerosene lamp.

"You've got to be dead on your feet," Casey whispered as she moved the sacks to one side of the table. "Why don't you go to bed? I'll unpack this stuff."

He studied her in the growing silence, his shadow covering her where she stood. Her hands trembled slightly. She was afraid. Of him? Resting his hands on his hips, he murmured, "Are you okay?"

"Yeah…sure I am…." Biting down on her lower lip, Casey busied herself taking the canned goods out of the sacks.

"You seem a little unsettled."

"I was worried...."

He ached to move forward and draw her into his arms. She seemed so tenuous and unsure right now. Reid hadn't seen her react like this before, so he wasn't sure what it meant. "Everything go okay here today while I was gone?" he demanded.

"Fine...everything was fine." Drawing in a ragged breath, Casey lifted her chin and met his burning gaze. "It's just that, well, I was worried for you, was all."

"Worried—how?"

Casey recalled Grandpa Henri's words about not throwing life away. If she was completely honest with herself, she'd admit that every moment spent with Reid was a delicious and happy experience, and she didn't want to lose him. "Well," she muttered, running her hand nervously through her hair, "about you, I guess."

"Me? Your Neanderthal guard dog?" he teased, a grin lapping at the corners of his mouth. Reid knew if he teased her, she'd relax. She always had before. Casey rallied instantly beneath his gentle nudging.

"Yes, Neanderthal Man. You. I was worried about you, okay?" Casey saw the warmth in his eyes and felt it encircle her as surely as if he'd embraced her physically with those very strong, caring arms of his.

"This is a red-letter day," he gibed. "Not only do you worry about me, but you touch me. I should go away more often."

She managed a nervous laugh. "Don't let it go to your head, jock."

Reid picked up the towel hanging on a nail near the door. He shared a gentle smile with her as he hesitated before going to the pool to bathe. "It didn't, good doctor. It went straight to my heart."

Chapter Eleven

"Play with us, Casey! Play with us!"

Children of all ages danced around Casey as she stepped away from the truck. They had just returned from their work site for the day. The children touched her hands, her arms, and jumped up and down in anticipation that she'd say yes. She tossed a merry look toward Reid. He returned her smile.

"Work's over for the day, Doc. Go play with your kids."

She warmed powerfully to the heated look in his eyes. "Okay, I'm gonna go play tag with them out there." She pointed to the savanna just outside the village. "Want to come with us?"

Chuckling, Reid turned off the key. "Nope, you go right ahead. I've got a few calls to make to Perseus." He raised his hand. "Have fun." Suddenly the fleeting, molten thought of Casey carrying his baby made him hesitate. Yes, he'd thought a lot about Casey from a lot of different angles and perspectives during the third month of their stay here at the village. And all of his thoughts were good. All of them fulfilled some empty, needy level of himself. But did she feel the same about him? He searched her radiant face and those emerald eyes that shone with obvious joy. Again he wondered if she'd have that look in her eyes as she held their newly born baby in her arms.

"Sure?" she baited him. "You've played tag with us before. It's always more fun with two adults being kids out there." She laughed delightedly. The look in Reid's eyes stirred her on some deep level. It was one he gave her often and it made her stomach curl deliciously with flutters of anticipation, man-to-woman. He made her feel special, needed and hotly desired. An ache began in her lower body, and as she stood there watching, that slow, heated smile tugged at his mouth. Casey found herself wanting to make hot, unbridled love with Reid. Lately her dreams had been torrid, and Casey was so afraid of waking up some night and finding herself climbing all over him. How embarrassing!

"Very sure, good doctor. Duty calls whether I like it or not." He met her smoky green gaze and studied her lips as they parted and beckoned him. "And stop teasing me with that come-hither look. It won't work."

Heat flowed into Casey's cheeks and she avoided his sharp, hungry gaze. "I can't even try feminine wiles on you, Hunter. I swear, you're immune to everything. Even Ebola."

Chuckling, Reid rested against the seat and simply absorbed Casey's presence. She was so good for him. She made him happy as no one ever had or possibly ever would in the future. He felt like a starving beggar, humbled to be in her sunny presence. "Believe me when I tell you this," he warned her in a growl. "You have more power over me than you'll ever realize."

Shaken by the low, intimate tone of his voice and that

smoldering gaze aimed directly at her, Casey swallowed hard. She felt the impatient tug of the children's hands. ''Er, I gotta go....'' And she was glad to escape, because for once, Reid had caught her tongue-tied. She didn't have a single blithe retort to parry his highly charged comment. As she turned, she waved to him.

Casey looked down into the velvet brown eyes of Gabriella, Henri's little four-year-old granddaughter, who looked beseechingly up in silent pleading as she grasped her hand. Where had three months flown to? she wondered as she scooped the child up into her arms.

Gabriella squealed in delight and threw her arms around Casey's neck. The other children hooted, laughed and shouted as she walked quickly down the slight incline to the now-withering grass. The heat had intensified, the rainy season was over and the once hip-deep grass had either been eaten by thousands of animals or was withering from lack of moisture. As she strode across the savanna, the grass crackled with dryness about her boots and pant legs. The children shrieked in joy and raced around her, their arms flying, their smiles wide and their eyes dancing with mischief.

Little Gaby nestled her face against Casey's damp neck. Casey smiled and slid her arm along the girl's thin back. Thanks to Reid, the girl was dressed in new red cotton pants and a white T-shirt with a Mickey Mouse emblem. Through Perseus, Reid had pushed to get the children of Henri's village new clothing and a number of large corporations had donated a great deal at Morgan's request.

Life was fragile, Casey decided as she moved beyond the village perimeter with the children dancing delightedly around her. Fragile but delicious. Was her newfound perspective a result of knowing Reid? Because of their mounting desire for one another? Casey smiled to herself. The sunlight was hot and felt good on her head and shoulders. All day she and Reid had labored beneath the dark roof of the jungle. Out here on the open savanna, the sky was a startling blue with a few white puffs of cloud.

Halting, Casey set Gabriella on the grassy ground and released her. "Okay, who's it?" she shouted in their native tongue.

Instantly, the children shrieked, pointed at her and took off like a startled flock of birds in every direction. Casey ran her fingers through her damp, short hair and laughed. She loved the children's laughter, their white teeth flashing when they smiled and their eyes dancing with unabashed delight. She took off after the oldest boy. The screams and shrieks heightened. several children, sensing they were no longer the quarry, rushed after Casey as she chased ten-year-old Charles around the savanna.

Charles was as tall and lean and as graceful as the gazelles that proliferated on the savanna, Casey decided. For his age, he was swift, and she had to push to catch up, reach out and touch his shoulder to make him "it." But Charles ducked and veered off to the left, giggling. Casey couldn't make the same tight turn because she was moving too fast. The dried vegetation wrapped around her legs. With a shout, she tripped and fell forward. In seconds, Casey was tumbling wildly in the dry, crackling grass. She came to an abrupt halt. The children laughed and encircled her, teasing her and pointing at her. Laughing with them, Casey let them pull the bits of grass out of her red hair and off her shoulders and back.

"You slow! You slow like a hippo!" they sang to her.

"Hippo lady," Casey agreed, laughing back at them as she got to her feet. Brushing off her pants, she grinned at them good-naturedly.

"Devil!"

Instantly, Casey spun toward the boy's cry of alarm. "Devil" meant only one thing to her: a black mamba had been spotted!

"Oh no…" she whispered, following the boy's pointing

hand. The children around her screamed in fear and took off at a run toward the village in the distance.

There, no more than three hundred yards away from them, was the largest black mamba Casey had ever seen. From where she stood, she would swear the snake was five feet high. And it was slithering toward her at an alarming rate of speed.

Gabriella burst into tears. She lifted her arms toward Casey.

Casey jerked her attention toward the crying child—who was directly in the path of the swift, deadly black mamba!

Without thinking, Casey closed the distance between them. She saw the boy who had spotted the mamba running wildly for the village, screaming "Devil!" at the top of his high, squeaky voice.

As she scooped Gabriella up into her arms, Casey turned to run. Her heart bounded hard in her chest, and she squeezed the child tightly. Casey knew that a mamba could race along at fifteen miles per hour. That was faster than she could run even if she wasn't carrying a four-year-old. Looking over her shoulder, she saw the cream-colored underside of the black snake as it zig-zagged with startling speed in her direction. She was the closest target. Luckily, all the other children were well ahead of her.

Drawing air into her lungs, she lunged forward. Gabriella shrieked. She threw her tiny arms around Casey's neck in a stranglehold.

"Hold on!" Casey rasped to the child.

It was a race between living and dying. Casey sucked huge drafts of air into her lungs. Boots pounding on the hard, unrelenting soil of the savanna, she plunged forward. Wind whipped around her. The dry grass threatened to entangle her feet once again.

Please, just let me get out of here! The thought was a prayer. Heart pounding in her chest, her breathing ragged,

Casey ran harder. Then terror shot through her and with a little cry, she skidded to a halt.

Somehow, the black mamba had not only outdistanced her, but had outsmarted her as well! The snake had placed itself between her and the safety of the village. Her eyes widened as she stood frozen, her breath coming in sobs. The creature was huge!

Everything went blank around Casey. All her attention, her focus, was on the black mamba, which was no more than six feet away from her. Though it was impossible to judge how large the snake was, right now it looked about ten feet long to Casey. Her heart skittered in fear. If she moved, the mamba would be merciless and strike out.

''Don't—move—don't move....'' she pleaded in gasps to Gabriella, whose tiny head was tucked tightly beneath her jaw, her face pressed into her shoulder. Oh, God, what could she do? Casey didn't dare risk looking around. Just the movement of her head could incite the mamba to strike. All her attention, her pulsing life force, was focused directly on that venomous snake standing like a thick, black-and-cream post in the yellowed grass. Its body shone and glistened in the hot sunlight. Its scales were a dark greenish brown, each lying neatly atop the next to form a seamless pattern. It had a flat, oval head and its eyes, round, large and intelligent looking, were lidless. The stare of its huge black pupils surrounded by olive green engaged Casey's own widening, terror-filled eyes. The snake did not look as deadly as she knew it was. Its eyes were glittering with such obvious curiosity that Casey would swear there was a human being staring out of them at her. There was nothing stupid or slow about this incredible reptile, whose terrifying reputation preceded it.

Breath tearing from her, her lungs burning from exertion, Casey gripped Gabriella even tighter as the little girl softly sobbed with fear. The world ebbed to a halt around them. Casey heard the throbbing of her heart in her ribcage, and each time her heart thudded, she felt her body vibrate. The snake advanced slowly, looking her over. Assessing her.

There was no way to escape. Casey knew one of them would die. It had to be her. She had to protect Gabriella at all costs. The black mamba moved again. There were fewer than three feet left between them now. Casey gulped. Her mind raced. Her heart, her love, was centered on Reid. Oh, why hadn't she loved him openly! Why had she been such a coward? She was going to die without ever telling him what she felt. Why hadn't she told him she loved him?

Bitterly, Casey held the snake's curious look. It seemed to be sizing her up like a quarry. *Probably deciding where to strike me.* Her arms tightened a little more. Whatever happened, she had to protect Gabriella. Could she move fast enough once the mamba lunged forward to strike her? Could she take the venomous, deadly bite instead of allowing Gabriella to be the target? Casey didn't want to die; she wanted to live. But death was standing erect and demanding, three feet away. There would be no escaping her fate.

"Don't move Casey."

She went rigid. Was she hearing things? Reid's voice! Low. Quiet. In control. *Oh, God!*

"Don't move a muscle."

No! Out of the corner of her eye, she saw Reid advancing slowly toward her. She saw the 9 mm pistol in his hands, the weapon pointed directly at the black mamba's head.

Her heart slammed into her ribs. *Reid! He's here!* It wasn't her imagination! She nearly cried out, but knew the mamba would strike if she even breathed. She had to remain perfectly still, as Reid said. She didn't even dare speak. Her gaze flicked to Hunter's sweaty, hardened features as he quietly closed in on the snake.

"Whatever you do," he rasped, "don't move, don't

talk, don't bat an eyelash…. I'm going to try and blow his head off before he strikes…." His breath was harsh, his hands held out from his body as he drew a bead on the huge black mamba. The snake didn't move. Its focus was entirely on Casey. Reid knew the snake must be aware of his presence, but it didn't seem to care. Coming to a halt ten feet away from them, Reid slowly aimed his pistol. He had one shot. One shot only. One chance… If he missed, the black mamba would strike out at Casey and kill her. Never had Reid felt so damn helpless. So enraged at the unfairness of it all.

Casey stood like a statue, the little girl held protectively in her arms. Her red hair moved with the slight, hot breeze. He saw the perspiration trickling down the sides of her face. Her eyes were huge, wide and frightened. All her attention was on the huge black mamba, which was at least thirteen feet long, its head held four feet into the air. The snake looked amazingly powerful as it began to move its body slightly from side to side. *Damn!* Reid blinked. Sweat burned his eyes and his sight blurred momentarily. He blinked savagely again. The snake was getting ready to strike. He *had* to take a shot!

As the mamba continued the slight, swaying motion, Reid tried to keep his gun sight on the reptile. It was a risky shot at best. The snake's head was huge, but as it moved, it became less of a sure target. Panic gripped Reid. He loved Casey! He'd never spoken those words. Why hadn't he? Why had he waited? As he stood there, legs spread apart for balance, his gaze locked on the snake, he cursed himself for his own cowardice in not telling Casey he loved her. When had it happened? How? He had no answers, only fear that she was going to die if he couldn't kill the black mamba.

His throat closed up with terror. His breathing shut off. His heart throbbed powerfully in his heaving chest. He'd run from the village, pistol in hand, when the children came back screaming, *"Devil! Devil!"* Now, his hands sweaty around the stock, his finger resting firmly against the trigger, he watched the mamba sway drunkenly. Any second now it was going to strike.

Casey couldn't breathe. She stood there, every nerve in her body screaming at her to run. She couldn't. She'd fallen under the power of the black mamba's lidless, hypnotizing gaze as it swayed gracefully from side to side, as if in some kind of ritualistic dance. Her mouth went dry. Her pulsed throbbed violently. She was going to die. Her life was at an end. She saw the pupils in the snake's eyes suddenly shrink to pinpoints. And then Casey knew. Knew it was going to strike. She tried to prepare herself for the savage attack, tried to anticipate where the black mamba would sink its fangs into her.

And then everything slowed down. Her heart pounded in slow, exaggerated beats. The world grew white around her; she no longer saw the blue of the sky. She felt the heat of the sun upon her. She felt Gabriella's tight, strangling grip around her neck. She saw the black mamba arch back into striking position. Her eyes widened enormously. Her lips parted in a soundless scream.

The black mamba lunged forward, its head moving at startling speed—right toward her legs.

The firing of a gun roared in Casey's ears. Pain from the sound tore through her.

She saw the black mamba's head jerk backward as it absorbed the shot. From somewhere, Casey heard Hunter's thundering voice. Her gaze was riveted on the snake, its head partially severed from its thick, powerful body. It thrashed forward, still lunging toward her, its dark green, lidless eyes still upon her. Still intent upon killing her.

Unable to move, Casey heard and then felt Reid's presence. She saw him dive between her and the thrashing reptile. With a grunt, he slammed his hands into her shoulders. The power of his thrust sent Casey reeling off her feet and flying backward, Gabriella shrieking in her arms. Before they slammed to the hard earth, Casey saw the thrashing black mamba strike out at Reid. A scream of warning tore from her throat. She saw the snake's lipless mouth open and snap like a rabid dog several times as it made contact with Reid's pant leg.

No! Oh, my God, no! Casey hit the ground on her back, all the wind knocked out of her. Gabriella went flying out of her arms and over her head.

Stunned, unable to move, Casey gasped for breath. She heard Gabriella sobbing nearby. *Reid! Where's Reid?* The black mamba had struck him! She'd seen it. *No! Oh, no!* Struggling, Casey tried to get up, but couldn't. Fear drove her to roll onto her side. She had to get to Reid! He'd stepped in front of her and saved her life. Sobbing herself, Casey couldn't get air into her lungs no matter how badly she tried.

Other sounds pummeled her. She heard the shouts and calls of villagers rushing to their aid. She saw Gabriella's mother pick her up and hold her fiercely in her arms. She saw the tears of gratitude in the mother's eyes. Forcing herself to her hands and knees, Casey fought the weakness she felt. Her shoulders ached where Reid had solidly connected with her and thrown her out of harm's way. *Reid!*

Hands—strong, sweaty hands—closed around Casey's arms and hauled her up. Up into Hunter's arms.

"Reid...!" she sobbed, as she helplessly fell against him.

"Hush, hush," he rasped, dragging her tightly against him. Reid sank to his knees with Casey in his arms. All his attention was still on the black mamba, which twitched in the dry grass no more than six feet away from them. Its mouth snapped open and shut in its death throes. "Are you okay? Are you all right?" Wildly, he searched her pale face, her wild-looking green eyes. Running his hand through her hair, down her neck and arms, he looked for any indication of a bite.

"Fine...." Casey gasped. "But you—"

"No...I'm okay...I'm okay," he said, burying his face against her sun-warmed red hair.

"But...I saw it bite...." Casey sobbed for air. She felt like a helpless puppet in Reid's strong, protective embrace.

"Sweet God, you feel good to me," he rasped, holding her so tightly he was afraid he'd squeeze the breath out of her. Her arms went around his waist and he shut his eyes. "I almost lost you.... Casey, I love you! Damn it, I should have told you that before." He ran his hand through her unruly hair, cupped her jaw and forced her to look up at him.

Sweat stood out on Reid's face, and his expression was hard and uncompromising. Casey gulped as she met and held his gleaming, dark silver gaze. He loved her. Was she hearing things? Was she hallucinating in the heat of the crisis? In the face of death? "W-what?" she stammered breathlessly. Without thinking, Casey lifted her hand and slid it along his hard, sandpapery jaw.

He laughed a little unsurely. "I said I love you."

Her heart exploded with joy. Quavering, she whispered, "I love you, Reid Hunter."

Casey saw his skin suddenly go pale. Alarmed, her eyes widening, she got to her knees. "Reid? Reid? What's wrong? Oh, no..."

Within seconds, Reid's arms loosened and went lax around her. She saw that burning gleam of life snuffed out of his eyes. She watched as his eyes rolled back in his head.

"No!" Casey shrieked. *"No!"* And she made a grab for him as he began to crumple to the dry, yellowed earth. "Help! Get help!" she cried to those who surrounded them.

Gasping, each breath painful, Casey quickly maneuvered Reid so that he lay on his back. He was completely unconscious. He *had* been bitten by the black mamba! Hands shaking badly, she tore at his right pant leg, where she'd seen the mamba strike at him as he'd bravely and foolishly placed himself between her and the reptile.

Grandfather Henri, who had just arrived, slowly bent down at Reid's feet. He dropped his cane, his weathered hands moving toward Hunter's leg.

"He's been bitten," Casey sobbed. She tore wildly at the pant leg and pulled it upward.

"There," Henri said heavily, and pointed to a faint scratch along the side of Reid's hairy shin.

Tears flooded her eyes. Casey sobbed. She stared at the scratch. "No!" she wailed. "I don't want him to die, Grandpa! Help me! Help me to save him!" Her sobs became louder. More desperate. "I love him! I love him, Grandpa. I don't want him to die! He can't! Damn it, he can't! I can't lose another man I love!"

Chapter Twelve

Casey was alone. Alone in a way she never wanted to experience again. Her face buried in her hands, she sat in a plastic lounge chair on the ICU floor of a Johannesburg, South Africa, clinic. The waiting room was deserted. The hours swam together, congealed into one long and horrifying nightmare. She tried to take in a deep breath, but her body shook with unreleased tears at her potential loss. Loss of Reid.

"Dr. Morrow? Casey?"

The deep, well-modulated voice gradually filtered through her state of shock into her spinning mind and tumultuous heart. Casey was reeling with so many raw feelings. Lifting her head, she rested her hands on the thighs of her coveralls. She hadn't changed clothes in twenty-four hours. Frowning, she looked up…up at a very tall man with dark hair and cinnamon-colored eyes set in a square face. He wore a white, short-sleeved cotton shirt that outlined his barrel chest and thick, broad shoulders. The dark blue jeans and tan work boots completed a picture of someone who was accustomed to being in the Outback, or on safari here in Africa. Somewhere, a memory stirred in her fogged, sleep-deprived brain. She knew this man. From where? Where?

"Yes...?" she answered finally, wondering if he was a doctor. A specialist off duty, called in because of Reid and his condition? Her mind simply wasn't functioning, over-run as it was with grief, shock and terror.

The man managed a thin, strained smile as he held out his hand. "We've met briefly a few times in the past, at the OID building where you work. Ty Hunter. I'm Reid's older brother. Remember me now?"

Casey gave a small cry of recognition. She pushed her-self off the plastic chair. "Ty...yes...of course I remember you now. I—I'm so sorry," she stammered, "this just isn't like me. Of course I remember you." She reached out and gripped his strong, heavily scarred hand. "I—uh, I'm just tired, and in a little bit of shock from all that's hap-pened...."

"Don't worry about it. Come on, sit down, Casey. You look pretty rough around the edges right now."

Casey shook her head and planted her feet. "No...listen, you have to see Reid. That's why you're here. I'm so glad you came, Ty...." Her voice cracked.

He gave her a compassionate look as he intently studied her. Gently, he put his arm around her shoulders. "How is he?"

Gulping back tears, Casey closed her eyes. Ty Hunter was so much like Reid in some ways. Warmth permeated from him just as it did from Reid, and she didn't fight his comforting embrace, instead leaning wearily against his very tall, heavy frame. Right now, Casey felt scared. Her mind spun with words, but she needed the right ones. She didn't want to scare Ty.

"He—Reid, that is—he's critical. He's in critical condition. They have him on life support.... Oh, God, Ty...he stepped between me and that black mamba. I had a little girl in my arms.'' Casey choked and pressed her face against his shoulder. How comforting his arm felt around her! How very tired she was. ''He saved our lives....''

''OID called me as soon as you contacted them. I was at the Perseus HQ in Washington when the message came through. They said he'd been bitten by a black mamba.'' Scowling, he said, ''I thought a person died in a couple minutes after being bitten?''

Sniffing, Casey nodded and wiped her eyes with a trembling hand, but remained in Ty's soothing embrace. ''Y-yes, they do. Reid had taken a shot at the snake and blew its head half off. When the snake went down, it was still snapping and lunging as it was dying. If Reid hadn't jumped between us, I'd be in ICU right now, not him.'' Casey lifted her head and look miserably toward the intensive care area across the hall from the waiting room. ''The snake hit Reid's pant leg in a glancing blow as he pushed me and Gabriella out of the way. It looks like hardly a scratch on his right calf, but some venom got in there. He didn't get a full dose and that's the only reason he's still alive right now.''

Grimly, Ty moved her toward the entrance. ''But enough to do this to him?''

''Yes,'' Casey whispered. ''I—I had to give him CPR off and on during the flight from Kinshasa. His heart would stop beating. I—I'd strike him in the chest with my fist and his heart would beat and he'd start breathing again. Once he became conscious, and I told him to cough. Every time he coughed, he would start breathing again.'' Wiping her eyes, she looked up at Ty's set features. He was looking at the ICU door. She knew he wanted to see his brother. ''The mamba's venom is a neurotoxin. It attacks the central nervous system. A person just stops breathing and dies. I told the colonel to fly us here because Johannesburg had the most modern facilities for snake bites in Africa.''

"I see," he rasped. "What have they done for him here, so far?"

"He's on full life support right now. He has to be. It's his only chance to pull through...."

Looking sharply down at Casey, Ty asked, "What is the prognosis? What'd the doctors say?"

Wearily, Casey lifted her shoulders. "They don't know. They've never had anyone survive a black mamba bite before, so they don't know anything about what kind of prognosis Reid has—if any." She waved her hand toward ICU. "I've been with him most of the time. I just keep talking to him, Ty. I keep telling him to come back to me."

"Has he regained consciousness?"

"No, not since we landed. The doctors say he's slipped into a coma...." Casey started to sob. "I'm sorry...I'm so torn up over this. I—I love Reid, and God...I just can't face it...I just don't want him to die.... I lost someone before and..."

Ty wrapped his large arms around her and brought her against him more firmly. He patted her shoulder. "Go ahead, cry," he urged roughly, his voice strained. "It's okay, just cry. I'll hold you. You love him, eh?" He managed a slight, strained smile. "I'll be damned. It finally happened...."

For the first time in twenty-four hours, Casey broke down. Earlier, she had to be the strong one. She had been Reid's only way to remain alive. How many times during the flight to Johannesburg had she given him CPR? Too many times to recall. And each time, she had wondered if he would start breathing on his own once again. Every time he stopped breathing, she'd wanted to scream out in terror at her sense of loss. The sobs came stronger and faster now. Tears poured from her eyes and she buried her face against Ty's shoulder. Just like Reid, he grazed her hair with his hand repeatedly, as if she were a small child to be comforted in her moment of terror. How alike the two brothers were!

After a few minutes, the storm passed from Casey. In a soft, tear-filled voice, she thanked Ty and withdrew from his embrace. Gripping his hand, she whispered brokenly, "Please, go see Reid. He needs to know you're here. He loves you so much. Over the past month he's told me so much about all of you...I know he'll hear you. I know he'll want you with him. Go...."

Reluctantly, Ty took a step toward the hall. "Are you sure?"

Casey waved him away. "I just needed a good cry is all. Go on. Reid needs you now, Ty."

Watching the big, tightly muscled mercenary move quietly down the hall toward the ICU nurses' station, Casey took out a tissue and blew her nose. With another tissue, she blotted her eyes dry once again. For the first time, Casey felt a trickle of hope. Ty Hunter was here. Family was with Reid. Family was so important! Casey sat down wearily, torn between sleep and continuing to pray for Reid's life to be spared. She leaned back in the plastic sofa and tipped her head against the beige wall behind it. Closing her eyes, she managed a soft, ragged sigh. Sleep came swiftly, and within moments, she nodded off.

"Casey?"

Casey groaned softly. She felt a hand gently squeezing her right shoulder.

"Dr. Morrow?"

Instantly, Casey's eyes snapped open. She jerked upright.

"Easy..." Ty Hunter cautioned as he leaned down over her.

Blinking rapidly, Casey came instantly awake. Ty Hunter was studying her intently. He kept his hand on her shoulder to steady her.

"Reid?" Her heart pounded. She shot a look up at Ty's shadowed face. *Reid!* "What's wrong?" She tried to get to her feet.

"It's okay...." Ty reassured her with a slight smile.

"Reid's okay, so relax. Just relax."

Casey crumpled. "Thank God." She looked toward the ICU. What time was it? Her neck hurt and she ruefully rubbed it. How long had she been sleeping in that impossible position?

"I've got good news," he said, managing a bit of a smile. "They took Reid off life support about two hours ago. All his vitals are coming back...slow but sure. How about that? When I came in here to get you, you were asleep. I figured you needed sleep more than me waking you up right then."

Casey leaped to her feet and staggered. If not for Ty rising to his full height and reaching out to steady her, she would have tripped over her own feet. She felt drugged, half in her body. "I've got to go to him," she whispered, pulling away.

Ty followed, his hand still on her arm to steady her as they hurried down the highly polished hallway. Casey saw early morning sunlight filtering in through a window at the end of the hall. Looking at her watch, she saw it was eight a.m. She must have slept three hours. Anxiously, she opened the glass door to Reid's room. The ventilator support machine had been withdrawn. Instead, she saw a cannula giving him oxygen. His color was no longer that pasty white, only pale, which was a decided improvement. She saw a hint of ruddiness in his cheeks. The IVs were still in his arms, but the beeps and sighs of the ventilator were gone. Only chirping monitoring machines remained. The turnaround was dramatic. Stunning.

Moving to his bedside, Casey slipped her fingers around Reid's still ones. Ty moved to the other side of the bed.

"Does he look better to you?" he asked hopefully.

"Yes, a *lot* better." She looked over at Ty. It was then that Casey realized how very tired he really was. He must have hopped the first plane across the Atlantic to get to South Africa. His face was darkly bearded, and it gave him a very dangerous look. Vaguely, Casey recalled that he was one of the top mercenaries at Perseus, a trained warrior who got the job done—or else. Off and on over the years Casey had had contact with Morgan and some of his highly trained employees.

"The doctors? What have they said?" She couldn't keep the anxiousness out of her tone.

Chuckling, Ty gripped Reid's other hand in his. "That Reid's one tough bastard and that he's probably going to pull through."

Her knees weakened. Casey closed her eyes and placed her hands on the bedside to steady herself. "Thank goodness...."

"They said he started breathing on his own shortly after you went to sleep." Ty smiled tiredly. "One nurse told me that you'd been with him constantly before I came."

A lump formed in her throat as she absorbed the sight of Reid's pale face into her heart. "If you love someone, you stick with them through thick and thin."

"Does he know how you feel about him?"

Opening her eyes, she gazed into Ty's dark, assessing ones. "What? That I love him? Yes." She was forever grateful they had shared that with one another before he'd lost consciousness.

"When did this happen? Reid never mentioned anything about it."

With a one-shouldered shrug, Casey whispered, "It just happened over time, Ty. I knew I loved Reid a lot sooner than I told him how I felt. I—I hadn't told him the truth because of my stubborn thickheadedness about the whole situation. I was afraid to, I guess.''

''Hmm, loving someone is a helluva risk. Biggest one any of us will ever take.''

''I know,'' Casey said softly. ''I know better than most.'' She nervously moved her fingers up and down Reid's damp forearm.

''I was hoping that someday Reid would get married,'' Ty continued in a low tone, ''especially after what happened to him. Getting left at the altar was damn hard on him. I was there. I saw how it hurt him. I felt so damn helpless for him, and there was nothing I or anyone else could do about it. He's the marrying kind, you know? He's got Husband and Dad written all over him. He cares so much and he's so damn responsible about everything and everyone.''

Wryly, Casey looked across the bed at Ty. ''Oh? And I suppose you're nothing like him?''

Grinning unabashedly, he looked up at the ceiling. ''Doctor, I'm a footloose-and-fancy-free kind of guy, like my other brothers. Yeah, I love women, but I haven't ever met one that makes me yearn to sink down roots and think about a family and things like that. I doubt I ever will. I'm thirty-one now, and I've had plenty of relationships. If it hasn't happen by now, well...''

''Reid said you three were the tumbleweeds of the family,'' Casey said, laughing a little for the first time in hours. She felt a huge weight beginning to lift off her shoulders. Reid was going to live! Her next worry was if he would suffer any nerve damage from the black mamba's deadly neurotoxin. Reid was such a graceful athlete. It broke her heart to think that his central nervous system might be somehow permanently affected by the venom. Sometimes she wished she didn't have so much medical knowledge. No one had ever survived a black mamba bite, so there was no way to tell from previous medical literature Reid's prognosis. One way or another, he was going to make medical history just because he had survived. Her heart swelled with such fierce joy and elation that Casey knew it didn't matter how Reid was affected. She would be there for him. She would be at his side every step of the way because she loved him.

"I have a confession to make," Ty admitted quietly. He glanced toward the door to make sure it was closed and no one could overhear them.

Frowning, Casey said, "About what?"

"I'm in touch with a homeopath. Her name is Rachel Donovan-Cunningham. It's a long story, but Rachel and I go back a long way. I was in Africa on a Perseus assignment three years ago when I caught Rift Valley fever. Most people who contract it die in a week or less after getting it. Morgan Trayhern, my boss, pulled me out of the mission clinic in Africa and had me flown to London for medical help because I was dying. I was taken to the Royal Homeopathic Hospital, where I was treated not only with traditional drugs, but with a homeopathic remedy, too. The MD on my case said the only reason I pulled through was because of the homeopathic intervention. The practitioner who cared for me was Rachel.

"I never forgot her or her magic potions or remedies." He smiled a little. "When I got word that Reid had been bitten by a black mamba, my first call was to Rachel, who now lives in Sedona, Arizona. I told her what had happened, and she told me to go to a homeopathic pharmacy in Washington, D.C., and get a snake venom remedy known as Lachesis Muta." He circumspectly pulled out a small glass vial from his jeans pocket and handed it to Casey. "Take a look at this medicine.

"Rachel told me that like cures like. If Reid was bitten by a venomous snake, then I'd need the homeopathic version of snake venom to save his life. She told me to put the pellets in some brandy to dissolve them, and when I got here, to place a couple of drops on the inside of his wrist—the one you're holding—and gently rub it into his skin. I did that.''

Blinking, Casey looked at the small, amber glass, which contained a clear fluid. "This contains snake venom?"

"Yes, from a South American bushmaster snake. *Lachesis* is the Latin word for the snake. Actually, there's none of the crude substance left in that bottle, if that's what you're worried about. It's the energy signature of the venom, is all. It's perfectly safe to handle."

Frowning, she looked down at Reid and then over at Ty. "I've only vaguely heard of homeopathy."

"I can fill you in more later," Ty said. He took the bottle and stuffed it back in his pocket. "Five minutes after I rubbed that remedy into his skin, Reid started moving around, and it scared the hell out of me." Grinning sheepishly, Ty said, "I called the nurses pronto. I didn't know what was going on. Reid started thrashing around and damn near tore out the ventilator. The nurses called the MD and he said Reid was breathing on his own and didn't need any life support. So," he said with a slight shrug as he studied his brother, "they took it out of him and upgraded him to serious but stable condition."

"Incredible...." Casey whispered. "That medicine—homeopathy—did it?"

"Must have." Ty chuckled. "I just got off the phone with Rachel. Woke her up in the middle of the night at her ranch and told her what had happened. She said to put one more drop on his wrist in about six hours, and that should pull him out of the most immediate danger."

Shaking her head in disbelief, Casey whispered, "That's a miracle, Ty."

He nodded somberly. "Listen, I was down for the count with that fever. I was starting to bleed out of every orifice in my body. The Catholic priest at the mission had already given me the last rites. When I got wheeled into that Lon-

don hospital, they said I was a goner, too—except for
Rachel. She was the only one on the medical team who
said I'd live.''

Releasing a breath of air, Casey leaned over and gently
threaded her fingers through Reid's damp hair. "He's perspiring. That's a good sign," she murmured. "Before, his
skin was cool and dry."

"Rachel said that this homeopathic remedy will engage
Reid's immune system to fight back and get rid of the
black mamba venom left inside him." Ty placed his hands
on his hips as he watched her move the back of her hand
against his brother's unshaved cheek. "I wonder if Reid
knows how lucky he is?"

Casey barely heard Ty's voice; all her focus, her love,
was directed at Reid. His lips were parted and badly
cracked. His lashes were dark, short and spiky against his
still-pale flesh. But just the way he was breathing made
her feel better, more hopeful.

"Morgan wants to transfer Reid back to the U.S. on a
Perseus jet that's waiting for us at the Johannesburg airport
whenever he's stable enough to transport."

Casey lifted her head. "This is a state-of-the-art hospital.''

Shrugging, Ty moved closer to the bed and placed his
large hand on his brother's gowned shoulder. "I asked
Morgan to fly Rachel Donovan-Cunningham to Bethesda
Hospital in Maryland. I want him there, to be cared for by
her. Think of it as a combination of the two best kind of
medicines in the world working together to help Reid pull
through this. They've got just as good a tropical lab department there as they do here."

Smiling a little, Casey straightened up. "You want
Rachel to treat him homeopathically, then?"

Ty nodded and frowned. "Absolutely. He's my brother,
Casey. I won't do anything less for him than what was
done for me when I was down for the count. And Rachel

was the only person who stood between me and death's door.'' He smiled a little. ''Are you game? Will you come home with us?''

''Sure,'' she murmured. ''But what about Black Dawn? We haven't seen *any* indication that they were in the area where we were hunting for the Ebola virus.''

Ty's dark brown brows dipped. ''Oh, that. Well, that's the good news—bad news, Casey.'' His full mouth thinned. ''We managed to intercept some comsat traffic from them out of Germany. We discovered they'd sent us on a wild-goose chase, making us think they were going to follow you into Africa to get Ebola if you found it during your research.''

''And they aren't here?''

''No. Instead, we found out just a few hours before I hopped a flight to come over here that they are actively nosing around in South America. They're scouting an outbreak south of Manaus, Brazil. An Indian villager managed to make it to the city and report that half of the people under his jurisdiction are either dead or dying of some bug. They're bleeding out, and I think it's one of the hemorrhagic viruses. But it could be a new one, too. No one knows yet. With them tearing up the rain forest and uncovering viruses that have been dormant or buried for thousands of years, anything is possible. And Black Dawn wants to get their hands on it. Whatever it is. If it's as lethal as that report that came out of Manaus indicates, we're looking at something that can be in the same class as Ebola virus.''

''It could be the Saba virus,'' Casey whispered worriedly. ''Well, what are you and Morgan going to do?''

Rubbing his jaw, Ty muttered, ''We're getting hammered in South America right now. Morgan's lead physician with Perseus is Dr. Ann Parsons, but she's down on a mission in Peru right now with Major Mike Houston. All hell's breaking loose down there because Eduardo Escovar, the most powerful cocaine drug lord in Peru, is going up against Mike and his team. Morgan can't ask Ann or Mike to leave, so he's sending me down to Brazil, to where the outbreak is occurring. OID has already sent their primary outbreak team ahead to help coordinate with local officials of the Amazon village that's being decimated by it, and to provide lab work and aid to the people who are dying of it.''

"I know Mike Houston very well," Casey murmured. "He's known as the jaguar god down in Peru. He's got one helluva reputation for going after the drug lords. He's been taking them down for ten years now. They all want his head on a platter, believe me." She shook her red curls. "I wouldn't want to be in that mess. I feel for Dr. Parsons. I met her a couple of times at the OID. Over the years she's taken a number of seminars with us on infectious diseases. What's a nice woman like her doing down in that sinkhole with Houston?"

Ty grinned a little. "Ann's an emergency room trained physician. She's always where the action is." Scratching his head, he added, "But I don't think she—or we—anticipated what's going on now. It's pretty bad. Morgan's worried about both of them, and generally he doesn't worry like I've seen him doing of late."

"Any chance of what's going on in Peru with Escovar spilling into Brazil?" Casey inquired.

Shrugging, Ty said, "Who knows? Our one link, our *only* one, is with a Brazilian green warrior by the name of Inca. I guess she and Mike Houston share a common, very mysterious and little understood heritage. Mike's part Quechua Indian, by the way. He and Inca are blood sister and brother." He smiled a little. "I've never met Inca, but believe me, her name is a curse and a legend in Brazil. The people who love her call her the jaguar goddess. Those that hate and fear her call her a green warrior."

"Green warrior is a name synonymous with people who

are trying to save the Amazon rain forest from the foreign loggers," Casey muttered. "Somehow, I think I'd like this Inca woman. Good for her. So, is Inca your contact when you go down to Brazil? It's her territory, right?"

"There's no official contact with Inca," Ty said. "She's like a ghost—you never know when she'll show up. Personally, I hope she does, but I'm not counting on it. The Indians of Brazil worship her as a goddess in human form. They say she's really a jaguar who turns into a human when she wants to. Where I'm going, deep in the Amazon basin, I'd be very happy to see Inca appear if we get into trouble with Black Dawn, jaguar or not." He grinned.

Casey nodded, thinking that the situation Ty was heading into was exceedingly dangerous. "Who's heading up that OID team?" she demanded. She was thinking it might be Catt Alborak, a medical doctor who worked in the hot zone with her at the OID labs.

"A gal by the name of Dr. Alborak, I think," he said, searching his memory.

"Ah, good. Catt's the best. Saba's her baby. She knows more about South American hemorrhagic viruses than anyone I know in virology. At least, in this hemisphere." Casey cracked a slight smile. "Well, Ty, I think you've met your match and then some." She chuckled a little.

"What's that mean?" he demanded darkly. "I hope she's not one of these prima donna virus hunters who's gonna be a pain in the rear to work with."

Casey's smile widened considerably. "No, unfortunately for you, Catt's a lot like me—a hellion *with* a cause, and she doesn't suffer fools lightly, either."

Managing a sour smile, he said, "Yeah? Well, I've had my share of women in my time, so I don't think there will be a problem. I know how to handle them."

"Oh, there won't be a problem." Casey grinned. "As long as you do things Catt's way, there won't be a problem at all."

Ty rolled his eyes. "Great. The two of you are a pair. You have a reputation yourself, you know. What did they do? Clone you over at the OID?" he said, laughing.

The laughter sounded good to Casey. She felt more than a little ray of hope now for Reid—and for herself. Just feeling Ty's stabilizing influence was a gift in itself. Reid had often said that when the chips were down, Ty would be there in a crisis. He was right. She gently stroked Reid's fingers, which were growing warmer. "I'm not a hellion, though. But Catt is world famous for that. It's a reputation she's earned over the years, and she's very proud of it."

Ty gave her an unhappy look. "What's your definition of a hellion?"

Chuckling, Casey said, "You're a smart man, Ty. You're asking the right questions." She smiled at him. "Hellion as in Catt gets the job done, is a fierce, good leader, doesn't back down, doesn't take no for an answer, will push when it comes to shove, is fearless in the face of the most deadly viruses known to us, has a short temper with idiots, is passionate about saving lives, is compassionate with the weak and the sick, will do whatever it takes to take down a killer virus or bacteria.... That's my definition of a hellion insofar as Catt's concerned."

"Phew," Ty muttered. "Where was she born?"

Casey's grin widened. "Texas. She's a Texas hellion, Ty. I think you kinda get the picture on Catt now, don't you?" She saw his scowl deepen.

"I'm supposed to be down there to protect her. Do you think she'll do as I ask?"

Casey rolled her eyes. "I forgot to add a couple of words about her—*pigheaded* and *stubborn*. But she was raised out in Texas cattle country and is the *best* person in the world to have at your back when all hell starts breaking loose."

"Great," he muttered. "Just great..."

Casey met his twisted grin. In her heart, she felt that Ty

might have a chance with Catt so long as he practiced a little patience and diplomacy with her. "You're getting thrown to the lions," she teased.

"Or maybe to a Texas hellion?" He grinned.

Casey felt lighter and more hopeful. "You'll find out soon enough, Ty. Just think of her as a modern day version of Joan of Arc. She's committed and can't be led off the scent." She gazed longingly down at Reid. "So, when can we leave?"

"The doctors have already given permission for him to be released to us. There's a Perseus doctor on board the aircraft, Dr. Jenny Hanson. She's an ER trained specialist. We've got a top medical facility on board the jet, as well as a trained paramedic—just in case. Reid will be in good hands." And then Ty grinned a little. "He's got you as his main cheerleader."

Casey nodded, sobering as she pressed Reid's limp fingers between hers. "You know what I wish for, Ty? As silly as it sounds?"

"No, what?"

"I wish," Casey whispered brokenly, "that Reid could recuperate at my home, north of Atlanta, as soon as he comes out of this coma. Silly as that sounds, that's what I wish. I wish he could be there with me...."

"So that you could care for him." Ty nodded. "I've always believed in miracles, Casey. If he keeps improving, I don't have a problem with Reid being with you."

Gratefully, she met Ty's thoughtful brown gaze. "Thank you.... You don't know how much that means to me...to us...."

"Yeah, I think I do." He gazed down at his brother. "Reid's a good guy. He's had more than his share of bad luck in his life." Lifting his chin, Ty studied Casey in silence. "It's time that changed. And my family and I are for anything that will help Reid survive this."

Casey fought back the tears. "Thanks...."

"And I know that you lost the man you loved before to Ebola. This has to be hard on you, too."

Ty's sensitivity and understanding were reassuring. She studied him for a long moment and then spoke. "You and Reid share a lot in common. I hope someday you find a woman who deserves what you have to give her."

He grinned carelessly and headed for the door. "That, Dr. Morrow, is a *lost cause....*" Then he swung out the door and into the hall, heading for the nurses' station to start the paperwork to get Reid out of there.

Chuckling, Casey remained at Reid's side. Even now there was more ruddiness flowing back into his cheeks. "You know what, Reid?" she said in a soft, amused tone. "I think your headstrong brother is going to more than meet his match in Catt Alborak. He's got a Texas hellion by the tail and doesn't know it—yet—but he will...." She laughed. How good it felt! As she gazed at his pale but improving features, she squeezed his fingers. *Home.* They were going home. Suddenly, her heart lifted and took wing. A fierce sense of love for Reid swept through Casey. He was going to live. Now the only question was would he come out of the coma? *One painful step at a time,* Casey reminded herself. *One at a time....* Still, she held the vision in her heart of Reid in the old brass bed she'd inherited from her great-great-grandmother, wrapped in the colorful quilt made by her grandmother, getting better every day he spent with her.

Reid swore he heard a robin singing. But he was in Africa. There were no robins in Africa. Again he heard the bird's melodic song. Frowning, he moved slowly, because it felt as if his hands and arms were encased in concrete. Struggling, he forced his eyes open to mere slits. Everything was white at first. Slowly, over the next few minutes, his vision began to clear.

Where was he? He was in a large bed, an old brass one

from the looks of it, with a light, colorful quilt thrown over him. There was a window not more than two feet away, hung with pretty, feminine curtains. The window was open and he could see a breeze gently moving the delicate white lace. Beyond it, he could see a big oak tree with thick Spanish moss hanging from the limbs. Somewhere in the tree, a robin was singing its heart out.

Reid liked robins. They always made a beautiful melody when they sang. Lying there, he tried to orient himself. His brain was sluggish as hell. He kept flexing his fingers and wriggling his toes. Looking down, he saw that there were IVs in both his arms.

Then he noticed soft classical music drifting in the partly open bedroom door—faraway, but nice to listen to. The odor of food wafted in on the breeze, or maybe it was coming from the door. Inhaling hungrily, Reid heard his stomach growl. Mouth dry, he looked around. He saw a pitcher and glass on the nearby bed stand. Pushing himself into an upright position, he found he was alarmingly weak. Thirst drove him to reach for water. To his surprise, he couldn't grasp the glass. It crashed to the wood floor, the sound echoing throughout the room.

"Damn," he muttered.

Footsteps sounded.

Frowning, he looked toward the door. He heard someone running down the hall toward him. Where was he?

Casey pushed open the door, breathless. Her eyes widened enormously.

"Reid!" It was a cry of surprise.

He looked at Casey strangely for a moment, shaken by her cry. And then his mouth pulled upward at one corner. "You're a sight for sore eyes. Do you know that?" His voice was rusty from disuse. He saw her eyes widen in joy as she stood poised at the door.

She flew to him, her heart pounding with relief. Sitting on the edge of the bed and facing him, Casey reached out and touched his face, then his shoulder, and finally gripped his hands. "You're conscious."

Her hands were warm and welcoming. Reid managed another one-cornered smile. "Alive and kicking. What the hell happened, Casey? And where are we? This doesn't look or sound like Africa."

Choking on a sob, Casey pressed one hand against her lips. Fighting to regain control over her shocked and unraveling emotions, she whispered, "We're home, Reid. In Atlanta, Georgia. This is where I live. You've been in a coma for three weeks." With trembling fingers she reached out and curved her hand across his stubbled cheek. "Welcome back, darling. I've missed you so much...."

"Come here," he coaxed brokenly, and he opened his arms to her. She came without hesitation, curving her arms around his neck and carefully pressing herself against him. With a groan, Reid closed his eyes and allowed his arms to wrap around her torso. "You feel so good to me," he rasped. "So damn good...."

Casey sobbed again and pressed her face against his. "I was so afraid, Reid. So afraid you'd die from that black mamba bite."

He opened his eyes. The sweetness of her perfume encircled him and he inhaled it deeply into his chest. "What bite?"

She eased away enough to look down at him. "Remember you leaped toward Gaby and me after partially shooting the head off that black mamba that threatened us? When it was thrashing around, dying, you stepped in front of it and pushed us out of its way. Somehow, it grazed your pant leg and one fang made a tiny scratch on your calf. You went unconscious about a minute after that." Taking a ragged breath, Casey closed her eyes, her voice trembling with tears. "Let me tell you, I've never been so scared. You nearly died five different times on that C-130 flight out of Yambuku to Johannesburg, where they got you stabilized.''

He felt new strength invading him and he raised his hand and grazed her damp cheek, touching the tears trailing down her flesh with his fingertips. "Helluva ride, wasn't it?" He watched her green eyes open and saw the gold of joy in them. Joy that they were here. That they were alive and in one another's arms.

"A helluva ride," Casey agreed. She sniffed, sat up and wiped away the tears. "I've got so many things to do now that you're conscious. Let me take care of you first, and then I'll make a lot of phone calls to a lot of people who are going to be jumping up and down to learn that you're awake and as feisty as ever. You must be thirsty?"

Reid wanted Casey to stay here, with him, but he understood. If he'd been in a coma for three weeks, he knew his family had to be contacted and a doctor notified, for starters. Brushing some of her silky red hair away from her cheek, he said, "I'm thirsty as a dog." Removing his hand, he looked down at the floor. "I just dropped the glass. What can I do to get another one?"

Casey smiled a little. "The old Reid is back. What a relief. I'll get you another glass—just hold on...." She hurried through the room to the bathroom. Her heart skittered. Rachel Donovan-Cunningham had given him a remedy three days ago and had said it would probably bring Reid out of the coma he'd been in since returning stateside.

Entering the bedroom again, Casey moved to the bed stand and poured water for him with shaking hands. Sitting on the edge of the bed facing him, she held the glass out to him.

"You're weak. Let me help you?" she said.

Casey looked pale. And she'd lost weight, he observed. Without hesitation, he placed his hands around hers and guided the glass to his lips. He drank the entire contents.

"More?" he croaked, and wiped his mouth with the

back of his hand. He saw the startled look and the tears in her eyes. Looking around and then back at her, he said, "When can I get out of these IVs?"

"Drink your water," Casey soothed as she poured him more. First she'd have to call Dr. Luanne Somers to come and check Reid over. Then she'd call his family, and then Rachel Donovan-Cunningham. All would be overjoyed to hear that Reid had finally come out of his coma. Relief burst through Casey. It was all she could do to sit quietly.

Reid's hands gained strength by the minute as he drank like a man who had crossed a desert. Water leaked out and dribbled down the sides of his mouth. Casey took a cloth and dabbed at the corners of his lips when he finished the second glass.

"I have to make some phone calls," she told him breathlessly as she stood up. "I'll be right back."

Studying her, Reid appreciated her once more. Her mop of red hair nearly touched her shoulders now, and in a light pink blouse with tiny rosebuds on the collar and beige slacks that fit her to perfection, she looked beautiful. "Before you leave, tell me where we are again?"

"My house in Atlanta, Georgia, Reid."

He looked around. "Your home?"

She hesitated at the door. "Yes." She saw the confusion on his features. The cloudy look in his eyes. It was obvious his memory wasn't functioning fully yet, but she had every hope it soon would. The neurotoxin? The coma? A little of both? She was unsure. "I'll be right back," she promised him in a husky voice. "And I'll fill you in."

As she moved quickly down the hall to her office, where she had a phone, Casey wondered if Reid would remember their love. Was that wiped out of his memory forever, too? How much did he recall? How much would he?

Reid felt incredibly restless. Strength was returning to him minute by minute and he wanted to get up. When

Casey came back she hesitated momentarily at the door and just stared at him.

"I'm real," he told her. Hungrily, Reid watched as she moved quickly back into the bedroom. He saw the flush staining her cheeks, the burnished red frame of her hair emphasizing her shadowed green eyes, the gauntness of her high cheekbones. She offered him a tentative smile as she carefully sat down at his bedside, and he moved his hand toward hers.

"I don't want to let you out of my sight," he croaked as his fingers clasped hers. The warmth in her eyes made him feel good inside.

"Me neither," she quavered. To hell with it, she decided, moving closer and leaning over. "I'm going to kiss you again, Reid Hunter, so get used to it...."

As her soft, warm mouth blanketed his, he felt her heat, her trembling, and he returned her searching, tentative kiss. Raising his hand, he placed it against her arm as she leaned over him. She tasted so good! She tasted of life. He could taste chocolate on her, and as they eased apart a few inches, he gazed up at her.

"Been eating chocolate?"

She smiled a little. "I just had a Godiva. My favorite." Easing her fingers through his hair, which had grown quite long compared to how he usually wore it, she asked, "Want one?"

"No," he whispered, one corner of his mouth pulling upward. "I just got all the dessert I could ever want right here beside me."

Tears flooded Casey's eyes. She lifted her hand and wiped them away. "It's been a long battle, Reid. You're back. You're alive and we're home. A lot of people's prayers have been answered, let me tell you."

Her words flowed gently through him. With each breath he took, he could feel strength returning to him tenfold. "How long have I been out? I remember the black mamba now.'' His eyes narrowed upon her flushed features. ''You okay?''

''Me?'' She smiled wryly. ''I am now that you're out of the coma.''

Scowling, he muttered, ''After you left the room I kept getting snatches of things, like photographs.''

''Rachel Donovan-Cunningham, the homeopath, said that would happen.''

He raised his brows. ''Rachel?''

''Yes. You remember her?'' Casey felt hope thrum through her. It appeared, at least on the surface, that Reid was fine. His mental state didn't seem to be impaired. Yes, he was weak, but that was to be expected. Her mouth tingled, reminding her how he'd returned her welcoming kiss. Just being here beside him, holding his hand and talking to him, made her world complete. Nothing else mattered.

''Sure, she saved my brother Ty's life. He contracted Rift Valley fever several years ago.'' Giving her a quizzical look, Reid asked, ''And she was here?''

Casey laughed softly. ''Let me start from the beginning and I'll tell you everything.''

He squeezed her cool, damp fingers. ''I'm all yours, good doctor. A willing patient who is eager for word from the outside world.''

Casey shook her head. Relief wound through her. The old Reid she knew and loved was back, humor and all. ''You're the first person to ever survive a black mamba bite and you're *still* a Neanderthal at heart!''

Her chuckle moved through him like a river flooding his chest. The heat and joy that came with it made him grin back at her. ''It's because I *am* a Neanderthal that I survived, good doctor, so let's not take my name in vain, shall we? Give me the long version of what happened. I've been gone three weeks.''

Gazing into his handsome face, Casey began the long, harrowing and ultimately happy tale.

Chapter Thirteen

Where was Casey? Impatiently, Reid forced himself out of bed, his feet touching the warmth of the golden-colored oak floor. In the past four days, he'd seen her only briefly between visits of his family from Colorado, and his brothers Dev and Shep. Ty was in Brazil and couldn't be reached. Reid wasn't surprised, given the fact that he was out in the middle of nowhere with an outbreak team from the OID.

Morgan and Laura Trayhern had even flown in to see Reid. And there was a parade of medical people who poked, prodded and drew blood from him, literally, in the last couple of days, too. With amazed looks on their faces, all had pronounced him cured and a hundred percent healthy. He was the first human being to ever survive a black mamba bite. And Reid knew he had not only the heroic efforts of traditional medical doctors to thank, but Dr. Rachel Donovan-Cunningham, with her homeopathic knowledge as well. Most of all, he was grateful to Casey.

Reid found out through Dev how constantly she had been there for him. Ty had told Dev about it in a phone call to the family before he'd left for Brazil.

On top of everything, Reid had had to begin a lengthy report for the Joint Chiefs of Staff on the mission to Africa. Casey, fortunately, had helped him fill in some blank spots in his memory as he typed the report on a laptop computer. She'd told him that the OID had sent another three-person team to Grandfather Henri's village to continue their active search for Ebola. Although there was no sign of Black Dawn around, the JCS had sent a fourth person, with a background similar to Reid's, to guard the group during the ongoing scientific investigation.

Sitting on the edge of the bed, he smiled a little. All the tubes and IVs had been removed shortly after he'd regained consciousness. That was a relief to him. He'd gained much of his strength back in the last week because Dev and Shep had pushed and cajoled him into getting out of bed and mobile once again. His brothers didn't tolerate weakness in any form, and Reid grinned a little, grateful for their assistance. He sensed that because of his brother's good humor and care, Casey was allowing his family to be more help to him than she might have otherwise. He missed her by his side, damn it. And that was going to change very shortly.

It was evening and the warmth of the early September dusk filtered in through the French lace across the window. Every time he'd seen Casey over the past few days, she looked sad. Why? Fear nagged at him as he stood up. Ever since her affectionate show of emotion, she seemed to have withdrawn from him. Normally her presence filled his life and his heart. He had eyes only for her—but she rarely visited him except to give him a tray filled with her wonderful home cooking three times a day. Why?

Compressing his lips, he glanced at the clock and saw that it was five p.m. Casey usually brought him dinner at six. He'd surprise her today. There was enough time to grab a hot shower, shave, put on some clean clothes and make his way downstairs to eat dinner with her tonight, instead. With a careless grin, Reid headed for the bathroom. Yes, tonight was theirs. All the company had come and gone. They were alone—finally.

Standing at the electric stove, apron tied around her waist, a fork in hand, Casey tended to the chicken frying in the skillet. She'd already made mashed potatoes, and the peas were warming up—all in preparation for Reid's dinner. Hearing the sound at the entrance to the kitchen, she turned around to see what it was and her breath caught.

Reid stood in the entrance of her sunny, yellow kitchen, staring at her. Wildly, her heart skidded beneath the heavy-lidded look that was charged with heat and longing—for her. Was she imagining his desire? How many nights had she dreamed of seeing that sexy gaze again? Her throat closed up. She stood there frozen, unable to speak.

Reid gave her a long, delicious look. How enticing Casey was in the soft lavender blouse that outlined her proud shoulders and small breasts. The narrowed waist emphasized the flare of her nice, wide hips—hips that could comfortably carry a baby. His baby, if he had anything to do with it. A slow smile tugged at his mouth. He saw the surprise in her green eyes and he savored the way her full, lush lips parted beneath his deliberate inspection. He was touching her with his gaze and he knew it. He wanted Casey to realize just how much he missed her presence, her voice, and most of all, her touch.

"Cat got your tongue?" he teased lazily as he leaned against the door jamb, his hands draped casually on the hips of the ivory chinos he wore.

Swallowing hard, Casey jerked her attention back to the stove. She quickly turned off the heating element and removed the skillet. Placing a lid on it, she moved to put the fork on the drain board. Nervously, she wiped her hands on the front of her red-and-white checked apron. "Uh, no... What are you doing out of bed? And how did you get down those stairs?"

His mouth curved more. "One step at a time?"

She avoided his hooded look, his gray eyes burning with desire. "I see...."

"Do you?" He saw the sudden nervousness in Casey's paling features. The way she rubbed her hands restlessly against her apron made him wonder if she was nervous about him. About what he thought they had together. Maybe they didn't have anything? He had to find out. Pushing away from the jamb, he eased his hands from his hips and moved with deliberate intent toward her.

"It's hell not having you around very much," he confided as he neared where she stood. Casey's eyes were huge and shadowed. He saw fear in them. And questions. And longing. For him, Reid hoped. Only for him.

Casey held out her hands and he reached for them. "We've had more than a little company," she said, her heart beating swiftly.

He gripped her hands. "Well, they're all gone," he growled in satisfaction. "Let's go to the living room, shall we? I like all those antiques in there," he told her in a conversational tone.

His fingers were strong and firm on the hand he still clasped. Casey trembled inwardly as she walked with him into the huge, semicircular living room. The dusky evening light shot through the windows covered with French lace curtains, highlighting the interior of the room. On the floor was an old, maroon Oriental rug from Turkey. The furniture was Victorian, mostly made from warm cherry wood. The fabric covering the chairs and sofa was a soft pink color with burgundy and cream woven throughout it in flower designs. The lamps, their rainbow of colors playing over each end of the huge old sofa she led Reid to, were Tiffany originals that she'd collected over the years.

"Sit down here," she said a little breathlessly.

"Sit with me?" Reid stood there looking down at her, and he refused to release her hand.

Her heart thundered momentarily. "Well…sure. Are you thirsty?"

He gave her a slow, heated smile. "Only for you."

Blinking, Casey slowly sat down. Her knee brushed against his. Reid kept her hand in his and rested it on his thigh. He leaned back and slowly looked around the huge room.

"I like all the live plants and palms you have in here. It makes it look like the room is breathing," he said in a low tone. Indeed, the living room looked more like a greenhouse. Casey had at least ten orchids, of the same species but different colors, located near the many windows. Most of them were in bloom, the spikes containing many orchid blossoms on each of them. Four palms almost touching the high ceiling graced the areas between the four huge windows, their branches looking like soft fern fronds. Classical music—Chopin, he guessed—was playing unobtrusively, adding to the peaceful environment she'd created.

His gaze came back to Casey, who sat stiffly and on guard next to him. "This room reflects you. And the peace I always feel whenever I'm in your presence," he told her quietly. With his thumb, he brushed the soft, warm flesh of her hand. Her fingers were roughened from being in water and, he imagined, from constant washing at the lab to keep them infection free.

"I remember," he said. "Today, when Dev left, I lay on my bed and I remembered, Casey…"

She tried to swallow the lump that refused to leave her throat. Her lashes swept down and she felt blazing heat in her cheeks. Did Reid know how much his touch affected

her? She ached to kiss him, to simply lean forward and
fall into his embrace. Feeling tears stalking her, she swallowed several more times. "What did you recall?" she
whispered raggedly.

His hand closed more surely over her cool, damp fingers. He saw the suffering so clearly on her face. "Princess?" he whispered, as he leaned over and cupped her
chin with his hand. He felt her chin tremble as he slid his
fingers along her flesh. He saw her lips part deliciously,
and he smiled knowingly as his shadow fell across her.
When he grazed her lips with his, she trembled violently.
"I remember us," he told her hoarsely, his mouth barely
touching hers. "I remember telling you I loved you before
I lost consciousness." He brushed her mouth again.
"Nothing's changed between us. Death couldn't take me
from you, Casey. And I'm not leaving you now, even
though I see the fear in your eyes that I will."

His mouth, warm and cherishing, closed once more
upon her lips. Hot tears slid down her cheeks as he took
her in a molten kiss. Casey felt his arm sliding around her
shoulders and drawing her to him just as she'd dreamed
about for so many nights. Oh! To kiss him in return! To
relish his strong, hard mouth against her own! With a small
cry, Casey flung her arms around his broad shoulders and
pressed herself unashamedly against him. Craving him,
needing him in every way possible, she forgot about everything except Reid and how much she loved him.

Their mouths met with hunger. She tasted his strength,
tasted him. His mouth was hot, cajoling, taking and giving.
His breath was warm against her skin. She felt his heart
thundering in his chest against her straining breasts. As his
hand moved surely down her shoulder and cupped her
breast, she gave a little cry of pleasure.

"You taste so damn good to me," he rasped against her
open mouth. "I'm hungry...starving for you. I want all of
you...in every possible way...."

"Yes...yes..." Casey said, tearing her mouth from his. His eyes glittered like that of a predator in that moment, and every cell in her body blazed to life beneath that hooded look. Her lips burned with the brand of his mouth upon them. She rose unsteadily, her hand held out to him. "Come...to my bedroom...over here...." She gestured toward the left, toward a hall directly off the living room.

He moved to her side, his arm around her waist in a claiming gesture. She leaned wearily against him, all her fear, all her terror, draining out of her, replaced with the bright light of love that she'd been so afraid of never being able to express or share with Reid. He remembered telling her of his love for her, and her telling him. Relief shuddered through her along with a euphoric joy that made her want to shout. Opening the heavy oak door to her bedroom, she gazed up at him. "Do you know how many times I've dreamed of us walking through this door together?"

He looked at the Victorian bed, the gauzy, pale lavender fabric stretching over the canopy and hanging down in feminine curls and coils around each of the thick mahogany bedposts. The sunlight was gone now, replaced with a dusky gold light that made the bedroom look as if it were covered in mist. Suddenly he felt as if he were in some mystical, sacred and magical place where dreams could come true. "No, but I do want to live out the dreams *I* had about you in Africa," he said, smiling gently down at her. He saw the flare of emerald and gold in her eyes. There was no mistaking that look—the look of a woman wanting her man in all ways. Never had Reid felt so powerful as in that moment when they stood just inside the bedroom door, swathed in the dusky gold light of eventide.

"Dreams are to be lived," Casey whispered as she turned and faced him fully. "I had love stolen from me once," she whispered brokenly as she began to undo his

shirt, one button at a time, "and I won't let it be stolen
this time...."

"I won't let it be stolen," Reid assured her huskily.

She smiled softly up at him. "And you have a heart,
Reid Hunter. A great and wonderful heart. I don't care
what Janet told you. With me, you're whole. Do you hear
me? Somehow, you let yourself be vulnerable and you
opened up to me. You're the greatest gift a woman could
ever have or want, believe me...."

Her fingers were like scorching brands sliding across his
chest. Wherever she touched him, his flesh automatically
tightened. Slipping his hands along her jaw, he lifted her
face so that their eyes met. "Listen to me, princess," he
rasped, "you and I are going to grow old together. There's
nothing on this earth that's going to take me from you
sooner. I promise you that. I fought like hell to come back,
and I'm here. I'm here because I love you. Love got me
here. It will keep me here...." Reid leaned down and
brushed her lush, waiting lips with his. He heard her moan
softly. Her hands flattened against his darkly haired chest,
splayed out and moved across it with luxurious slowness.
It felt so good to be worshipped by her. To be touched
and explored by her.

As he continued the sweet assault on her lips, she
opened her mouth even more and he teased her with his
tongue. When her fingers came to rest on the waistband of
his chinos, she opened them with trembling, fumbling
hands, and it was his turn to groan. Her fingers were warm
and searching. A low growl reverberated through him as
she discovered his male hardness. Sliding his fingers
through her hair, he captured her commandingly against
him and took her hotly, her mouth moist, opening and
ripening beneath his. In her eyes, he was a man with a
heart, with a soul. Someone who was whole. Someone she
wanted. The joy of that discovery shook him as nothing
else ever had and released whatever misgivings or worries

he had left over from his past. His fears all melted away beneath her fierce, passionate kiss as she clung like the bold-hearted lioness she was to him. In every way she met and matched him, and it made him feel stronger and more masculine than he ever had before.

With delicious slowness, she divested him of his clothes, dropping them in a heap around their feet. Now it was his turn to undress her. As he began to ease each button open, her lashes swept downward. The cleavage of her breasts was shadowed, caressed by the golden light that spilled through the windows. Easing off her blouse, he allowed it to flutter away as if on the wings of a bird. She wore no bra, he saw with pleasure, but a thin silken camisole of pale ivory. Moving his hands across the material, he cupped her breasts and felt her tremble violently. She swayed. He caught her.

"Come," he urged in a low voice, and drew her to the bed, where she lay down at his side. The apron was next. It fell to the floor. He eased her soft leather sandals off her long, delicate feet and then slid her white silk slacks off her long, beautifully tapered legs. The silken ivory briefs outlined her wide, curved hips, and he lightly traced his fingers across the top of them. Casey's eyes closed and she moaned. As he turned on the bed to look at her, to ravish her with his gaze, Reid moved his hand slowly, lightly, up her right calf to her knee and her curved, firm thigh.

"You are so exquisitely beautiful...." he rasped as he eased himself to his knees. He placed one hand near her shoulder and continued his assault upon her. A soft moan escaped her as he moved his other hand across the top of her firm thigh to that intimate place between her legs. With a growl of satisfaction, he slid his fingers deeper into that moist, beckoning cleft. She arched against him. He felt her hands grip his arms in a pleading gesture. Giving her a very male smile, he absorbed the pleasure radiating from her—from her sultry, dark green eyes to her parted, lush mouth. "Yes..." he whispered as he leaned closer "...just feel the pleasure, princess. It's yours...all yours.... Don't be afraid to take it...."

A sob broke from her lips just as he claimed them with his. He moved over her carefully, for he didn't want to hurt her with his superior weight. Easing across her, he placed his knee between her thighs, resting his elbows on either side of her head. She opened like a hothouse orchid to the sun. There was such beauty, such promise in her gesture of utter trust in him. Gazing deeply into her cloudy, pleasure-filled eyes, he smiled a little.

"You are my dream come true, lady. And if you ever doubted it, you won't anymore...." He moved lightly against her. He felt the hardened nipples of her breasts against his chest, felt her hips arch to meet him and her hands range demandingly across his damp shoulders. The moment he met her heated warmth, he froze with pleasure, with anticipation of the treasure that each was going to bequeath the other in the delicious moments to come. Closing his eyes, Reid found his breath growing ragged as she not only met him but twined her long legs around his own. No one would ever accuse Casey of being cowardly, of not facing danger. Not even the danger of loving once again.

Heat scorched his body as she brought him inside her. He groaned. She cried out. Her hands opened and closed against his shoulders. She felt so damn good to him. So tight, hot and willing. He couldn't still himself, or the rocking motion she established with him. Her mouth was wild, searching and hot against his jaw, his neck and chest. He felt her teeth scrape his nipples and he gripped her hair in his fists, his lips curling away from his clenched teeth. He wanted to wait, to give her pleasure as well, but she was untrammeled, taking him fiercely. Fine. He would match her equally....

Leaning down, Reid captured her mouth and drank of her sweetness. Thrusting his tongue deeply, he rocked forward, moving into her sweet womanly depths. He felt a cry reverberate through her and he absorbed it greedily. It was a cry of utter pleasure, of surrendering to him in all ways, on all levels. Their breathing became ragged. Their heartbeats soared and thundered. Their wild, hungry kisses became flames of heat licking across their straining, slick bodies. Death had almost claimed him. He wanted to renew himself within her. He wanted to love her so deeply, so profoundly, to touch her soul and drink of the sunlight and honey within her. Every second was molten, sliding into the next. She rocked in unison with him. He felt her power, felt her nails digging into his back. Felt her cries of joy with each thrust as he took her harder and plunged deeper within her yielding body.

Ripe, golden sunlight hurtled out of him and into the dark vastness that was the mystery of womanhood. In those hot, explosive moments, Reid felt his heart burst with such powerful love for her that he could only lay there frozen with pleasure, grasping her shoulders, his face buried in her hair, his teeth clenched, his nostrils flared. And yet she continued to rock her hips with a such graceful, unbroken motion, pulling him even more deeply into her, that he could only sob for breath. Just when he thought he could bear no more of the razor-edged pleasure shearing through him, he felt her arch. Air rushed from her lips, and he slid his arm beneath her hips and lifted her slightly. Then he thrust deeply, repeatedly into her and absorbed each of the cries of pleasure that bubbled up that long, exquisite throat of hers. He felt her grow soft in the aftermath of her own release as she surrendered completely to his arms and to his body and to him. She felt as if she was boneless as he rolled over on his side and took her with him, so that she lay completely against him, her head rest-

ing on his left shoulder, her arm limp across his hip, her
breathing broken and shallow.

He tried to smile, but he was too weak to even manage
that. All he could do was hold Casey and feel the wild
beating of her heart fluttering against his thundering one.
Her breasts were soft and pliant against him. Their hips
met and fused. Her long legs were entwined with his. It
was perfect. So perfect that Reid wondered if he wasn't
dreaming again.

Weakly, he touched her flaming cheek with his fingers.
"I dreamed of this, but not like this—the wildness…your
heart.…" His voice trailed off in wonder and awe at their
lovemaking. He closed his eyes and flared his nostrils. He
wanted to drink in her womanly scent, the fragrance of her
damp skin, and he leaned over and gently bit her shoulder.
She tasted good to him, slightly salty, her flesh firm and
warm. Easing back, he ran his tongue across her lower lip.
"You taste like honey no matter where I kiss you.…"

Forcing her eyes open, Casey met and held Reid's silvered gaze. She felt like an animal. A wild, untamed, lib-
erated animal at his side. Like that lioness that Grandfather
Henri had always said she was. She recalled hazily that
Henri had told her she would one day claim her lioness
heart, and that when she did, she would know it. She knew
it now.

Reid was primal. There was nothing tame about him as
a man. How had she been so fooled by that military veneer
of his? Smiling carelessly, she slid her fingers up his darkly
bearded cheek. That dangerous male, predatory quality
was clear to her now. Her body sang because of it. Her
heart was exploding with such joy that she found herself
breathless, her voice soft and rich with emotion. "You're
more lion than even Grandfather Henri realized. You *are*
a lion in a man's form, do you know that?"

Reid caught her hand, kissed her palm slowly and then
ran his tongue in a circle around it. Casey sighed and

moaned. She pressed her hips insistently against him. Amazingly, she felt him hardening once more at her teasing gesture.

"Grandfather Henri knew *exactly* who I was," Reid growled, a smile playing at the corners of his mouth.

Giggling, Casey felt like a schoolgirl in his arms, in his powerful and protective aura, which surrounded them. "Well, if he did, he sure didn't let on to me!"

Reid's eyebrow moved up. "Why would he?"

With an unladylike snort, Casey said, "You Neanderthals all stick together, don't you?"

Chuckling indulgently, Reid gently moved her onto her back and placed her arms above her head, capturing her wrists. Then slowly, with his free hand, he began to trace the curve of her left breast. He watched as her lips parted in reaction.

"I may be a Neanderthal, good doctor, but sometimes that's just what the lady needs." He leaned over and drew the hardened tip between his lips. When he began to suckle her, she moaned and tossed feverishly against him. Lifting his head, his eyes glittering, he met and held her burning gaze. Settling his hand across her abdomen, his darkly tanned fingers against her pearl white flesh, he rasped, "And you're mine. Now. Forever."

The force of his comment flowed through her like a bolt of white-hot heat. Casey felt the strength of his hand upon her rounded abdomen; she felt so loved, so protected. Yes, Reid was like a lion claiming her, his lioness mate, forever. Her lower body warmed beneath his captive hand. She fearlessly met and held the challenging look gleaming in his hooded eyes. "Yes," she whispered softly, "I want to carry your babies in me. I want to feel them grow deep within my body—our children that we'll make as we lie here loving one another...."

Her words were joyous and so alive with life. Whispering her name roughly, Hunter brought her into the protec-

tive haven of his arms and held her so tightly that he was
worried he'd crush the breath out of her. Instead, she
wrapped her arms deliciously around his sweat-slick shoulders and embraced him with the strength of a lioness,
which was really what she was in his eyes and heart.

Moonlight shifted brokenly through the French lace curtains. Reid awoke with a jerk. He'd had a nightmare about
the black mamba striking him, its fangs sinking deeply into
his calf. Forcing his eyes open, he felt the strong, supple
warmth of Casey lying next to him. She was in his arms.
He was alive.

Sweat trickled down his temples. He blinked away the
burning perspiration that flowed into his eyes. Breathing
roughly, he sat up. The thin sheet fell away, exposing his
naked upper body as he turned to the woman he loved.
The moonlight caressed Casey as she slept. One hand was
beneath the goose-down pillow, the other stretched outward, her fingers slightly closed. Hands that had loved him
earlier. Had held him. Had pressed against his fingers as
he'd caressed her rounded abdomen. *Babies. Yes, life.*

Running his fingers through his damp hair, Reid looked
around the quiet room. The moonlight chased away the
darkness. His gaze returned to Casey as she slept. She'd
chased away the darkness that had haunted his heart for
so long. A tender smile tugged at his mouth as he reached
out, his fingers sifting lightly through her mussed red hair.
She was part tomboy, part woman, part fierce lioness—
and all his. The strands of her hair felt strong and sleek
between his thumb and forefinger. Like her. She was such
a brave woman. Did he really deserve someone like her?

Reid lay back down and fitted his body against the back
of hers. He rested his head on his arm and allowed his
hand to trail across her waist, hip and thigh. Her skin was
cool and yet so alive and inviting to him. He was alive.
He'd survived. And she loved him. What a fierce heart she

had! But Reid had known that all along. He didn't know many people who would brave the killer Ebola virus, look it in the eye and gaze fiercely back at it like Casey did on a regular basis. She had braved going back to Africa, even with the threat of terrorists, the possibility of being killed like her cohorts, or worse, being kidnapped by Black Dawn, just so she could settle the score on Steve's account. She had gone for revenge against Ebola and had found Reid—and love. His hand stilled on her hip and he smiled a little as he watched the moonlight play through her hair. Casey had even braved the likes of him. And won his heart…his soul.

Closing his eyes, Hunter felt the fingers of sleep tugging once more at him. Tomorrow was a new day—for both of them. One that he eagerly looked forward to, with Casey. What a team they were going to be! She was a leader in so many ways, and so was he. Reid could imagine the healthy discussions they'd get into from time to time, but that would never dim the love and admiration and respect he felt toward her. No, any relationship with Casey was going to have its fair share of fireworks. Reid felt more than up to the challenge of it all because the bottom line was the love they held for one another.

The idea crossed his mind that perhaps it was time to leave the Marine Corps. He felt far less vulnerable, emotionally, and the possibility of being a civilian seemed less risky than before. He knew it had to do with Casey's love for him. It would be very easy to get a job with Perseus, perhaps in their Intelligence section so that he didn't have to go overseas like most mercenaries did. Morgan could use someone with his knowledge, since black biology was a looming threat and would be, unfortunately, for decades to come. Reid would discuss this idea with Casey and see what she thought. He knew she'd tell him to jump ship and don civvies in a heartbeat. He grinned at that. Besides, he could live here, with her, and still do his job. Perseus had a satellite office in Atlanta, so it would not be a problem. No longer would he use the military as a way to hide, to shield himself from his emotions. Leaving the corps would be a symbol of his resolve to learn how to live with his feelings daily, like Casey and many other people did.

Sighing heavily, he allowed his hand to remain on her hip. She felt damn good against him. She smelled good to him, too. There wasn't anything not to love about Casey. He liked the way she loved him, like a fierce lioness claiming her mate with equal veracity and powerful intent. Yes, they were a good match. And in the very near future, he wanted to ask her to marry him. She wouldn't leave him waiting at the altar, he knew. No, not Casey. She'd beat him to it and demand that he arrive there on time or else!

Joy floated through him over that last thought as he drifted toward sleep. Somehow, Reid knew that his fears about being only half a man, a man without a heart, were now laid permanently to rest. Casey had brought out his heart and revealed its vulnerability. She had held it tenderly, without judgment, and had showered him with nonstop love in so many different and wonderful forms. Reid had learned a lot from her. She had so much more to teach him. He recalled Grandfather Henri's words that a strong woman made a man feel weak. Only if the man refused to learn about and respect the woman he loved, for that woman could turn out to be one of his greatest, most loving teachers.

A careless smile crossed Reid's mouth. Somehow, he knew that Grandfather Henri already knew that. He hadn't told Reid because he'd wanted him to discover this incredible treasure in Casey on his own. And he had. The heart of the hunter had been captured, opened and lovingly tended by a woman who was as strong and fierce as a lioness, who knew herself and wasn't afraid to stand whatever tests he'd thrown at her. Casey had passed them all and become not only his teacher, but his guide. As he gently moved his hand down across her firm thigh, his eyes glimmered with tears. His wife-to-be was an incredible woman who led with her heart, first, last and always. He was looking forward to learning how to do that himself. Casey would be more than happy to show him the way.

Life had never look so good to Reid.

Epilogue

Casey moaned and slowly turned over on her back. Sunlight was bright outside the window, and she wrinkled her nose and lifted her hands to her eyes. A slight breeze moved the curtains. As she grew more alert, she realized with a start that Reid had left her side. Pushing herself up on one elbow, she looked around for him. The bedroom was quiet, and he wasn't around. A sudden stab of fear plunged through her heart. Throwing off the sheet, she got to her feet and reached for her pink silk robe. All kinds of awful thoughts assailed her as she quickly padded barefoot out of the room and into the hallway.

"Reid?" Her voice sounded hollow. Fearful. She pulled at the collar of her robe as she headed down toward the kitchen. Halfway there, she sniffed the odor of freshly perking coffee. Entering the kitchen, she saw Reid at the stove. She halted. Laughter bubbled up her throat as she leaned lazily against the door jamb, her arms crossed. He stood there in his jeans and a red polo shirt, a checkered green-and-white apron wrapped haphazardly around his waist. The look on his face was one of pure frustration. In his hand was a spatula. In the skillet were eggs burning.

"I didn't think Neanderthals could cook," she murmured wryly. "Although I've gotta give you an A for effort."

He twisted around and gave her a slow, welcoming grin.

Holding up the spatula in defense, he muttered, "Well, I *had* good intentions. I woke up early and thought it would be nice to serve you breakfast in bed." Giving the eggs in the skillet a doleful look, he removed them from the stove. "Best laid plans, you know?" He liked the drowsy sensuality mirrored in her face, the remnants of sleep still lingering in her green eyes as she walked slowly toward him as he stood at the sink.

Touched beyond words, Casey lifted her arms as he laid down the utensil and turned to meet her. There was a bashful, little-boy look on his face and it endeared him to her even more. "Somehow," she murmured as she slid her hands over his shoulders and curved them around his neck, "you give new meaning to the word *apron*."

Chuckling, Reid felt heat nettling his cheeks. Just the way Casey's body fit with his made everything right in his world. He embraced her and brought her solidly against him. She lifted her chin, her eyes slumberous, her lips parting, asking…. He didn't disappoint her. Sliding his mouth commandingly across hers, he felt her give a little moan as she surrendered entirely to him. She tasted of sleep, of a woman in love with him, a woman who wanted him all over again. Her fingers threaded through his dark hair as he continued to worship her mouth. Never would he get enough of her. Not ever. Nostrils flaring, he drank in the sweet fragrance that was hers alone. Moving his hand from her waist to her cheek, he angled her jaw just slightly so he could drink even more deeply of her honeyed offering.

"Mmm..." he rasped against her lips "...this is better than scrambled eggs...." Reid felt her laugh.

Lifting her lashes, Casey met his silvered gaze and that heated, predatory look that lingered in his eyes. Her stomach curled in anticipation as his strong arms encircled her and held her captive against his tall, lean frame. "My kiss had better taste a helluva lot better than those crispy-critter eggs you just destroyed, Hunter."

Chuckling, he caressed her smiling mouth. "Just a little, good doctor...."

Her body burned hotly with a renewed hunger for him, for his masculine touch. Casey kissed his mouth, his cheek, and then nibbled teasingly on the lobe of his ear. She felt him stiffen, then grip her hips and pull her demandingly against him. She reveled in his male hardness. "What can I do to get a cup of coffee out of you?" she asked huskily, lifting her chin and meeting his amused, hungry gaze.

"Bribery will get you everywhere."

She laughed and said, "I'm torn between you and the IV of coffee I need first thing in the morning."

He raised his brows. "There's no contest here. I should win that one hands down."

Her lips curved more. "There goes that Neanderthal ego again...."

Casting a rueful look over at the coffeemaker, Reid tried to pretend he was hurt. He wasn't, of course, but he enjoyed teasing Casey because she was so easy to laugh with. Finding a woman with a good sense of humor was worth gold, in his opinion. "Coffee—over me? How could you?"

"Hmm, let's see," Casey whispered, falling into his arms and resting her brow against his neck, "do I want you or the coffee worse?"

He moved his fingers through her mussed red hair. "As if you'd even think there was a choice." He laughed deeply.

Casey laughed with Reid. She felt joyful and free in his arms. Sobering a little, she gripped his arms, pushed away just enough to look up at him. Despite his loss of weight, Reid would bounce back quickly, she knew. "I think," she murmured, giving him a coy look, "that I really ought to make us a huge breakfast of grits, ham, fried eggs and the best Southern biscuits you've ever tasted. I have to keep the man I love in peak health because—" she grinned impishly "—you're gonna need all the stamina you own, Captain, to keep up with me in bed. You thought humping hills was tough. Just wait and see...."

"I always did like a challenge, Doctor." He grinned and framed her face. "I love you, Casey Morrow. In every way possible. In sickness. In health. I'm yours and you're mine. Forever, if you want?"

Her smile dissolved. Tears pricked at her eyes and she blinked them away. Standing captive in Reid's embrace was the only place she ever wanted to be. Placing her hands over his, she held his dark gray gaze as he mercilessly probed hers for an answer. "Yes," she whispered softly, choking back the unexpected tears. "Yes to anything and everything you ever ask of me, Reid."

The tears leaked from her eyes and down her flushed cheeks. With his thumbs he removed them. "Marry me? Be my mate for life? My best friend?"

"In a heartbeat," Casey whispered brokenly. "You won't have to ask me twice. And I won't leave you standing at the altar, either."

Reid believed her as he heard the low, fiercely spoken words slip from her lips. Leaning down, he cherished her mouth in gentle adoration. "No altar this time," he said against her wet, soft lips. "Let's get married here, in this beautiful old, antique house with an old-fashioned woman who has stolen my heart."

She nodded her head, unable to trust her voice as they

stood in one another's arms, their brows pressed together. "I like it...."

"You name the date, I'll be there, princess."

Just then, the phone rang. Casey jumped.

Reid scowled and his gaze shot to a red phone that hung near the kitchen door. "Who?" he demanded.

Hesitating, Casey said, "It's my office. The red phone is only used if there's a problem. Usually on biohazard level four, the hot zone. I have to get it...." She felt his arms fall away as she hurried over to the phone.

Reid rested his hips against the drain board, his arms wrapped across his chest as he watched Casey talk in a low tone on the phone. He saw the flush drain from her cheeks. Her fingers pressed to her mouth. And then she turned to him. Her green eyes were dark.

"Morgan Trayhern is on the phone. He just got done talking to my immediate boss, Dr. Jonas Hawthorn. This is about your brother Ty and Dr. Catt Alborak...." She choked. "It sounds like all hell's breaking loose down in Brazil." She held the phone toward him. "Morgan wants to speak with you...."

Casey stepped aside. She felt fear for Ty and Catt. Worriedly, she remained at Reid's elbow as he talked in a low, dark tone with Morgan. From the man she'd known minutes earlier, Reid had switched back into his military officer mode once again. But Casey understood the need for him to assume that role.

Sighing, she turned and moved woodenly back to the drain board. Right now, she knew, they both needed a fortifying cup of coffee. As she poured the steaming black brew, she heard Reid say a terse goodbye and hang up the phone. Turning, she handed him a mug of coffee. His brow was wrinkled. His eyes were a flat, dark gray. She felt his anguish and worry.

"Thanks," he murmured, and took a quick sip. Casting a look at Casey, he saw the fear lurking in her eyes. "Morgan was calling to update me. He was trying to contact Ty to let him know I'm among the living, and he finally got ahold of him.''

"Yes," she said hollowly, "Jonas said Ty and Catt were working in a small village three hours south of Manaus, in Brazil. He said the village had a bad outbreak. They still don't know what they're dealing with down there. No one has been able to identify the virus. It's killing people right and left." She gripped the mug with both hands and looked over the rim at him. "What are you going to do?"

Raggedly, he said, "Pray? Ty is good at what he does. And from what you've said about Catt, she's the best in her field. You couldn't have two better people in the breach as far as I'm concerned."

"What about Black Dawn? Any hint they're around the outbreak area?"

"Morgan said there's nothing conclusive so far. He thinks they're trying to work with the drug lords in South America now, since scientific labs around the world refuse to sell them the bacteria and viruses they want. Now they'll go to the black market, he thinks." Grimly, he added, "And Morgan suspects they're trying to get in touch with Eduardo Escovar right now."

"The man Mike Houston is up against in Peru?"

"Yeah, the same." He sighed softly. "Morgan just said that Dr. Ann Parsons is missing...."

"What?" Casey tried to sound less strident. "You mean kidnapped?"

"Morgan doesn't know yet. The nuns at the clinic in Lima called him. Ann didn't show up for work this morning. They're worried. Mike's not around. He's chasing some of Escovar's men up in the highlands far north of the capital city."

Hearing the frustration in Reid's tone, Casey wrapped one arm around his waist and led him out of the kitchen toward the living room. "I know enough about Morgan to

know he won't let one of his men or women be taken like
that, Reid. Perseus is a very tight, family-oriented agency.
Everyone knows everyone else. He cares deeply for his
people. They aren't just employees to him, they're family.
He'll rip up earth and heaven to find them. I know he will.
And I know Mike and Ann. They're resourceful people.
What an awful situation, though.''

"Yeah, and it's worsening in Brazil and Peru simultaneously,'' Reid said worriedly. "Morgan's really concerned that a vial of that unknown killer virus from Brazil
will fall into Black Dawn's hands. They want that virus in
order to sow their ugly seeds of destruction somewhere
else in the world. And if Black Dawn is serious about
making a pact with drug lords…well, that's one helluva
powerful alliance for any government or agency in this
world to battle.''

Casey felt some of her happiness returning despite the
somber news. How like Morgan to keep Reid in touch
about his brother. She admired his loyalty to all his people.

Moving across the living room, Reid placed his arm
comfortingly around Casey's slumped shoulders. "Morgan
knows I'm here,'' he rasped. "He'll call us if there's any
news, or a change in the situation down in Brazil with Catt
and Ty.''

Nodding, Casey slid down on the couch beside Reid.
Elbows on his thighs, hands locked around his coffee cup
he sat there, staring straight ahead, lost in thought. She
saw pain in the way his mouth had tightened up. "After
we drink our coffee, maybe you want to call your family,
let them know what's going on?''

"Yes, I will,'' he said, sounding preoccupied. Sipping
the coffee, he straightened and then leaned back on the
couch. Giving Casey a warm look, he said, "One thing
about all of this, we got lucky. Black Dawn didn't hit us.''

Closing her eyes, she concentrated on the warmth of the

cup between her cool, damp hands. "Yes...just a snake bite was all...."

Reid reached over and moved his hand up and down her bare thigh where it peeked out of the silk robe she wore. "Ty won't go down easy. He's a fighter. I've got to think they will outwit the terrorists...."

Managing a partial smile, Casey added, "Catt is no weak sister, either, Reid. She's one helluva fighter when the chips are down."

"Better than you?"

She placed her hand over his where it rested on her thigh. "Listen, you know what her nickname around bio-hazard four is?"

"No. What?"

"Valkyrie."

He raised his brows and clung to her feisty gaze. "Then there's hope.... Ty's not someone you want to come up against, because he'll take you down with his last dying breath."

Shivering, Casey placed her cup on the antique coffee table in front of them. She leaned back and wrapped her arm around Reid's taut shoulders. She could feel the tension, the anguish, thrumming through him, though he was trying so hard not to show it. Gently running her hand across his neck, she laid her head on his shoulder and whispered, "I love you, Reid Hunter. Hell can freeze over, but nothing is going to take how I feel about you away from me." She kissed his cheek. "When Ty and Catt get back, let's set a wedding date, okay? What do you say?"

Reid loved her fiercely for her courage. For her faith. Right now, his military mind was running at the speed of sound with possibilities. With worry, with anguish. Just the fierce light in Casey's eyes made him feel something else: hope. "Do you always hold out hope for the hopeless, good doctor?"

She grinned carelessly and ruffled his short hair. "That's

what docs do best, isn't it? Feed hope to the hopeless? Help them heal? Help them renew their faith in themselves and the fact that they can heal?'' Her voice grew husky. ''I've stared death in the face too many times myself, Reid. I know the value of life, just like you do. And so does Catt. She worked with me on Ebola. She knows the risks. She's just as much a fighter as your brother Ty.'' Sliding her hand down his cheek, Casey caught and held his stormy gaze. ''No, life's too precious to Catt. She's seen death. She's faced it too often herself. Believe me, Ty couldn't have a better partner to face Black Dawn with than Catt. She may not be a trained mercenary, but she's smart and doesn't miss a trick.''

Buoyed by Casey's care and nurturing, Reid heaved a sigh, set the mug aside and took her into his arms. One moment he was on top of the world, the next, shattered. Still, he had more than most men would ever have. Bussing her hair as she lay against him, he rasped, ''Life's precious—you're precious. We'll get through this together, princess…and at the end of this dark tunnel, we're getting married.''

''Promise?'' Casey whispered, closing her eyes and savoring his heartbeat against her ear, his strong, protective arms.

''I promise I'm going to love you forever and one day after that.…'' And he would.

*   *   *   *   *

"This is probably the sorriest decision I'll ever make, Houston, but I'm sticking it out down here for six weeks. With or without you. I honor Morgan's commitments. I go where he sends me."

Ann watched a slow grin crawl across Mike Houston's face at her decision to stay on the mission with him. He had such a strong, chiseled mouth. A beautiful mouth, she admitted. One that she wanted to feel against her lips again and again....

"Well," she challenged, her voice husky, "are you going to stand there gawking at me or are you going to buy me that espresso you promised?"

Snapping out of it, Houston slid his arm around her upper arm and guided her forward. "No ma'am, I'll buy you that well-deserved cup of espresso." As Ann walked with her own lanky stride at his side, breath-stealing elation raced through him. This time, she didn't seem to mind

his hand on her arm. Indeed, it was as if she liked it there.
But Houston didn't fool himself. They'd just been through
a very intense life and death situation together. He found
it normal that *medicos* automatically drew close to one
another for emotional support after the crisis was over. It
was only human, he warned himself. Still, his fingers tingled wildly as he felt the slip and slide of her blouse and
the firmness of her flesh beneath it. Grinning recklessly,
he said, "This has been one wild ride so far, Dr. Parsons
and the day is young yet...."

She raised one brow and glanced at him as they walked.
"I'll give you that," she replied, her pulse speeding up.
The undisguised happiness in Mike's eyes affected her, left
her aching to kiss him, to feel his hands slide around the
curve of her torso as he pulled her uncompromisingly
against his body.

When Mike glanced down at Ann, he realized in that
split second that her guard was down. To hell with it, he
thought, throwing all caution aside. "Come here..." he
murmured huskily as he drew her out of the traffic in the
busy corridor. He placed her against the wall and leaned
close to her. He read the need for him in her eyes. He felt
it in every fiber of his being. The connection between them
was as palpable as the feel of his fingers as he grazed the
slope of her flushed cheek.

"I need you," he rasped, placing his hand against her
cheek and guiding her face upward. He saw her eyes widen
momentarily, heard her breath hitch. Smiling tenderly
down at her as he lightly brushed her parting lips with his,
he saw the fear dissolve in her eyes. Yes, she wanted this
as much as he did.

For one heated moment out of time, all her surroundings
dissolved from Ann's awareness. All she'd longed for was
finally happening. Somehow, Mike had known she'd
needed him. It was all so crazy. So mixed up. Yet as she

lifted her chin and felt his strong mouth settle upon her lips, nothing had ever felt so right. So pure. So devastatingly beautiful. His strong arms moved around her back and she felt him pull her against him. There was no mistake about his gesture; it was clearly that of a man claiming his woman.

Her lashes swept downward and the ache inside her intensified as his mouth skimmed hers. How good he tasted! She inhaled his very male scent, slid her hands upward against his barrel chest, marveling in the strength of his muscles tightening beneath her exploration. His mouth slid surely against her lips, rocking them open even more, his tongue thrusting boldly into her mouth. A moan of sweet surrender trembled throughout Ann as she lost herself in the fiery, hungry mating. All that existed in that moment was Mike, his maleness, his tender domination of her. Oh, how stupid she had been not to give herself to him sooner!

As Houston began to ease his mouth from hers, she cried out internally, not wanting to cease contact with him in any way. Yet, she knew they must. She was sure they were making a spectacle of themselves in the corridor. People were probably staring at them. But for once, Ann didn't care. Mike had somehow dissolved all her fears; her need to be proper and prudish out in public. He tore away her doctor's façade and stripped her naked to her hot, womanly core of primitive needs and desires. As she looked dazedly up into his narrowed, gleaming eyes, she never felt so protected or so desired in all her life.

Gradually, ever so gradually, Houston forced himself to ease from Ann's lips. Lips made of the wild honey he'd found only in the jungle of Peru. Honey that was so sweet it made him dissolve beneath her searching, innocent mouth. There was no question he needed her. None.

Houston cupped her shoulders and gently moved her away from him. Once Ann could confide in him, he vowed to tell her all that had happened to him in the jungle years ago. But even as he made the decision, another part of him warned that he was crazy for allowing her to get too close to him. Did he want to put her in that kind of danger? How could he?

But Ann would know the truth about him very soon, one way or another. Then she would have to make her own decision about whether she could love a man like him....

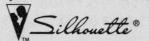

Silhouette®SPECIAL EDITION®

AND BABY MAKES THREE: THE NEXT GENERATION:

The Adams men and women of Texas all find love—and parenthood—in the most unexpected ways!

Bestselling author Sherryl Woods continues to captivate with her popular series about the headstrong heroes and independent-minded ladies of charming Los Pinos, Texas:

November 1998: THE COWGIRL & THE UNEXPECTED WEDDING (SE #1208)
Could fit-to-be-tied cowboy Hank Robbins convince mule-headed mother-to-be Lizzie Adams to march down the aisle?

December 1998: NATURAL BORN LAWMAN (SE #1216)
Justin Adams was a strictly by-the-book lawman—until he fell in love with a desperate, devoted single mom on the run!

February 1999: THE UNCLAIMED BABY
(Silhouette Single Title)
The family saga continues with a passionate, longer-length romance about a fateful stormy night that changes Sharon Adams's life—forever!

March 1999: THE COWBOY AND HIS WAYWARD BRIDE (SE #1234)
Rancher Harlan Patrick Adams would do just about anything to claim stubborn Laurie Jensen—mother of his infant daughter—as his own!

Available at your favorite retail outlet.

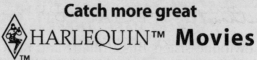

Silhouette® SPECIAL EDITION®

Newfound sisters Bliss, Tiffany and Katie
learn more about family and true love
than they *ever* expected.

A new miniseries by
LISA JACKSON

A FAMILY KIND OF GUY (SE#1191) August 1998
Bliss Cawthorne wanted nothing to do with ex-flame
Mason Lafferty, the cowboy who had destroyed her
dreams of being his bride. Could Bliss withstand his irresistible charm—the second time around?

A FAMILY KIND OF GAL (SE#1207) November 1998
How could widowed single mother Tiffany Santini be
attracted to her sexy brother-in-law, J.D.? Especially
since J.D. was hiding something that could destroy the
love she had just found in his arms....

And watch for the conclusion of this series in
early 1999 with Katie Kinkaid's story in
A FAMILY KIND OF WEDDING.

Available at your favorite retail outlet. Only from

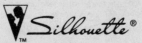

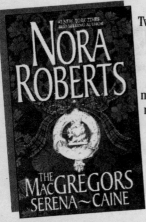
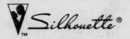

FORTUNE'S Children™

*The Fortune family requests
the honor of your presence at the weddings of*

Silhouette Desire's scintillating new miniseries,
featuring the beloved Fortune family
and five of your favorite authors.

The Honor Bound Groom—**January 1999**
by Jennifer Greene (SD #1190)

Society Bride—**February 1999**
by Elizabeth Bevarly (SD #1196)

And look for more **FORTUNE'S CHILDREN:
THE BRIDES** installments by Leanne Banks,
Susan Crosby and Merline Lovelace,
coming in spring 1999.

Available at your favorite retail outlet.

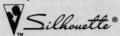

Look us up on-line at: http://www.romance.net   SDFORTUNE

COMING NEXT MONTH

#1219 A FAMILY KIND OF WEDDING—Lisa Jackson
That Special Woman!/Forever Family
When rancher Luke Gates arrived in town on a mysterious mission,
he had everything under control—until he lost his heart to hardworking
ace reporter Katie Kincaid and her ten-year-old son. Would Katie still
trust in him once she learned a shocking secret that would forever alter
her family?

#1220 THE MILLIONAIRE BACHELOR—Susan Mallery
During their late-night phone chats, Cathy Eldridge couldn't resist
entertaining a pained Stone Ward with tall tales about "her" life as a
globe-trotting goddess. Then a twist of fate brought the self-conscious
answering-service operator face-to-face with the reclusive millionaire
of her dreams....

#1221 MEANT FOR EACH OTHER—Ginna Gray
The Blaines and the McCalls of Crockett, Texas
Good-natured Dr. Mike McCall was only too happy to save
Dr. Leah Albright's ailing kid brother. And, as an added bonus, the
alluring, ultrareserved lady doc finally allowed Mike to sweep her off
her feet. But would their once-in-a-lifetime love survive the ultimate
betrayal?

#1222 I TAKE THIS MAN—AGAIN!—Carole Halston
Six years ago, Mac McDaniel had foolishly let the love of his life go.
Now he vowed to do anything—and *everything*—to make irresistibly
sweet Ginger Honeycutt his again. For better, for worse, he knew they
were destined to become husband and wife—for keeps!

#1223 JUST WHAT THE DOCTOR ORDERED—Leigh Greenwood
A hard-knock life had taught Dr. Matt Dennis to steer clear of emotional
intimacy at all costs. But when he took a job at a rural clinic, struggling
single mom Liz Rawlins welcomed him into her warm, embracing
family. Would Liz's tender lovin' care convince the jaded doctor he
truly belonged?

#1224 PRENUPTIAL AGREEMENT—Doris Rangel
It was meant to be when China Smith blissfully wed the only man she
would *ever* love. Though Yance had proposed marriage for the sake of
his son, an enamored China planned to cherish her husband forever and
always. And she wasn't about to let a pesky prenuptial agreement stand
in her way!